Blood Stained

Blood Stained

CJ Lyons

CANELO

First published in United States in 2012 by Legacy Books

This edition published in the United Kingdom in 2018 by

Canelo Digital Publishing Limited
57 Shepherds Lane
Beaconsfield, Bucks HP9 2DU
United Kingdom

A CIP catalogue record for this book is available from the British Library.

Print ISBN 978 1 78863 262 1
Ebook ISBN 978 1 910859 66 7

Look for more great books at www.canelo.co

Printed and bound in Great Britain by Clays Ltd, Elcograf S.p.A.

Prologue

An accountant from Lawrence, Kansas has a wife who is constantly cold. Summer or winter, she wears long sleeves and wraps her neck in silk scarves. Secretly he wondered if she was still self-conscious about the scars left by a car accident that almost killed her right after they first met in college.

Back then, when she vanished without a word for three weeks, he'd been angry she didn't have the courage to break it off face-to-face, but also afraid he'd done something wrong and frightened her off.

Being a freshman in college, away from home for the first time, left him intoxicated with his first taste of independence, yet terrified of facing the future alone. But then she returned, their passion rekindled stronger than ever before. Three months later they married. Five months later the baby came—scandalous to any who bothered to do the math, but given the birth was premature and the baby so small, he thanked God for a miracle.

Life was good. She opened an antique store and he delighted in lavishing her with silk scarves whenever he saw any that matched her beauty.

Sometimes nights were bad. She'd cry out in her sleep, pummeling him as if he were a stranger. He'd hold her tight until she quieted. Those nights he'd stare into the dark, not quite daring to pull back the curtain on their perfect lives. Nevertheless, stray suspicions would slip into his mind.

What kind of car accident left those scars? And the child. Pronounced "fey" and suffering from "bad blood" by his great-aunt who at a doddering ninety-four said anything she damn well pleased, why did the child stare at them both, not as parents or elders or even fellow human beings, but rather as if they were playthings?

Just as sleep overtook him, a strange voice whispered treachery: *Was the child even his?*

Then morning would wake him with its smells of coffee and pancakes, all doubts erased, thankful to be living such a perfect life with such a perfect wife and child.

Until their child was taken. Their little Morgan. Only eleven. Vanished.

Witnesses said Morgan had gone off with a boy, just a little older, much taller. Police, state and local, searched. The FBI helped. Even the milk carton people. A private investigator ate through their savings, but produced neither answers nor comfort.

Finally, enough time passed they felt permitted to relinquish hope and accept grief.

That night as he held his wife, he didn't see sorrow or despair in her face. Instead he saw a relief that mirrored his own.

They slept peacefully as they never had before. They woke the next morning, moved on with their perfect lives.

That was two years ago...

Chapter 1

FBI Special Agent Lucy Guardino was used to dealing with life and death situations. Gangs, human traffickers, domestic terrorism, hostage takers, sexual predators, two serial killers.

She could handle all that.

Now that she was a Supervisory Special Agent in charge of the Pittsburgh FBI Field Office's Sexual Assault Felony Enforcement squad, Lucy's world held more challenging threats.

Like the everyday quarrels of a multi-agency squad fueled by adrenalin, long on ego and short on patience. A mountain of paperwork on her desk grown so tall, if she leaned too far forward the topmost sheet wouldn't give her a paper cut, it would decapitate her.

And condescending defense attorneys aiming to crucify her on the witness stand. Like the one pacing before her now.

"You carry a gun, don't you Special Agent Guardino?"

"Yes. I'm required to."

They were in the federal courthouse on Grant Street. An old building with high ceilings, dark oak paneling, marble floors that were killers on the arches as you stood waiting because there were no benches or chairs in the spacious hallways, and wicked drafts. Even in her best wool suit Lucy still had goose bumps.

"So you carried your weapon with you on the night you coerced—"

"Objection." The Assistant US Attorney sounded bored. "Supervisory Special Agent Guardino did not coerce Mr. Plushenko into giving a statement."

"Sustained." The judge barely looked up from whatever he was reading. Probably the crossword from the way he paused, scratched a few letters, then paused again.

The defense attorney gave an elaborate "says you" shrug, but bowed his head graciously to the judge and continued, "You were armed when you intimidated my client—"

"Objection. Your honor—"

"Sustained." Now the judge did look up. "Counselor, please control your rhetoric to the facts established."

"I'm sorry, your honor. I guess I'm at a loss how to characterize Ms. Guardino's need to bring a forty caliber semi-automatic pistol to a simple conversation with a sixty-seven year old legally blind retired plumber as anything other than intimidation."

"You've made your point. Move on."

Nothing like being talked about as if you weren't there. Lucy was used to it, but she could see the jury getting restless. She shifted slightly in the hard wooden chair of the witness stand, smiled at the jury in sympathy, kept her posture relaxed. A little shrug and head tilt, let her hair graze her shoulder. So sorry this bozo is wasting your time.

The defense attorney hastened to stand in front of the jury box, bringing their attention back to him and his client, who sat in a Sunday suit complete with frayed cuffs and an out of date striped polyester necktie. Simple workingman, just like the folks on the jury. Old. Wearing the dark glasses of someone who recently had eye surgery. He coughed into his fist. And sick.

Anything but a child molester.

This was why Lucy hated court. Everyone playing a role. Nothing to do with the truth. And very little to do with justice.

"Special Agent Guardino." The attorney pivoted abruptly as if accusing Lucy. "Didn't you kill a man two months ago? And aren't you scheduled for a mandatory psychiatric evaluation?"

"Objection!" Now the AUSA was interested. Unfortunately, so was the jury. They perked up; suddenly realizing this FBI agent was *that* FBI agent, the one all over the news in September. "Relevance."

"Goes to the witness's state of mind when she interrogated my client."

"Supervisory Special Agent Guardino *interviewed* the defendant months before the incident the counselor is referring to."

The judge nodded. "Sustained."

Technically the good guys—Lucy and the prosecutor—were winning. But the defense had definitely steered the jury where he wanted it: believing Lucy a trigger-happy vigilante who terrorized his client into making self-incriminating statements.

Lucy refused to play along with the lawyer's games. She smiled at him. Ever patient. Looked over at the jury again, took a moment to make eye contact with each of them.

The man she'd killed threatened her daughter, Megan, and murdered four people. Lucy had no regrets. Except that afterwards the powers-that-be curtailed her forays into the field and chained her to her desk where a dutiful Supervisory Special Agent living up to her title should be.

She missed being out in the field.

Until a few weeks ago she had the excuse that she was the only woman in her squad certified in undercover work. The FBI took its UC ops very seriously. There was a special training course, exhaustive testing, and, of course, reams of paperwork.

Now she was the one filing the paperwork to send her people into the field. Including a new addition to the team, Jenna Galloway, a female postal inspector certified for UC work. Replaced by a glorified mailman. Mailwoman. Whatever.

"The night you raided my client's home," the defense attorney continued, "how many armed men were present?"

"The evening of July tenth as we executed a routine search warrant of the premises, I was accompanied by a Special Agent with expertise in computer forensics, the Immigration and Customs Enforcement agent who originally intercepted the defendant's child pornography and traced it back to his home computer as part of the Innocent Images Initiative, and two evidence recovery technicians."

Of course she didn't mention that if Plushenko owned any weapons or appeared to pose any threat to anyone other than seven-year-old boys, a fully armed strike team would have accompanied them.

Lucy continued, "That's two male federal agents carrying their service weapons as required by law, two unarmed technicians, also both men, and myself. At no time did anyone draw their weapons." She snuck the last in before the attorney could cut her off, earning her a scowl.

He could have objected but it wouldn't have looked good to the jury, so he changed tactics. "If you were a sixty-seven year old man blind with cataracts would you have been intimidated by such an overwhelming show of force?"

The AUSA jerked his chin, ready to protest the request for her to speculate. Lucy shook her head and he kept his mouth shut. He stared at her suspiciously. Lawyers never liked it when a witness took control of the proceedings. They preferred to be the only ones with a script.

"In deference to Mr. Plushenko's age, I personally escorted him to the kitchen and made him a cup of tea while he read the search warrant. In fact, that's where our conversation took place. At the kitchen table." Lucy folded her hands on the horizontal ledge of the witness stand and leaned forward earnestly, her posture open. Unlike the defendant who had slumped so far down in his chair, he threatened to slide under the table.

Lucy loved kitchens. It was amazing the things people would say in the comfort of their own homes, especially to a petite, pleasantly smiling woman with a sympathetic ear. Someone who never judged, who let them talk openly, honestly about the urges that taunted them day and night, urges they could never confess to anyone.

She wasn't allowed to reveal the contents of their conversation—the defense had seen to that, although he couldn't suppress the fact a confession had been obtained. That little fact made it to the newspapers, which forced him to address it here in court. If the AUSA had been allowed to play the recording Lucy had made of her conversation with Plushenko, this trial would have been over days ago.

The defense attorney turned back to his notes, gesturing to his client to sit up straight. Lucy smiled at the jury. Just a tea-making, good-listening, Italian-American soccer-mom here.

What the jury didn't realize, of course, was how absolutely relieved men like Plushenko were to have someone to talk to. They wanted—needed—a chance to talk. Not to brag, not usually. Most often it was as if they sought absolution. Or at the very least acceptance. Some indication that what they did, what they *wanted* to do to little children, was okay. Not perverse.

When she was a kid, Lucy's dad loved to take her fishing. Together they delighted in teasing trout from their shady hiding places along the banks of the Loyalhanna. He always said fishing was all about the art of dangling bait. Showing them what they wanted but not ever letting them have it.

Dad was right. That's all her job was, a different kind of fishing. And Lucy was a good fisherman. She lived for that instant when the line snapped taut, ready to break, adrenalin stretching the moment, time holding its breath until she took control and finessed the fish into shore— right where she wanted it.

Just like Plushenko and his attorney. The attorney shuffled through his legal pad of notes, then turned to the judge. "Given the late hour, your honor—"

The judge took the hint. "Let's take this up again tomorrow. Nine o'clock. Until then court is adjourned."

Lucy would have preferred to stay and see Plushenko buried once and for all. But one good thing about leaving early, she'd be able to get over to Megan's soccer practice before it finished.

She waited until the jury departed before she left the witness box. She wanted to leave them with the impression she was in no rush; she'd be happy to answer any and all questions if the defense attorney only let her. Several of them smiled at her as they gathered their coats and sweaters and the bailiff led them out.

Just as she was slipping into her own coat, a utilitarian parka, the doors to the courtroom opened and a tall black man in his early fifties entered. Walden, her second in command.

"What's wrong?" she asked when he met her mid-aisle. She kept walking, knowing anything serious enough to get Walden to come across the river from the Federal Building on Pittsburgh's South Side was going to require her presence somewhere other than an empty courtroom.

"You got a letter. Sender didn't realize we open and screen everything." He handed her a photocopy. A single page. Words centered. Not that there were many of them.

There didn't need to be. Because the sender used the one word Lucy could not ignore.

Megan's name.

She had to force her gaze back to the top. Her chest burned before she remembered to take a breath.

> *Dear Lucy,*
>
> *I've missed you. You blamed the wrong man for my work in New Hope. That wasn't very nice of you.*
>
> *You need to make this right. Or I'll be forced to take drastic action.*
>
> *Hugs to Megan—I hope to meet her someday. I'm sure she's growing up to be a beautiful teenager.*
>
> *See you in New Hope.*

Signed,
A disappointed fan

Lucy's fingers went numb, barely able to fold the letter and shove it in her pocket. New Hope. Christ, she'd prayed that nightmare was dead and gone forever. She leaned against the marble wall beside her, not feeling the cold as she pretended to search her pockets for her cell phone when really she was busy squelching the sudden nausea that threatened to topple her. She looked up. Walden wasn't fooled by her cover actions, but he was kind enough to not say anything.

"I need you to get a car over to the soccer fields off of Braddock," she instructed as she fumbled her cell phone from her pocket and impatiently waited for it to power up. Damn court rules. She began down the hallway, long strides for such a short woman, heels clacking loud enough to make several court officials and bystanders glance up as she rushed past. "And Nick—"

"Galloway's already headed over to his office." Jenna Galloway was the new addition to the team, the postal inspector.

Damn. Nick wasn't picking up. Must be in with a patient. She didn't leave a message. What could she say? Some nut job sent a letter threatening their daughter?

She'd never told Nick about New Hope. Prayed like hell she'd never have to. The man responsible for the kidnapping, rape, and killing of at least eleven women was supposed to be dead.

Not sending her letters. Letters using Megan's name.

"Forensics?" Going down the investigative checklist helped keep her emotions from running wild.

"Working on it."

She dialed her mother. No answer there either. "I need someone to locate my mother."

Walden finished talking with the Pittsburgh Police Zone Commander who oversaw the region where the soccer fields were. "On it."

They cut down one of the restricted access corridors, were waved through security, and emerged behind the post office. Lucy's personal vehicle, a blue Subaru Impreza, was parked beneath the overhang near the employee exit, protected from the November rain. "I'm going to Megan. Call me when you know anything."

Walden touched her arm as she opened the driver's door. "You know how many of these letters come through every day? And half of them are addressed to you—especially after all the press in September."

"None of them threaten my family by name." She shook his hand free. Walden hadn't worked New Hope; he didn't understand. He would as soon as he read the file. "Call me."

She slammed the door, grateful for the safe haven of her car. She turned the ignition on and pulled past the guardhouse out onto Bigelow Avenue. November sleet and wind rocked the car in a staccato beat the windshield wipers struggled to keep up with. The radio was cranked high, as usual, and Mudvayne came on with "Scream with Me."

As Lucy swerved between sedate, carefree drivers oblivious to her need, she followed the title's command. One ear-splitting release of noise before silencing the radio with a stab of her finger.

If only Plushenko's lawyer could see her now.

—

Somehow Lucy made it to the soccer field without crashing. She climbed out of the car and waved to the officer waiting in the police cruiser. He nodded, flashed his lights, and took off to return to his duties.

She hugged herself against the cold. Her parka was unzipped and beneath it she wore her "court" suit: navy skirt and jacket and black pumps that sank into the soggy gravel of the parking lot. The week after Thanksgiving and it had already snowed twice in Pittsburgh, leaving slushy mounds to ambush unsuspecting pedestrians. Thick clouds, heavy as steel, pressed down against the waning sunlight, trying to squeeze the life out of the city, promising more snow to come.

Happy squeals came from the soccer field where kids in colorful uniforms chased a ball covered in mud. The other parents lined up beneath bright golf umbrellas along the sidelines, clapping and cheering despite the weather. These were the top players in this age range invited for a special intersession all-star skills camp and their parents were the district's top soccer moms and dads.

Lucy didn't join them. She didn't have an umbrella. She needed both hands free. She didn't raise her hood. Too restrictive. Cut off her peripheral vision. Resting one hand on the gun at her hip, she remained behind the crowd at her car. From there she could keep Megan in sight, target the crowd as well, plus the car provided cover and escape.

A whistle blew. Lucy jerked upright, hand falling to her Glock.

Hyper-vigilant, Nick had diagnosed her. Normal after almost dying two months ago, after seeing her daughter placed in harm's way. As if there could be anything normal about that.

Megan vanished from sight as two fathers arguing about the Steelers' offensive line blocked Lucy's view. Her heart skidded, lurching into overdrive, pounding louder than the sleet drumming against the car roof. She ran two steps forward. Hands. She needed to see all of their hands, even as she scanned for Megan.

It wasn't until the whistle blew again and she spotted Megan's form bobbing through the crowd of players that she realized she'd drawn her gun.

Tears streaked warm down her chilled cheeks, a counterpoint to the embarrassment and fear flooding her. She hadn't raised her gun, hadn't pointed it at anyone. But that didn't matter. Her emotions overpowered her training.

Thankfully the rest of the crowd remained focused on the players. Lucy turned away, needing both trembling hands to re-holster her weapon. Nausea left her mouth dry and skin clammy. Leaning against the car, she focused on the not-so-simple act of breathing, tried to force back her panic.

It never left. Never entirely. Not since September. But she could control it.

She had to. If she let herself fall apart, who would protect her family?

Chapter 2

Adam Caine got off the Greyhound in New Hope, PA with seventeen cents in his pocket. He wore everything he owned: ragged tennis shoes with a hole in one toe and a broken lace, jeans, a t-shirt, flannel shirt, Penn State sweatshirt with a rip in the hem, and his father's oversized denim jacket. He was fourteen, hungry, cold, and his home was no longer his.

The bus stop was the curb in front of Thomson's Hardware. There was no depot. If you were lucky enough to be leaving New Hope, "No Hope," the kids called it when Adam was young, you bought your ticket from the clerk inside the Safeway at the other end of the parking lot.

No hope of Adam leaving anytime soon. But that was okay. It was nice to be back. He'd spent the past eight months on his own, foraging for food, standing up to street bullies. Kids as alone and scared as himself, psych patients left to fend for themselves on the streets, plus other kinds of predators, the ones with money in their pockets and need in their eyes. To Adam, New Hope lived up to its name, simply by still being here.

No worries about predators in New Hope. Unless you counted Adam.

This was one of those November days where the sun didn't set so much as fade away without even a whimper of surrender. There were only four cars in the Safeway's lot and he recognized three of them. One of them was Mrs. Chesshir's bright yellow vintage VW bug. He edged through the hazy gray light, wincing when he stepped into a mound of slush and ice, the cold water rushing into his shoe. The icy wet made him walk funny as if he had a limp.

A familiar form approached from the bright lights of the store, a woman juggling two cloth shopping bags and a large paper bag. Mrs. Chesshir. The last teacher he ever had. Back in fourth grade. The perfect fish. All he had to do was reel her in.

Adam hesitated. Not because he was afraid. No way. That churning in his stomach was just hunger. Even if he was afraid—and he wasn't, of course he wasn't—he wouldn't ever let it show.

His dad had hammered it into him: never admit fear. Deny it. Smile. Make eye contact. Offer help or a compliment. Get them to say yes—to anything. Hunch your shoulders so you don't look so damn tall and intimidating. Be polite. Never say "I" always say "we."

Seven steps to getting just about anything you wanted. All you had to do was follow Dad's rules.

Mrs. Chesshir stopped and nodded to the leg he hobbled on, ice water squishing between his toes. "Are you okay?"

She startled him. He forgot all about the approach he meant to make. "Mrs. Chesshir. You remember me?"

"Of course. It's good to see you, Adam."

She recognized him right away even though he'd been gone four years. The thought swept through him like a fever. She hadn't changed—still the bright smile that lit her eyes, the glossy dark hair that swung below her shoulders. Back when he was a kid, he'd kinda fallen in love with her.

Fantasized she'd be the one to rescue him. Adam knew better now. He needed to rescue himself.

"Here. Let me carry those." Treat her like a fish. Follow Dad's rules. Before she could protest, he lifted the brown paper bag and one of the canvas ones from her arms.

"Why thank you. Are you home visiting?" She didn't ask about his dad and he didn't volunteer. Never volunteer information, Dad always said.

"Yes ma'am. Got an uncle and cousins over in Huntingdon, but when the bus stopped here, well, I couldn't resist—"

Too late he realized his mistake. Huntingdon was too close. There was a good chance she knew he didn't really have relatives there. Stupid. Barely off the bus and he'd already screwed up. Good thing Dad wasn't here to see it.

Adam shuffled his feet as she opened the trunk of her VW, the bag crinkling restlessly as he hugged it. He bowed his head as he thought hard about how to fix his mistake.

"Such a shame about your mother. She was a brave woman," Mrs. Chesshir filled in the silence. "You came to pay your respects?"

Adam swallowed hard and nodded. She patted his hand and looked away as if she thought he was crying. He wasn't, but after he placed the groceries into the trunk he swiped his bare knuckles, white with the cold, across his cheeks. Dad could cry on command—so could Morgan. Adam never mastered the trick.

"Do you need a ride?" she asked. "I don't mind. It's on the way."

A lie. The churchyard where his mom's marker stood— they'd never found her body or any of the others—was a good two miles out of her way. But that was just the way folks were here in New Hope. A third of the population was Amish or Mennonite, the rest farmers and merchants or folks looking to get out of the city and live in the middle of nowhere. There was no industry except the fruit stands and craft fairs that popped up during summer tourist season. Not that they ever brought the town much revenue. The only tourists who found their way to New Hope were hopelessly lost, usually took the wrong turn on their way to a Penn State football game or tailgate party.

"No. Thanks. I'd—I'd rather walk."

"I understand." She clasped his hand, folding a five-dollar bill into it. "You know you can call me anytime. If you need anything."

Stunned by the unexpected kindness, he nodded and said nothing. He wouldn't be calling her. He didn't have a phone. Too easy to track, Dad said. Although he let Morgan keep the smart phone Morgan lifted from a Starbucks they'd been walking past. Like watching a magic trick. Morgan laughing, telling a story, hands gesticulating. The phone on a table, then in a hand, zip, it went in the backpack and vanished. Dad had smiled.

He never smiled like that at Adam. Not anymore. It was always Morgan, younger than Adam, but perfect in Dad's eyes. Unlike Adam.

Not for long. He was going to make Dad notice. Make him proud.

"Welcome home, Adam," Mrs. Chesshir said. Then she got in her car and left.

Adam stood in the mostly empty parking lot of the Safeway, snow melting through the hole in his shoe, fear making his insides shiver.

Five minutes back in New Hope and he was already falling apart. Maybe Dad was right. Maybe Adam was hopeless.

He wondered, not for the first time, if he'd been wrong about everything.

-

The whistle blew. Megan ran over from the sidelines, lifting her muddy cleat against the Subaru's front bumper to retie it. "You made it. Any word from Dad?"

No one else would have noticed the undercurrent of longing in her voice, but to Lucy it was louder than the firing range during recertification week. "Sorry, sweetie. He's working late again."

Two months ago it would have been Nick making that excuse for Lucy's tardiness. But when the VA clinic cut back its staff, Nick's private practice contracted to take their overflow. With more and more soldiers needing Nick's expertise, he just couldn't refuse.

Megan bobbed her head, focused on her shoelaces. "Okay. Did you see me take that penalty kick? I nailed it."

"You sure did." Despite the rain and mud covering Megan, Lucy pulled her into a quick hug. "I'm so proud of you." She wasn't talking about soccer and Megan knew it.

Over the past two months Megan had become Lucy's anchor, keeping her connected to the outside world, despite Lucy's ever-growing litany of damn good reasons to stay inside, lock the doors, and keep the guns loaded and at the ready.

"What's wrong?" Megan asked suspiciously. Hard to fool the daughter of a FBI agent trained in both undercover work and interrogation techniques. Even harder to fool the daughter of a psychologist specializing in post-traumatic stress. And Megan was her father's daughter in so many ways: extroverted, trusting, smart, empathic.

Too bad Nick wasn't here to see it.

"I came to take you home. Something's come up."

"Mom," Megan said with a well-practiced adolescent whine that reminded Lucy of the defense attorney who tried to skewer her testimony an hour ago. "I'm one of the only girls invited. I can't leave early."

This really wasn't the time or place to explain, and last thing Lucy wanted was to have a public confrontation with Megan. She opened the passenger door to the Subaru, hoped Megan would take the hint. "I don't like this. You playing in the cold. You'll get sick."

Megan was merciful, sparing Lucy an eye roll. Instead she sighed, as if she were the long-suffering mother, patted Lucy's arm, and said, "I'm fine." She dribbled an invisible ball with her feet, impervious to the freezing rain and wind. "You can watch from the car if you want. Or go home. I'll catch a ride with Danny."

As if Lucy would ever trust her thirteen-year-old alone with a twenty-something soccer coach. Especially not one who encouraged his athletes to call him "Danny."

Her phone rang, distracting her just as the whistle blew again.

"Gotta go." Megan raced into the crowd of parents and players before Lucy could grab her.

Lucy kept Megan in sight as she answered the phone. It was Walden. Hopefully good news.

"Guardino," she answered. "What have you got?"

"No trace on the letter. The envelope, about what you'd expect." Of course. Send a threatening letter through the US Mail and you'd tie up fingerprint analysts for days with the number of random partials. "Taylor's at your house, just finished clearing it."

"Nick?"

"He's fine. Still at work. Galloway is with him, will see him home. He's not too happy about the whole thing. Especially us monitoring his mail."

"I'll take care of it." It wasn't the monitoring or the security detail that bothered Nick. It was the fact that Lucy's work placed her family at risk. Again. She didn't realize she'd sighed out loud until it echoed back to her through the cell phone.

"I think I calmed him down," Walden added. A big guy, intimidating as hell when he had to be, but whenever they needed to play good cop/bad cop, Walden was always the good cop, the sane one. The sight of a six-two, two-twenty black guy being unable to control a petite white woman fifteen years his junior got a subject's attention, fast. "We had a little heart to heart."

Lucy shook her head. Nick and Walden, talking about her. She so didn't want to know. "Thanks, Walden."

"Finally found your mom as well. She's with her gentleman friend. Said not to worry about her."

That warranted another sigh, but Lucy swallowed it before Verizon could broadcast her feelings to the world. She pulled her copy of the anonymous letter from her pocket and scanned it again for clues. "What does he mean, we blamed the wrong man? I saw the killer die."

"No body was ever recovered. Plus, we never identified the Unsub. Makes it easy for crackpots to try to grab credit." Walden, logical as always.

"He mentions Megan by name. And he knows how old she is."

"Your name's been in the news a lot lately."

"My name." Lucy used her maiden name everywhere, but Megan was Megan Callahan, Nick's name. "Not Megan's. Or her age."

"Taylor says any kid with a smart phone and five minutes online could find Megan's name and age. Said he could get her shoe size if you gave him ten minutes." Taylor was their resident whiz kid when it came to computers—when it came to almost anything except people. He was thirty-four, a recent graduate from the High-Tech Computer Crimes Taskforce before attending Quantico, and would be called "kid" until the day he retired.

Walden dropped his voice. "The New Hope case was four and a half years ago. Maybe you mentioned Megan to someone back then? Trying to bond with local law enforcement or a witness?"

"No. I never talk about my family with anyone on a case. Not my real family, at any rate." Part of Lucy's job was to slip into roles. Pretend to understand and offer forgiveness for the pedophile's urges while interviewing them at their kitchen table, the computer screensaver flashing porn from the countertop as they sipped iced tea. Playing at being a lonely pre-pubescent girl or boy in Internet chat rooms. Going undercover as a mom offering her child's services as a "model."

Lucy understood the kind of persona needed for a given situation. Just like in court today. And she was very good at slipping them on and off again, like trying on outfits in a dressing room. Sometimes Nick said she was too good at it, that she liked to push the edge to get the result she wanted. She couldn't really argue with that. Nick was also good at his job and his job was to see the truth behind the veil of lies.

"I skimmed the case file on New Hope," Walden said. "Didn't see anything out of the ordinary. Other than the fact we had no DNA to compare."

"What did Greally say?" John Greally had been one of her field supervisors when she graduated from the FBI Academy and was now Assistant Special Agent in Charge of the Pittsburgh field office. But he hadn't been involved with the New Hope case. She wished he had been. Hamilton, her supervisor on New Hope, was an asshole. More interested in headlines and commendations than the truth. "Is he going to move my family into protective custody?"

It was Walden's turn to sigh.

"They can't blow this off—"

"They're not. Galloway's opening a case file. She'll handle it personally since it comes under the Postal Service's jurisdiction."

Lucy was sure Jenna Galloway was perfectly competent with a letter opener, but with her family involved she'd rather have someone she knew and trusted—a *real* agent—on the case.

Walden continued, "Greally doesn't have the manpower or funding for a full security detail. He also suggested since you were up for your semi-annual eval next week that you do it tomorrow, then take some time off. Mentioned that Cancun is lovely this time of year and you have plenty of vacation coming."

Like Lucy was going to lie on a beach sipping margaritas while her team did the heavy lifting and her family was at risk. "He's at least re-opening the New Hope case, right? Are we taking the lead on it?"

Silence.

"Walden—"

"He tried, Lucy. But like you said, witnesses saw the killer die. Case closed. There's nothing in that letter someone couldn't find reading the news accounts of the case."

"We never found his body. Or maybe he had a partner." Still, it made no sense. Why come after her, announce his presence, after all this time? No. This was about something else. She was sure of it.

Walden echoed her thoughts. "Maybe it has nothing to do with the New Hope case. It could be someone out to sabotage your career by casting doubts on your work."

Lucy thought about that. She had risen through the ranks quickly and inadvertently made enemies along the way. Including her former supervisor. It would also explain why the letter was so vague on specifics. A true sociopath looking for glory would have built his case, boasted about the details the original investigation had gotten wrong. Whoever wrote the letter seemed like he wanted something, and it wasn't fame or credit.

He wanted something from Lucy. He'd succeeded in frightening her, but to what end? More importantly, how much danger was her family in?

Walden continued, "Greally couldn't sign off on a protective detail but there's no way in hell either Galloway or Taylor will leave their posts."

Her people. Loyal—to a fault. She had to protect them, so if things went bad they didn't get caught in the crossfire. "Thanks, Walden."

"You can thank me tonight. Nick invited me to dinner. Said you were getting pizza from Travanti's. I like mine with mushrooms and black olives."

Lucy hung up the phone. Her family was safe for tonight. But what about tomorrow?

Chapter 3

Five dollars wasn't enough to buy everything on Adam's list, so he did what he planned to do in the first place: steal what he needed.

He hated doing it. It was clear from the half-stocked shelves and empty aisles Mr. Cooperman wasn't doing well. Adam promised himself he'd pay back everything after he found his dad. Dad always had money; that was never a problem. The problem was getting him to spend it.

Adam splurged and spent part of the five dollars on a luxury item not on his list: a container of chocolate milk. By the time he left the Safeway, it was almost six and already full dark. The wind cut through the narrow street, teasing him with the threat of snow, but he was warm enough in his layers. Except for his hands and feet. He wasn't sure if those would ever be warm again.

He could have stolen a car, but didn't want to risk it. It was only a mile or so. He walked through downtown on Main Street, actually the only street that ran through the three blocks New Hope called downtown.

Downtown—heck, the entire town—was never what you'd call busy, but it was different now.

The real estate office had closed. The colors on its flyers in the window had faded from time and the glare of the sun, as if it'd been a joke to start with. Henderson's florist's shop was now a coffee shop, and from the lights on the second floor of the century old brick building, they'd either rented out the apartment there or they'd left their nursery and moved into town. He hoped it wasn't the second. He remembered running through their fields of lavender, swishing the fragrant stems, his palms smelling like fresh beginnings.

He drank his milk and ate a shoplifted Slim Jim. Wondered how many times his dad had been out on these streets alone at night, heading into the darkness. Adam was glad he hadn't taken a car. Dad always said cars were nice when you needed them, but no one ever got arrested for walking.

Following in Dad's footsteps. That was his plan. Tonight he would set up camp in his hidey-hole. The letter should have reached Lucy by now. Hopefully she and the other cops would be here by tomorrow—the next day at the latest. Then the TV and reporters.

And finally, Dad. Dad would hear the news, know it was Adam. He'd come and get him, take him back.

Maybe even smile that secret smile that said he was proud of his boy. Adam would about kill for a glimpse of that smile.

As he walked, imagining the look of pride on Dad's face, Adam didn't feel the cold anymore.

He reached the end of the sidewalk and began walking along the curb, one foot in front of the other, balancing, arms stretched wide, like he had when he was a kid.

Then he came across something surprising: A traffic light instead of the old four-way stop sign at the intersection of Main and Route 4004. The new light blinked amber in one direction and red in the other.

It seemed out of place given the only traffic as far as the eye could see was Adam walking west and the taillights of a truck headed south. But somehow it fit. That was New Hope, never giving up on tomorrow.

He crossed the street, no longer Main Street, now just a nameless county road, and found another change. The old Dairy Treat had been remodeled. It boasted a large sign out front: Huntingdon County Sheriff's Department. The lights were off, the parking lot empty. Only one lone streetlamp between the front door and the curb lit the squat cinderblock building.

Adam stepped over a mound of snow at the edge of the lot and crossed over neatly plowed macadam to the front door. It had the sheriff's star in gold, shining against the blackness beyond the glass door. *Office hours 8am to 4pm, closed weekends and holidays. In case of emergency call 911. Please ring bell for assistance.*

They never had a police department in New Hope. Never thought they needed one. Not until four years ago. Then he spotted the small brass plaque mounted on the wall beside the door. It read: *In memory of Marion Caine.*

It didn't list any of the other dead women. They never found the bodies, so he guessed they couldn't confirm their names. But Lucy had had a list of possibilities.

He traced his fingers over his mother's name. The people of New Hope thought she was a hero. The cold stung his eyes as anger mixed with grief. He pounded his fist sideways against the plaque, punching his mother's name so hard the embossed letters embedded themselves in his flesh.

He loved his mother. He missed his mother. But she wasn't a hero. She'd chosen to go there, even though she knew what she was risking. She'd chosen. Chosen to leave Adam. Chosen death.

Her voice wove through his anger, calming and soothing as it always did. "I can't help myself, baby," she said in that singsong she used whenever she wanted his forgiveness. "Can't help what I do. I just love the man so much."

They'd hug and cry and he'd forgive her. Because he knew exactly what she felt. Like her, he'd do anything for his dad.

He just loved the man so much.

–

Most nights Lucy loved walking into their house, a renovated Victorian on a decent sized lot, nestled in the slopes of West Homestead. So much so, that some mornings lately, it took everything she had to force herself to leave the safe haven of her family.

Tonight as she pulled past Taylor sitting in a gray Taurus, blending into the rain and mist, she felt anything but tranquil. Her teeth ground together while she turned the ignition off, searching the premises for any danger before leaving the vehicle.

Megan, of course, had no such anxieties. She bounded from the car with her usual noise and energy. Lucy lunged across the seats to stop her, but it was too late. All she could do was grab the pizzas and hustle after her daughter, one hand on her weapon.

Not exactly the homecoming she'd envisioned when she left for work this morning. She walked inside the kitchen, following the trail of discarded clothing and soccer equipment Megan left in her wake. Megan made it as far as the hallway before succumbing to the need to fall on the floor and play with Zeke, her new Australian shepherd puppy. Boots, the orange tabby Megan had adopted, looked on in disdain.

"I still don't get why I couldn't go with everyone else. Just because I'm the youngest shouldn't mean I can't hang out with everyone else on the team," Megan said when she came up for air.

"Please come clean up your mess." Lucy sidestepped another argument as she deposited the pizzas on the counter and put her guns away. She used to safe the Glocks first, but after September, she now left one loaded on top of the refrigerator and the other in her bag. She kept another in the nightstand upstairs. Nick hated having loaded weapons in the house, but Megan was a better shot and more responsible about them than he was. He refused to do more than learn how to handle a pistol safely, so he suffered in silence.

"In a minute." Megan's voice was muffled by puppy slurping.

"Now, please. Your dad will be home in a few minutes and he's bringing company."

"Company? Who?"

"Walden."

"Cool. I like his stories." Everyone Lucy worked with fascinated Megan, although she acted terminally bored if Lucy dared to mention work herself. Megan appeared in the kitchen, puppy in arms. "He really misses his wife, doesn't he?"

"Yes. She died over Thanksgiving, so this is a tough time of year for him."

"Then he should come to dinner more often. He promised to teach me how to make sweet potato pie." She reached for the top box of pizza but Lucy shooed her away.

"Feed the animals, pick up your clothes, and get cleaned up."

Now came the inevitable eye roll. "Yeah, yeah, yeah."

"Homework?"

"Done." Megan poured food and fresh water for the animals, then scooped up her discarded items on her way past Lucy, shoulders slumped as if the dirty shin guards and sweatshirt weighed more than Sisyphus's boulder.

Lucy couldn't resist. She grabbed Megan from behind, planted a loud kiss on the top of her head before she could escape. "Love you, Sugar Lou."

"Mom." Megan pulled free. "I'm not a baby anymore."

"I know," Lucy whispered as Megan clomped up the stairs, leaving Lucy alone with the gobbling puppy and the cat eying the pizzas.

–

"Exactly how serious is this?" Nick punctuated his question by waving his slice of pepperoni-sausage-onions in the air. "All this was just routine precaution, standard operating procedure, right?"

Lucy exchanged glances with Walden. He shoved another bite of pizza in his mouth, leaving her to break the bad news. Probably better that way, anyway.

"Nick, Megan," she began. Megan looked up, still sulky from being forced to skip the after-practice get together with her soccer teammates. "I'm not trying to scare you, but we need to take this seriously."

"But you guys get threats all the time," Megan protested. "Like you always say, the world's filled with crazy people." She caught herself. "Sorry, Dad. You know what I mean."

"This one's different. I think we should go away for awhile—"

Megan stood so fast she almost knocked her plate off the table. "No! Mom, I'm not missing soccer. It's not fair! You can't make me."

"Megan Constance Callahan," her father admonished in a voice he seldom used. "Sit down and listen to your mother. She knows how much soccer means to you, but your safety comes first."

"Can't we move to a hotel or something?" Megan asked in a calmer voice, hands folded together, mirroring her father's posture. "And you could give me a bodyguard. How about Taylor? He's cool. No one would ever think he's with the FBI."

"Hope you never tell him that," Walden said with a smile.

Taylor prided himself on being a "G-man" and dressing the part. No matter it made him look more like a junior advertising exec than a federal agent.

"This isn't like the movies, Megan," Lucy protested.

"Wait. She has a point. We could move out of the house. My office has plenty of space."

Lucy stared at her husband. He often accused her of falling into the psychological trap of denial, but now who wasn't facing facts? Thankfully Walden took this one.

"That might be problematic. It's the first place anyone would look for you."

Nick straightened, his posture rigid. "I'm not abandoning my patients."

"Nick—"

"Not negotiable, Lucy. This family has sacrificed a lot for your job. Moving, changing schools, even—" His Adam's apple bobbed as he glanced in Megan's direction.

Lucy reached across the table for his hand, knowing he was remembering September.

He slid free of her grasp, grabbing his napkin instead and wadding it into a tight rock. "Even missing time with you because of your devotion to your victims and their cases. You can't ask me to be any less devoted to my patients. They're counting on me to be there for them and I'm not letting them down."

There was nothing she could say to that except guilty on all charges. She had uprooted them time and again because of her job. When she took the promotion here in Pittsburgh, she promised them she would be home on time and take less risks—exactly what the FBI wanted of her as well. Yet here she was, putting their lives on the line. Again.

She couldn't ask more of them. And, as much as she'd like to, she couldn't keep them locked up forever. The best she could do was find the bastard behind this, whether it was someone inside the Bureau gunning for her job or some psycho-nut out on the streets taking potshots at her.

"Okay," she surrendered. For now. She'd figure out some way to keep them under surveillance.

Nick jerked his chin up, eyes narrowed in suspicion. Megan hopped up from the table and leapt to Lucy's side and hugged her.

Walden caught her eye as he calculated how to free up manpower to form an unofficial protection unit, and took another chomp out of his pizza. "We'll make it work," he said after he swallowed.

Lucy pushed away her half-eaten slice, no longer hungry.

Chapter 4

Once he left the road and entered the shelter of the Stolfultz's cornfields, Adam's fear eased. No one could hurt him, not once he made it to his special spot, his thinking cave.

He was only ten when he first found it, running away from a pair of bullies who chased him on their bikes from the school playground on the other side of the farm. Using the terrain to his advantage, he ducked over and under fences, letting the July-high corn cover his tracks, and finally escaped into the woods.

New Hope lay in the narrow end of the valley, sand-wiched between two forks of Warrior Ridge. Limestone caverns riddled the ridge, some of them extending for miles beneath the surface. Grownups warned kids all the time not to go into the caves. There were terrible campfire stories about kids who wandered inside the mountain, never to return.

Like the two teens that broke into Echo Cavern on a dare, climbing over the wrought iron padlocked gate that guarded its entrance. Adam had only been eight at the time, but he still remembered the look of stricken grief on the faces of the adults when they brought out one kid on a stretcher, his leg bent at a horrible angle, crying for his friend who'd fallen down a crevasse.

They never found the second boy's body.

Adam was a cautious kid. The bullies called him scaredy cat because he liked to think about all the angles before committing himself to action. His dad just called him slow. But on that July day, running through the woods even though his pursuers had long ago given up, he'd done something brave and bold. Like his dad. He went into a cave.

Not just any cave. This one was hidden. Secret. Its entrance blocked from view by a tall rectangular boulder. You'd never guess if you ducked your head and held your elbows by your side that two steps later you'd be in a wide open space, cool and sheltered and safe.

That was just the antechamber. The foyer, Adam called it, liking the idea of his cave being a home. There was the master bedroom—his room—just off the foyer, the floor smooth and sloped up just enough so it was never wet even when it was storming outside, a rock the perfect size to use as a table or bed, natural ledges in the walls to store his stuff.

His cave wasn't as big or deep as Echo Cavern, but it was perfect for Adam. Beyond the foyer was a tiny stream. Depending on the time of year, anywhere from a trickle to wide enough you'd have to jump across the cold, fresh water. Crawl over and around some boulders and rock ledges and you could follow the stream down to a wider cavern inside the belly of the mountain. There were giant stalactites and deposits of zinc sulfide that glowed, making the whole place spark with magic.

The stream was wider here, rushing and noisy, and a tiny bit dangerous—enough to make the journey an adventure. If you crossed over to the other side and scrambled up through a hole in the wall, there was a second entrance.

This one shielded by a wall of tumbled boulders too high for Adam to climb when he traced the outside opening, but it was nice to have the additional sunlight coming in from above. Inside the second entrance was a sudden drop off, a trap for the unwary.

Adam spent most of one summer—his last summer in New Hope, although he hadn't known it then—exploring that pit. He'd been obsessed with it. With the possibilities of an endless chasm that could transport him deep to the center of the earth, just like in the books he loved to read, old ones by Jules Verne and Edgar Rice Burroughs and Arthur Conan Doyle and HG Wells.

He'd been disappointed to find it was only around ten feet deep. Just a shimmy down a strong rope he eventually replaced with a ladder borrowed from Stolfultz's barn. That was okay. Other adventures waited at the bottom of the pit. He'd found a bunch of arrowheads, a mound of charcoal, the outline of a man's hand in what appeared to be dried blood, and a bone that looked just like the shinbone on the human skeleton in the science classroom at school.

Lying on the cold, hard floor of the pit, his head filled with amazing stories: Indians using his cave as their last outpost against a warring tribe, or maybe settlers defending themselves against marauding Indians; outlaws chased by a posse, only to starve to death down here when they couldn't climb back out. Adam dug for treasure, but the floor was hard, unyielding, and he did little more than scratch at it.

He never did find any other bones—another mystery that made the pit irresistible.

Adam stockpiled his cave with survival necessities. He used his mom's Space Age Air Tite storage bags to protect his stash: a sleeping bag, matches, disposable lighters, a bunch of candles of all sizes and shapes, comic books and books and magazines, a whole bag of Hershey's miniatures he was saving for a special treat, cans of soda, bottles of water, cans of his favorite foods: tuna fish and Dinty Moore and baked beans and Spaghettios, a notebook and pencils, spare clothes, one of his dad's pocket knives, a couple of flashlights with spare batteries, and the neatest thing of all: a little radio/flashlight that you powered with a hand crank. The only station it got was one that talked about the weather and then only outside the cave, but still pretty cool.

At least he thought so when he was ten. Now he just hoped those space age bags really had protected his stuff—and that no one had taken it—so he could get a good night's sleep, nestled warm and safe inside his sleeping bag.

Maybe even read one of his old *Mad* magazines. Would they still be funny?

He stopped at the edge of the woods. He trusted himself not to get lost, but the forest that seemed so welcoming and friendly when he was a kid now looked dark and menacing. He risked turning on the tiny keychain LED flashlight stolen from the Safeway but it didn't help.

Was anything the way he remembered it? It was as if he'd lost himself during the past four years. Not just grown up. Like he wasn't who he thought he was and never had been. It was all a dream—no, not a dream, he'd definitely been awake, had the scars to prove it—maybe a mirage?

Guided by the narrow beam of light, his footsteps crunched through dead leaves and tinder, releasing the scent of hemlock and pine and decay.

If he wasn't who he thought he was, then who was he? With each footstep one answer echoed through his mind: his father's son.

His father would disagree. Had disagreed when he left Adam, abandoned him as a failure and ran off with Morgan in tow.

This was Adam's last chance to prove him wrong.

—

"We shouldn't have included Megan in our discussion." Lucy grabbed the mouthwash and rinsed while Nick flossed beside her at the bathroom sink. He always had so much more patience than her. Would floss each tooth twice then brush for the full two minutes, no cheating. Lucy used a kid's toothbrush with a noisy timer to keep her honest. But her dentist said it helped keep her TMJ symptoms down, especially since she kept losing or breaking night splints.

Nick pulled the floss free. "After September, we need to give her some sense of control over her life. Besides, she's thirteen now—"

"That doesn't make her an adult—"

"You don't think *I'm* adult enough to have been included in our discussion." He snapped the floss one last time, the string so tight his fingers went white. "You wanted me to cave in, do whatever you damn well wanted."

She yanked the toothbrush from her mouth and spat. The motor kept whining, flinging toothpaste all over the mirror. She turned it off. The sudden silence made the small room feel even smaller.

"Doing what I damn well wanted would ensure your and Megan's safety. I don't see how that's a mistake." She wiped her face on one of their mismatched towels. Her jaws were clenched so tight, lightning crackled along the nerves into her ears. So much for controlling the TMJ.

Nick saw it too. He dropped the floss into the waste can and stood behind her, his fingers expertly massaging the tension away from her neck and jaw. Slowly the pain eased. "I know you want what's best for us, but being locked away in a jail of our own making isn't going to keep us safe. Especially not Megan, not at her age. The more you try to protect her, the more she'll try to fight free."

She leaned back into his healing warmth. "Maybe. But the New Hope case—"

Her shoulders tightened and he laid his palms down on them, pressing gently until the muscles relaxed.

"You never told me what happened." He sounded hurt.

She opened her mouth then shut it again. She didn't want to make an excuse. And she wasn't ready to dissect those memories.

Their eyes met in the mirror. His calm, waiting. Hers tight with worry.

"Have you considered that maybe the emotions you associate with the New Hope case are making you over-react?" His work voice. She hated when he used it on her. Not because he might treat her like a patient, but because when he got all calm and reasonable, he was usually right.

"You think I overreacted?" The thought hadn't even occurred to her. Although Lord only knew, she was prone to jumping in first, figuring out the details later. She trusted her gut instinct. It's what kept her alive and successful as a street agent. Now that she sat behind a desk, her greatest strength had become her greatest liability.

Maybe she had overreacted. She abandoned all thoughts of dental hygiene and sat down on the toilet. "What do you think of the note? Professionally?"

He thought about it for a long moment. His eyes turned paler than their usual gray as he focused on a distant point, chin tilted so a stray lock of sandy colored hair fell into his face. "From what I read in the papers, the man behind the New Hope case was some kind of mastermind, able to elude police for years, getting away with kidnapping, rape, and murder. When you cornered him, he killed himself, taking his last victim with him rather than let you rescue her... Classic malignant narcissistic personality."

"What if the letter's right and that wasn't really the killer down in that cave?" Impossible. She'd seen the man plunge to his death, taking Marion Caine with him. But her job was to explore every possibility—no matter how remote.

"Then the New Hope Killer was even more brilliant if he was able to fool you and escape. First of all, why call that to your attention after all this time? Second, look at the letter. Whoever wrote it has the emotional IQ of a child Megan's age. There's no evidence of true narcissism or sociopathy. Despite the melodramatic language, the intent seems almost the opposite. It's not about 'look at me, I fooled you, I'm brilliant.' This letter is more like a cry for help.

"My bet is you'll get another letter in a few days telling you the real reason they need help. Then another hinting at their location or identity. Breadcrumbs to get you to come rescue them. Whoever sent that letter is no killer. That much I'm certain of."

She traced the hexagonal black and white tiles with her toe. Nick was right. The letter was childish. Attention-getting more than threatening.

"You said it sounded like a kid. If so, I know who sent it."

"Who?"

"Adam Caine."

"The boy whose mom died?"

She nodded. It had to be Adam. He'd be what, fourteen, now? And she may have mentioned Megan to him while trying to comfort him in the aftermath of his mother's death.

"But why?" she asked. Adam could have easily picked up the phone, called her. There was no reason for playing games.

Nick misunderstood her question. "Lucy, you're a hero. Who else would he send it to?"

If only he hadn't said that. Not that way, his voice filled with pride. She looked away, her gaze zeroing in on the corner below the tub where the grout had turned dingy gray because she never took the time to properly get into the tight area when scrubbing and do the job right.

Just like she hadn't in New Hope.

"Hey, what's wrong?" Nick said. He crouched down to her level and tipped her chin towards him.

Tears choked her throat. She swallowed them without allowing any to come to the surface. Shook her head. Blinked hard as her gaze scoured the rest of the tiny room, seeking out further evidence of her housekeeping failures. Looking anywhere except at him.

"I'm no hero," she muttered, pushing to her feet and marching out to the bedroom, leaving him behind. She dreaded the day when she'd have to finish the sentence, tell him the truth about what happened in New Hope. Everything that happened. And didn't.

The day when she'd confess she was a coward.

Maybe that's why Adam sent the letter. He finally realized Lucy was to blame for his mother's death.

Chapter 5

The cave was a constant fifty-six degrees year round, so Adam didn't bother with a fire. Especially after finding his stuff sealed up just fine, except for a few books animals had nested in. Huddled at his table in his bedroom, wrapped in his sleeping bag, he examined his belongings. Everything he needed. Unless he had to stay here more than a few days.

Dad said never plan too far ahead. "It'll only break your heart."

Better to learn how to improvise, go with the flow. Something Dad relished. Morgan, too. Sometimes the two of them would start riffing and lie to fish just for the fun of it. Adam couldn't do that. He liked to have a plan—at least the inkling of one—and he craved routine, security.

Two things Dad scoffed at. "You guys are the luckiest kids in the world," he'd proclaim as they left one town for the next. "I'm giving you the whole wide world. How many fathers do that for their kids? No one. No one except me."

He'd honk the horn to punctuate the sentiment and smile expectantly at Adam and Morgan. That smile was a starter gun, triggering a competition to outdo each other with their thank-yous. Morgan always won, of course.

Adam liked Morgan, but he liked it better when it was just him and Dad. Until two years ago when he took a growth spurt and started scaring the fish. That's when Dad began checking in on his other kids. They even came back here to New Hope—although Dad made sure no one saw them—before Dad decided it was time for Morgan to start learning the family business.

They didn't come back to New Hope after that. Adam wondered how the kids here were doing. He was their big brother. He should make sure they were all right. Dad would want that. Family was everything to Dad.

He glanced at his watch in the light from the wind-up flashlight. Almost midnight. A good time to check on the kids without anyone seeing him. He was tired but the more he thought about seeing his half-brothers and sister, the more he wanted to. It had been months since he felt a real connection to anyone, especially a bond like what he had with Dad. He missed that so much, his insides ached as bad as when he got food poisoning after dumpster diving in Cleveland.

Adam re-dressed in his layers, adding a black Steelers knit cap turned inside out to cover his light hair. The cap was a little small—he'd been ten when he last wore it—but it stretched enough to fit.

While he sorted through the old clothing, he found the first paracord bracelet he ever made. Mrs. Chesshir had taught the class how to weave the special knots. Some of the other boys laughed, saying it was like knitting. Knowing how to make the bracelets kept him alive in Cleveland. Not just selling them for a few bucks on the street, but having something to do. A purpose.

The bracelet had been too big for him back then. He'd used about ten feet of paracord, way too much. Now it fit just right. And it was red—Dad's favorite color. That had to be a good omen. He slipped it on, then grabbed his knife and the duct tape he'd taken from the Safeway, the roll smooshed flat to fit in his pocket without making a bulge.

Be prepared, Dad always said. Just like the Boy Scouts.

–

He came out of the woods behind the elementary school and headed west along Pine Avenue. He didn't pass a single soul on the way and only saw the headlights of one car in the distance, but it turned before drawing near.

Marty and Darrin lived a couple of blocks away from each other, but their houses were very different. Marty and his mom had a brick ranch house with a small yard and carport and a rope swing dangling from a big old maple in the backyard.

Darrin lived up the hill in a house that stood all alone, surrounded by forest as it glared down at the town below. Darrin's house was built in layers like a wedding cake cut in half and welded to the side of the hill, all glass and wood and steel beams jutting out.

No one in New Hope liked Darrin's house. Or Darrin's mom's husband who built it.

When Adam was about Darrin and Marty's age, six, Mom got sick for the first time and had her surgery. Then chemo. Dad stayed home, took care of her, worked only local deliveries during those two years before she was strong enough to handle him leaving on long-distance hauls.

Adam still remembered her crying the first time Dad left. But he came home with a new fish and things changed. Mom had something to do, taking care of the fish when Dad was gone. Sometimes there was more than one. Then she began to go fishing with Dad, leaving Adam home alone. He figured out at the time it had something to do with Mom not being able to have any more kids.

Kids were so very important to Dad. Even though half the time he accused Adam of not being his. Usually when Adam messed up. So Adam tried harder to get things right, to do them just like Dad would, make Dad proud of him.

When he did… it was better than Christmas and Easter and summer vacation all wrapped up into one bright moment. He treasured each of those moments, reliving them in his memory, trying to figure out what he did right and how he could win Dad's smile again.

Checking on the little kids, taking care of them for Dad, that would definitely be a step in the right direction. Not as big as reeling in a fish, but close.

He started with Marty's house. Marty's mom's Honda made ticking noises as the engine cooled in the carport. She must have just gotten home from her shift at the hospital. He slid between the brick wall and the hemlocks that lined the front wall of the house. A perfect hiding place to see inside through the wide picture window.

To his surprise, Marty was up. It was way past a little kid's bedtime. Even worse, his mom was yelling at Marty. "Go to bed, young man."

"When's my Daddy coming home? I want my Daddy!" Over and over and over he cried, his wailing so loud, Adam thought the window would shake out of its frame.

Marty's mom hugged him but he fought free. When Marty stopped screaming long enough to drag in a breath, she shouted, "He's not coming back, he's never coming back! Now go to bed before I give you a spanking."

Marty froze. His mouth wide open, his eyes wide. The same look of sheer terror the fish got after Dad hooked them. He ran from the room, his little feet thump-thumping loudly even after he vanished down the hall.

His mom took one step after him.

Anger surged through Adam. She had no right to yell at a little kid like that. Of course he wanted his daddy. Who wouldn't?

If she went after Marty, he'd break in and stop her. He'd been hit too many times. No way would he let his little brother get treated that way. Dad wouldn't stand for it.

But she didn't go after Marty. Instead she collapsed onto the couch, buried her face in her hands, and cried. Adam couldn't stand watching that. He hated women crying—just like Dad—so he left to go check on Darrin.

—

It was a climb up a lonely gravel drive to get to Darrin's house. House, not home. There was nothing warm and homey here. The hill was steep, although nothing compared to the mountain looming above it. Leaving the house always in shadow.

Lights were on in every window. Still it felt gloomier here than down the hill at Marty's home. Colder, too.

Before he chose Morgan, Dad visited Darrin's house more than any of the others. He always came away pinch-eyed and angry. Maybe because Darrin's mom's husband was so rich. Or maybe because he was never home with his family. A lobbyist in DC, he worked there most of the week then would fly his plane back home for the weekend.

Adam once asked Dad why Darrin and his mom didn't live with her husband. And why he'd built such an expensive house way up the side of the mountain when he was never home to use it. Dad said it was because the SOB wanted to build the perfect prison.

That created more questions than answers, but when Dad got that look on his face, you knew better than to keep asking, so Adam shut up and watched as Dad showed him where the security cameras were and how to tell if the alarm was on or not. Every time they checked on Darrin, the alarm had been off, but Adam didn't take any chances. He shimmied his way through snow-covered pine needles to shine his light through the basement window. If he angled his body just right, half way down the window well and stretched to the left, he could see the alarm box. Green light. It was off.

Adam brushed off the dirt and leaves and pine needles then trudged up the hill alongside the house's foundation. The cement blocks stepped up as they formed the wall, but there were no steps for Adam, just a rain-washed patch of dirt. Finally he made it to the rear of the house where the kitchen opened onto a wide deck notched into the side of the mountain. There was no view here, unlike the front of the house that was shaped like a glass boat keel and looked out over the valley. There was also no sunlight except right at noon, making the deck, with its hopeful wooden swing set and playhouse, a dark and dreary place.

Adam heard shouting, just like at Marty's house. Only this time it was a man. Adam climbed over the deck railing and peered in through the kitchen window. A little boy stood beside an open cellar door, his arms filled with sheets. His pajama bottoms were wet. And he was crying.

No frank sobs. But tears shone in the overhead light. He bit his lip, his entire body trembling. And he stood there. Silent.

The man yelling at him wasn't tall, but he was big. Adam smiled at the sight of his belly hanging out between the waistband of his boxers and the bottom of his undershirt. The only times he'd ever seen Darrin's mom's husband before was when he came to town around election day to talk with the farmers. He always looked out of place with his spiffed-up suit and city-shoes. Without the fancy clothes, he looked like anyone else in New Hope. He even had a tattoo: Daffy Duck, hunched forward, hands on his hips. Angry just like his owner.

Mr. Daffy moved his hands up and down as he yelled. Darrin's gaze never left those hands. He knew where the real danger lay.

"Look at me when I'm talking to you! You bedwetting little faggot. You get down there and wash those sheets and filthy clothes so your mother won't have to." He pointed to the open doorway behind the boy and the darkness that lay beyond. The way down to the cellar. Darrin cringed and edged away from the steps.

The man blocked his escape. "Get down there right now. You hear me?"

A woman came in from the front of the house. Darrin's mom. She never left the house, so Adam had only seen her from a distance. Up close, he saw she was younger than Daffy Duck. Dark hair hanging down past her shoulders. Skinny, but big breasts. A good fish. Just the way Dad liked them.

She wore a fancy silk robe and kept twisting the belt as she shuffled into the kitchen, eyes always aimed at her feet, so Adam couldn't really see her face. In the hallway behind her, he caught a glimpse of a girl, about his age. The big sister. She should take better care of her little brother, he thought, glaring at her even though there was no way she could see him in the shadows.

The girl flattened herself against the wall, listening but poised to run away. No fight in her. Just another fish.

"Are you deaf, boy?" The man thundered, raising his fist.

The mother shuffled faster, still not looking up. "Darrin." Her voice was soft but carried. "Listen to your father now."

She joined the man. Together they formed an impenetrable barrier. Darrin looked up at both of them then looked behind him to the dark stairway. The man pointed. Stood there like the grim reaper.

Adam couldn't hear Darrin's sigh of surrender, but he felt it. The way the boy's expression crumbled to the ground as he inched along the fancy tiled floor, focusing on his feet as they climbed down. As soon as he'd gone three steps, the man slammed the door shut behind him and bolted it.

At the noise of the lock clicking, the girl in the hallway sprinted out of sight.

"That will teach him." The man marched down the hall. The woman looked at the cellar door for a long moment. She reached out her hand. Adam thought she might set Darrin free, but she clicked off the lights and followed the man upstairs to bed.

Adam waited until the house went quiet. The back door had a simple spring lock that was no match for his knife. He quietly tiptoed across the kitchen, moving by memory, not daring to use his flashlight, until he bumped into the basement door. He eased the latch, muffling the squeak with his hands, then opened the door.

There was one feeble bulb lighting the space at the bottom of the steps. Directly below it, still in his wet pajamas, was Darrin curled up in a ball. He didn't even look up when Adam came down the steps. The washing machine churned away in the corner and beside it a dryer stood waiting. Unlike the empty, uncluttered kitchen, the space down here was filled with boxes and plastic garbage bags and wooden crates haphazardly jumbled around the floor like someone just kicked them down the steps in any direction. It was too dark to see what was inside any of containers but something smelled bad. Like a small animal had crawled down here to die.

"You okay, Darrin?" Adam crouched down beside the boy and gently touched him on the shoulder.

Darrin tensed but didn't open his eyes. Instead he lay there, holding his breath, waiting for something very bad to happen. How often had Adam lay like that in the group home in Cleveland? Waiting for Rick the Prick to tiptoe into his room, into his bed?

Adam shivered. It was okay. Rick the Prick was never going to touch him again. In fact, once he found Dad and told him, Rick the Prick was going to be missing his dick, real quick.

"I'm not going to hurt you," Adam whispered. "I'm here to help."

Another long moment passed.

Darrin opened his eyes. "Help?"

"Sure. That's what brothers do. They help each other."

"I don't have a brother. All I have is a sister."

"Wrong. You have a lot of brothers. More sisters, too."

Darrin sat up, scrunching his face in confusion. "No. I don't."

"Well, we're half-brothers. Hi, I'm Adam." Adam thrust out his hand. Darrin shook it. He stood and Darrin did as well.

"Is this a dream?"

"Nope. It's all real. But you have to promise not to tell anyone I was here. Can you do that?"

Darrin's face wrinkled even tighter. Then he nodded.

"Good. Then I can stay and help you." Adam looked around the grim space. Darrin hadn't moved from the small circle of light. "You're afraid of the dark, aren't you?"

"Just down here," Darrin admitted. "At night."

"Yeah. I know what you mean. This place creeps me out." Adam went to the dryer. It held a load of freshly washed clothing. He pulled it out. Lots of women's stuff. But then he came to a flannel shirt. Probably the sister's, not Daffy Duck's. Way too big for Darrin, but it was nice and warm. "Here. Put this on and let's throw those wet PJs in the wash."

Darrin turned his back and quickly changed, then shyly handed Adam his soiled pajamas.

"It's okay. Nothing to be ashamed of."

"Dad says I'm a fag because I still wet the bed." Darrin shuffled one bare foot against the rough-hewn cement floor. "He says I'm stupid and my brain is messed up, that's why I never learned how not to."

"You know he's not your real dad, right?"

Darrin nodded, looked over his shoulder towards the stairs. "Yeah. I'm not supposed to talk about my real dad."

"Why not?"

"My mom says he was a bad man. He was killed."

Typical fish. Too stupid to know how lucky she was. She could've ended up like Adam's mom. Dead.

"What if your dad—your real dad—wasn't killed? What if he was on his way here right now to come and get you and take you away? Would you want to go?"

Darrin looked even more frightened. Adam understood that. Hard not to be scared when there was a whole wide world out there and you were stuck in a place like this. But then Darrin nodded. Slowly. Up. Down. Up. Down. "Where?" The single word emerged like a peep from a baby bird.

"Anywhere. Everywhere. You name the place."

"Disney World? We were supposed to go last year but Dad got busy."

"Sure. Disney World."

Darrin looked down again. "I guess. Maybe."

"Good." Adam was half afraid to say anything, but even if the kid talked, who would believe him? "You keep wishing, keep thinking about going to Disney. Keep an eye out for me. And I'll keep an eye out for you."

"But… why? Why are you here? Why are you helping me?" The poor kid sounded empty as if he didn't know the meaning of the word hope. Because nobody ever taught it to him.

Adam crouched down to look Darrin in the eye. He planted both palms on Darrin's shoulders, centering all his attention on the little boy. "Because, Darrin. We're family. And you don't need to worry about Mr. Daffy Duck or wetting the bed or any of that stuff anymore. It's no big deal. Like our dad, our real dad, always says, 'There's always another sunrise waiting around the corner.' Sounds good, don't it?"

"Yeah." Darrin didn't seem totally convinced.

"You just remember. Family first, last, and always. That's our motto." Adam pulled him into a hug. "And you're my family. Never forget that."

Darrin crumbled in his arms, tears wetting Adam's jacket. Adam didn't care. Not at all. Darrin was family.

Chapter 6

Lucy let Nick hold her until he fell asleep. He didn't press her about New Hope but she knew he was hurt by her silence.

She couldn't help it. All she saw every time she thought about the case that built her career was the image of a ten-year-old crying out as he lunged into the blackness, almost moving too fast for Lucy to stop him from following his mother into the abyss.

No kid should have to see that. And it was her fault. Her fault Marion Caine died. Her fault the killer took her with him. Her fault Adam had been there to see it all.

Now it was coming back to haunt her.

As soon as Nick began making the tiny raspy noises he insisted weren't snoring, she slipped out of bed and walked barefoot downstairs, avoiding the creaky one four steps down. Light spilled out from the kitchen. There, feet propped up on a chair, sat Jenna Galloway, the team's newest addition.

Lucy paused in the doorway, not sure she liked how at home Jenna made herself. The same way the postal inspector had waltzed into their office—Lucy's office—and acted as if she'd been there forever. Jenna was young. Late twenties. Thin but not skinny, and had dark red hair, a shade that made men look twice and women envious.

She seemed competent, which was what mattered most to Lucy. Able to carry her weight and not put any of her team at risk.

She was withholding judgment on any more than that. Like Jenna's undercover capabilities, for instance.

"Did you need something?" Jenna asked without looking up from her laptop. She typed with one hand and drank a cup of coffee with the other.

"Thought you were replacing Taylor outside."

"In an hour. He's enjoying some quiet time in the car."

Didn't sound like Taylor. He was more ADHD than Megan's fellow middle-schoolers. "Quiet time?"

Jenna nodded, her coffee mug joining in on the motion. She still didn't look up from her typing. "Actually alone time might be a better word for it. Phone sex with his girlfriend."

Lucy felt a blood vessel at her temple begin to dance. "While on a protective detail? On my family?"

"Hey, it keeps him awake. Not like he's not looking at the street while she's whispering in his ear."

Lucy straightened, ready to step outside until she realized two things. First, she was wearing an old t-shirt and flannel robe and nothing else. And second, Jenna was pulling her leg. Maybe there was hope for the mailman—mailwoman—after all. "Good one."

"Almost had you, didn't I?" Jenna glanced up, a smile crinkling the button nose that matched her creamy skin and ponytail. Jeez, could she be any more all-American girl if she tried? No way in hell she could pass for anything but a sorority girl slumming if she was out on the street undercover.

"Almost." Lucy moved to the refrigerator. She hadn't eaten more than a few bites at dinner and now her stomach rumbled. She grabbed a slice of pizza and poured herself a glass of milk. As she joined Jenna at the table, she saw that the postal inspector had a Pennsylvania map laid out. "What's this for?"

"My trip to New Hope in the morning. I don't trust my GPS." She'd used a pink highlighter to trace her route from Pittsburgh to a small town on the New Jersey border.

Lucy hid her smile with a gulp of milk. Should she tell her? Keeping silent would be the best way to keep Jenna out of her hair while Lucy went to New Hope—the right New Hope.

No. Jenna was part of her team, like it or not. "You might want to re-think that route."

"Why?"

"It's the wrong New Hope."

"No, it's not. There's only one New Hope, PA listed in the zip code directory."

"Sorry, Zippy, but our New Hope is unincorporated. It's under the zip code for Alexandria. And it's smack dab in the center of the state. Here." Lucy pointed to a spot.

Jenna bent over to scrutinize the map. "There's nothing there. I mean literally nothing. Except for one squiggly little road, State Route 4004."

"Where are you from, Jenna?"

"L.A." She turned her attention from the map to her computer. "Wait. I found it on Google Earth. Wow, there are some houses there."

"And an elementary school and some farms, churches, a few shops, a hardware, a grocery store. Believe it or not, folks living in even smaller towns drive into New Hope to do their shopping."

Jenna looked up. "Too small for a police force?"

"Covered by a county sheriff. He and seven deputies cover eight hundred seventy-five square miles."

"That's spread pretty thin. Perfect place for a serial killer to hide."

"Not to mention the limestone caves riddling the mountains. Entrances scattered all over." Lucy pulled the laptop closer. She hadn't tried this before, but given the publicity the New Hope case had gotten, it was a good bet photos had been uploaded to the web. A few keystrokes later she had a selection of images for Jenna.

"That's the padlocked entrance to the cave on Stolfultz's dairy farm. In the old days, their family actually used the front caverns to store their milk and cheese. If you keep going the cavern connects to another system that comes out here."

She clicked on a picture, revealing a nondescript pre-fab hanger. The kind used to store farm equipment or hay bales. Easy to erect, easy to overlook. Except this hanger backed onto an opening into the side of the mountain.

Jenna enlarged the picture, then clicked through to the others, revealing the inside of the hanger with the blue minivan and the cave entrance, taken from just beyond the crime scene tape.

The next image was lit with a flash that made the cave walls look like burnished copper. The light sparked off steel chains bolted into the stone, giving them a festive glow. An overturned five-gallon bucket could be seen on the rough rock of the cave floor. Along with a smear that looked black but Lucy knew was actually blood. Her blood.

She wrapped her arms around her belly, her pizza forgotten.

Another picture showed the ledge above the chasm where Adam's mother and the New Hope Killer plunged to their deaths. The bodies were never recovered, presumed washed into unknown parts by the underground river the chasm opened into. One more showed the collection of MREs, water bottles, night vision goggles and cameras, along with the knives, stun guns, and other instruments of torture the killer used. Lucy wondered who leaked that one. They removed all that as evidence long before any civilian entered the scene.

The next picture was the famous one. The one every newspaper carried. A bit blurry, taken as it was by a cell phone without time to focus, but that only made it more evocative. A skinny boy, face crumpled in grief, supporting Lucy, helping her from the cavern. Her service weapon dangled from one hand, the other gathered to her side, trying to staunch the bleeding.

Jenna made a small noise deep in her throat. Lucy reached past her and clicked the window shut. The postal inspector had replaced the official desktop background with a picture of a young girl riding a horse, jumping a high fence, bright red ponytail streaming from below her helmet. She looked wild and ecstatic and fearless.

"How the hell did you become a mailman?" Lucy blurted out.

Jenna didn't answer. Instead she traced the horse's face with her finger. In the picture she looked around Megan's age—and just as defiant. "Long story. Let's just say it wasn't the path I expected."

Lucy nodded at that. Somehow seeing that picture of the younger Jenna, she started to like the postal inspector. Enough to trust her. A little, at least. "You hooked into NCIC?"

The National Crime Information Center was the clearinghouse for all law enforcement, local, state and federal. Jenna nodded, clicked a few keys. "Sure. What do you need?"

"Run a name for me. Adam Caine. Age—"

"I've got his DOB from the New Hope file. Why him?"

"He sent the letter."

"No shit. He's the kid in the photo, the one whose mom was killed?"

"Yes. Last I knew he and his dad still lived in New Hope."

"Not according to this." Jenna tapped her fingernail against the computer screen. French manicure, of course. Probably had her toes done as well. The last time Lucy had time for a pedicure was two years ago, an anniversary treat from Nick. "Picked up for vagrancy and attempted theft in Cleveland. Put into a group home when they couldn't find any family. Ran away eight months ago. Has a warrant on him. Assault and battery on a counselor."

So Adam was a fugitive. Damn. She'd wished better for him after what he'd been through. "Run his dad, Clinton Caine. He was a truck driver."

The computer did its business. "Nothing. He's clean." Jenna tried another database. "No address listed except a PO Box in Altoona, PA 16601. Want me to dig deeper?"

Four years ago Adam clung to his dad, they seemed so close. She'd only met the man once, but she still remembered the awkward way Clint tried to comfort his son, ignoring the tears streaming down his own face after Lucy told him what had happened to his wife.

Why would Adam run away from his dad? And what did he want from Lucy?

Something was off here. Something that made Lucy's gut instincts do a creepy-crawly dance down her nerve endings.

"Yeah. Start digging. Find Clinton Caine."

Jenna continued typing as Lucy stared at her cold food, one hand massaging the scar on her belly. The wound had been minor, but sometimes it still burned like frostbite. Four years and not finished healing.

Just like Adam Caine.

—

Adam felt pretty good when he left Darrin's. They finished Darrin's laundry while Adam told the kid stories about all the wonderful places Dad had taken him. Then they snuck upstairs, re-made Darrin's bed, and the kid finally fell asleep. As Adam left, he locked the door to the cellar again. Let the fish figure that one out.

He thought about going home to his cave to sleep, but decided to check on Sally first. She and her mom lived in the trailer court just outside of town, not too far out of his way. Besides, he liked Sally. She was the youngest of all his brothers and sisters, hadn't even been born when he and Dad left New Hope. Dad said he wasn't having any more kids, making her the last of the Caines.

As he walked, he found himself whistling an old tune. Something about the moon and stars. A silly song that made him feel light. He couldn't remember hearing a song in his head for such a long time. Couldn't remember feeling anything but fear and anger. Now a new feeling crept in. He was almost afraid to name it; it made him feel dizzy just thinking about it. But talking to Darrin, promising him all the wonderful adventures they'd have when Dad came to get them, had sparked something bigger than fear or anger.

Hope. It felt good, but it also was a little scary—like holding a sharp knife when your fingers were numb with cold. You know you could just as easily cut yourself.

But he hadn't. He'd used the knife to open a door and save Darrin. Just like Dad would've wanted him to. Just like a big brother should.

He arrived at the trailer park and approached Sally's single-wide from the woods behind it. He peeked through the window in the door and saw light flickering like someone watching TV in the dark.

Sally's mom lay across the couch, her shirt open, naked beneath it. A man with dark hair wearing jeans and no shirt lay across her, his face between her breasts. Both passed out. Below the woman's hand a glass pipe had burned a hole in the lime green shag carpet. There were a bunch of holes near it as well.

Adam wrinkled his nose against the sharp stench of cat piss. Crank. Smelled like they were making it as well as smoking it.

He knew about methamphetamine. In Cleveland he'd seen how a binge of meth could lead to a deep crash, folks sleeping for days.

Who was taking care of Sally? She'd only just turned four.

The master bedroom was at the end of the trailer. He couldn't see anyone through the window there except a rumpled bed and clothing thrown everywhere like someone had gone through a frenzy and emptied every drawer and closet. He walked around to the front of the trailer, keeping his footsteps silent despite the gravel coated with frost.

And then he saw her. Sally sat on the cement block steps leading up to the trailer's front door, her knees drawn to her chest, arms hugging them to her body. She wore a pink nightgown, a pink fleece bathrobe, and pink fuzzy fake fur slippers.

"Sally," he said.

She didn't respond at first. Her eyes were open but not focused. He shook her gently. She was freezing. Her face was white, lips dusky, teeth chattering.

Adam sat down beside her. The cold from the cement blocks burned through his jeans. He took off his jacket, then his sweatshirt and bundled Sally inside them both before gathering her onto his lap. A bedraggled stuffed cat that once was white fell from her arms. She'd been hugging it tight to her body as if more worried about it getting cold than herself.

Between the cold bundle in his arms and the night air surrounding him, he was shivering as well. Without moving her, he reached behind him, up to the doorknob and tried to turn it. Locked. "What are you doing out here so late?"

She pointed to the stuffed cat at her feet, her hands lost in the sleeves of his sweatshirt. Adam scooped up the cat. One of its glass eyes was missing, the space left behind colored in with blue marker to match the remaining eye. He handed it to her.

"I woke up," she said, not looking at him but focused on the cat. "Miss Priss was gone. I went to look for her. She was hiding in Mommy's car." She nodded to a Chevy Impala parked beside a black Ford F-150. The truck was shiny, even in the moonlight. Chrome accents, fancy toolbox. The Chevy listed to one side, its front tire flat, and had more primer than paint holding it together.

"You got locked out?"

She nodded. It couldn't have been too long ago or, dressed the way she was, she'd be dead.

"Didn't you knock?"

"No one answered. I hit it as loud as I could, rang the doorbell. Mommy and Bert are asleep. They didn't wake up." She looked up at him with wide eyes so big they could have swallowed the moon reflected in them. "Do you think they're okay?"

Something stung Adam's cheek. He reached a hand up and realized it was a tear. Just the cold, he told himself. He stood up, taking Sally and Miss Priss with him, and carried them to the truck. The doors were open. He slid Sally into the passenger seat. It was a little warmer in here and she was out of the wind.

A few seconds later he had the engine running and heat blasting from the vents.

"How would you and Miss Priss like to come home with me?" he asked, tickling the cat under its chin. Sally giggled at that, the color already returning to her face. "My name is Adam. I'm kinda your big brother."

She yawned, covering her mouth after the fact, and curled up with her head resting against the back of the seat. "What about Mommy?"

"I'll leave her a note so she won't worry."

"No. I mean, who's going to take care of her?"

"Don't worry. I'll come back and take care of her. That's too much work for a little girl like you. You just leave it all to me."

Another yawn. This time she didn't even bother to cover it. Instead she let her eyes drift shut.

"Stay here in the truck. I'll be right back." Adam left her half asleep and walked around to the back door. Another spring lock, cheap and easier to pop than the one at Darrin's place.

The stench of ammonia was worse inside. The woman and man didn't stir. He walked down the hall, keeping his knife at the ready just in case, and entered the small second bedroom. Sally's room had no bed, just a mattress on the floor. There were a few toys, all well loved, and tons of drawings on every kind of paper imaginable: old newspaper, brown paper bags, wrapping paper, packaging. A KFC bucket was filled with crayons, their wrappers torn off, some worn down to tiny stubs.

A few plastic milk crates formed a pseudo-dresser. Beside them was a pink Hello Kitty backpack. Adam took it, shoving clothing, barrettes, a hairbrush, and a few Barbie dolls, coloring books and a handful of crayons inside. Then he added a pair of sneakers. He grabbed Sally's coat, pink fake fur, along with her blanket and pillow.

He'd get her new crayons tomorrow. No way in hell she was ever coming back here.

When he returned to the main room the man and woman were still sound asleep, one of them snoring. He walked past them, crunching a meth pipe beneath his foot. A pair of nice black leather cowboy boots stood beside the end table. Hanging from the back of one of the kitchen chairs was a matching leather motorcycle jacket with padded insulation. Adam slid the jacket on and tried the boots on for size. A little loose, but better than his sneakers.

He left the sneakers in their place. Then he raided the kitchen, using Sally's pillowcase as a bag. Other than the ingredients to cook meth, there wasn't much. But now with two mouths to feed, he'd need more than what was stashed at the cave. He grabbed a box of instant oatmeal, a few cans of soup, Pop Tarts, and some Girl Scout cookies he found in the freezer. In the freezer he also found a wad of cash wrapped up in rubber bands. He took that as well as the two sets of car keys hanging from a hook beside the front door.

He opened all the doors and windows before grabbing his stash. Feeling like Santa Claus with everything bundled up in Sally's pink blanket, he returned to the truck. Sally was still asleep, but she smiled and squeezed his finger when he took her hand. Nice and warm and pink. Just the way it should be.

He hoped like hell it was cold enough to freeze the fish he left behind.

Chapter 7

Adam woke to a finger wiggling in his ear. It tickled. Then came a little girl's giggle. She removed the finger and patted his face like a blind person. It was dark enough in the cave—she probably felt blind.

He smiled beneath her palm. She giggled again. Adam flicked on the flashlight—the tiny LED one so it wouldn't fill the room with shocking light—and handed it to her. Bright streams edged in blue danced through the darkness above them.

The pink blanket jostled from his body as he sat up. He wrapped it around Sally's shoulders. "Good morning."

She bounced, excited by the play of light. "Hey, Adam," she sang out, as if she woke up next to strangers every day. Given what he'd seen in the trailer, maybe she did. She turned, the light held between them so he could see her face. "Where's the potty?"

Whoops. Hadn't really planned for that. Not with a little girl in mind, anyway. He hastily converted a bucket into a makeshift toilet for her in a far corner of the cave, behind a rock formation for privacy. She didn't complain about the primitive conditions, but Adam felt embarrassed. Now that he had cash, he could do better. He began a shopping list.

They ate breakfast outside, listening to the weather radio and watching squirrels chase themselves through the trees. Sally clapped and cheered her favorites, tossing them crumbs of Pop Tarts in reward. The guy on the radio said it would snow today. The cave would be warm enough, but Adam decided to stock up on more food, maybe a way to cook it—he doubted Sally would like cold Chef Boyardee straight from the can like he did—and a lantern that would last if the snow kept them inside for long. Maybe one of those fancy Coleman ones. Or he could borrow a kerosene lantern from the Stolfultz's barn. They had tons there. Wouldn't miss one or two. He added it to his list.

"Do you have school?" he asked Sally. He couldn't take her into town. She'd be safe in school.

She shook her head, zooming Miss Priss around like she was a flying squirrel instead of a cat. Miss Priss managed to look offended by the indignity of it all. "No, silly. I'm only four. But I get to go next year. Like the big kids. I'm gonna learn how to read real books."

Okay. No school. "I have to go into town."

"To check on Mommy? Sometimes she's hard to wake up in the morning." Sally's voice dropped. "Some mornings she wakes up okay but she's real cranky. Then you have to be very, very quiet. No cartoons. But coloring's okay."

"I'll check on your mommy. She'll be real proud of what a big girl you're being on your first adventure."

"I'm Dora the Explorer," she proclaimed. "Where does Dora go potty when she's in the jungle 'sploring? Does she have a bucket, too?"

Adam had no clue what Dora did although he'd seen her on one of Sally's coloring books. A book with every page, every margin, even the inside covers filled with pictures. "I'll bet she does. But not a cave. Not one as nice as this."

"It's good to go 'sploring with friends." She took Adam's hand, intertwining his fingers with hers, and swung it back and forth.

"How about if I show you another part of the cave? A very special part? You can wait there and color and play while I go check on your mommy."

She curled Miss Priss into her free arm. "Can Miss Priss come, too?"

"Sure. We'd never leave Miss Priss behind, would we?"

"Okay. You get to be Boots." She jumped to her feet and tugged Adam to his. "C'mon, Adam. We're 'splorers!"

–

During the night Lucy kept reliving those three days she spent in New Hope four years ago. In her dreams, she walked step by step through her part of the investigation— which at the time had been considered a wild goose chase, not an official case.

No one expected her to find anything in New Hope, much less a serial killer's lair. And then, after it was all over, she was considered a victim. Not a professional.

None of that was what her sleeping mind had focused on. Instead she dreamed of Adam Caine and their journey into the mountain. Nightmares filled with darkness so black you breathed it in and it grew inside you, filling your veins.

Slashing pain, screams, and the staccato image of Marion Caine, lit only by a trembling flashlight beam, being pulled into the crevasse by her abductor, a man whose face no one except Marion ever saw clearly.

From the clock, Lucy knew her nightmares had lasted no more than a few minutes. But each time she woke, it was as if she had lived through days of terror.

The next morning when she arrived in her office and found her boss, John Greally, sitting at her desk, she knew her plans of finishing the Plushenko trial and heading out to New Hope were about to go up in smoke.

"I've got good news and bad news," John said, drinking coffee from one of Lucy's mugs. He said Lucy's coffee was better, but really he often came down to chat—usually when he had a problem that needed untangling without going through official channels.

Lucy slung her bag onto the conference table and leaned against it. She'd worn her only "power suit" for court this morning. It was crimson—dark enough to be business-like, red enough to be intimidating. She hoped it would keep the defense attorney on the Plushenko case on the defensive.

"Good news is Plushenko pled out," John continued. "Guess your testimony yesterday put the fear of God into him."

That was good news. No court. She could head out immediately for New Hope. Except... "And the bad news?"

"Well, maybe not bad news. Actually, I pulled a few strings to make it happen. I got your psych eval scheduled for today."

Lucy gave him a slow blink. Something she'd learned from Megan. Less offensive than an eye roll of disgust, but almost as effective. "I feel like all I've been doing these past few months is talking to psych services. Surely they can use those evals for my semi-annual review?"

"Doesn't work like that. You know everyone working this unit has to undergo evaluation every six months. It's an easy day, Lucy. Go in, do a little moaning and groaning, tell them what their damn ink splots mean, then the rest of the day is yours." He opened his hands as if giving her a gift. "It's Friday. Gives you all weekend to relax. Did you think about my offer of taking some vacation time? It's slow enough around here right now."

John had never worked sexual assaults or crimes against children. He had no idea how rigorous the psych evals were. Probing into every nook and cranny of your subconscious, trying to weed out potential head cases, the agents close to snapping who might decide to take justice into their own hands against the Plushenkos of the world.

Not her idea of an easy day. But his heart was in the right place, so Lucy smiled and nodded like a good Supervisory Special Agent should. "Guess I better change if I'm going to be lying on a couch for most of the day."

"Great. I'll start pushing through paper to give you next week off." He grabbed his coffee and got up to leave. He stopped when he came shoulder to shoulder with her. "Sometimes it's important to remember why we do what we do. Go someplace fun. Put a smile on Megan's face. Take long bubble baths. Hell, stay home and turn off the phones for all I care. But, Lucy, I need you to come back in a better place."

She jerked her chin to face him. She'd spent the past two months doing everything the brass asked. "Are you saying I can't do my job?"

"I'm saying doing this job and taking care of a family requires a tightrope walk. Consider this vacation your safety net."

What the hell did that mean? It wasn't like John to play word games. He was a friend, an old friend. "John—"

"Don't say anything. You're the best at what you do. But sometimes that doesn't translate well on paper. The brass are looking at this unit under a microscope. They'll soon get bored and move on and life around here can get back to normal. But until then, you need to stay off their radar, understand?"

"No, I don't. I almost died for this job. My people almost died. My daughter almost died. If they don't like the way I did things, then—" Anger scorched her words into dust. Her hands clenched into two fists as the muscles at her jaw spasmed.

Greally raised one of her fists and forced it to unclench. He slid the warm coffee mug into it. "Take the time off, Lucy. This job isn't everything. In the long run, despite all the good we do, it isn't anything. Not compared to family. Sometimes we need to remember that."

—

Sally had actually enjoyed exploring the rest of Adam's cave. She called him Boots and ordered him around as if he didn't know where he was going. And she wanted him to make goofy monkey sounds, so he did. It was worth it to make her laugh.

The only time she flinched was when he scooped her up to ride piggyback down the ladder into the pit. At first he thought she was afraid of heights, but once they were on the bottom, she scampered back up and down the ladder fearlessly while he set out her toys and coloring books on her blanket. That's when he realized what had frightened her. Poor kid never had anyone give her a piggyback before.

"You're sure you'll be all right alone here?" he asked after they sat and colored together for a while. Long enough for the wind-up light to start to fade. Before he could do anything, Sally cranked it back up just as he'd shown her.

Even with the light, the pit was still rimmed with shadows. But in a few hours the sun would be high enough to add light through the overhead opening.

Sally kept on drawing. He had the feeling she spent a lot of time alone in the dark. The thought made him angry and sad.

"I'll bring you back more crayons and coloring books."

She nodded eagerly. Then surprised him by jumping up and giving him a hug. "I like having a big brother, Adam," she whispered into his ear as she clung to him.

Now he was the one startled. Not sure how to respond. Slowly he wrapped his arms around her, careful not to squeeze too hard. "You're my favorite little sister in the whole world." Reluctantly he released her. "I'll be back as soon as I can."

She tickled his face with Miss Priss, and then returned to her earnest activity. He'd never seen anyone take coloring so seriously.

As he left he was already worrying about her. About how he was going to take care of her. Because now she was his.

How had Dad done it? So many years of taking care of him and Mom and even the fish. Adam stepped out from the entrance of the cave and sucked in a bracing breath of November air. Time to be a man.

He marched into the woods, determined, for once in his life, not to screw things up.

Chapter 8

Lucy changed into her regular work clothes of khakis and a button-down and slid her suit into a garment bag. It was only 8:20; her appointment with the shrink wasn't until ten.

New Hope was a two-hour drive. No matter how she tried to ignore it, the thought kept ricocheting back. She had a go-bag in her office closet with extra clothes, toiletries, winter gear. Not that she'd need it. She could be to New Hope and back before Megan came home from soccer.

To hell with the shrink. Making sure Adam was okay would do a helluva lot more good for her psyche.

She grabbed her travel duffle, hid it by folding the garment bag over top her arm, smiled at everyone she saw on the way out, and left without saying a word.

She'd just reached her car when an official unmarked vehicle, a gray Taurus, pulled up with Jenna Galloway at the wheel. "Get in," the postal inspector shouted through the window.

Lucy opened the passenger door but didn't get in. "Where you off to?"

"New Hope. Thought you might want to ride with me."

"I told you. I'll take care of Adam Caine. You get back on Operation Roundup."

"Taylor's got it covered. And the threatening letter you received falls under Postal Service jurisdiction. You've got no standing to investigate it even if you weren't a principle. Plus, I'm the new guy here. How's the team gonna feel if I let you waltz off and something happens?"

Lucy hesitated.

"I'm going with or without you. C'mon," Jenna wheedled. "This place isn't even on the map. Wouldn't want me to get lost, would you?"

"All right. But on two conditions."

"What?"

"I drive." Lucy threw her stuff into the backseat.

"Sure." Jenna hopped out of the driver's seat before Lucy made it around the front of the Taurus. After they were both belted in and headed towards the security perimeter, Jenna asked, "What's the second condition?"

"You do not document Adam's name in anything without clearing it with me first. Kid's had it rough enough. I'm not about to ruin his life because of some misguided cry for attention."

"I can live with that."

Lucy waved at the guard as they drove past, then turned onto Carson Street. She smiled and eased back in the driver's seat, effortlessly navigating around the civilians on their way to work. Not even nine o'clock and she was risking her career to do what her gut told her was the right thing. To help a lost kid who needed her. Just like she had two months ago.

Finally, life felt good again.

Adam had left the truck parked in the staff lot behind the school, so he headed there. Perfect timing to catch a glimpse of Marty and Darrin. Since the district was so large geographically, the buses had to make two trips, leaving kids from the early routes time to play before the bell rang.

Or sometimes not to play. As Adam drew close to the rear of the school where the playground lay, he spotted Darrin and Marty. They were the two kids everyone ignored, herded into a corner by four boys twice their age. Bullies.

He hated bullies.

Adam skirted the waist high fence that surrounded the playground. The boys were in the far corner near the staff parking, away from the teachers manning the bus drop off, where the security cameras couldn't see them. He ducked behind between the car parked in the first row.

Usually when bullies targeted Adam, he simply let them do what they wanted, kept quiet, showed as little pain as possible, and eventually they'd get tired of tormenting him and leave.

But this time he was the one with the power. He was the big brother. No way in hell was he going to let these skinny snot nose punks pick on his little brothers.

"I said, give me the watch, bitch," one of the older boys said when Adam got close enough to hear. He was the smallest—skinny but in that weasely, dirty-fighter way— and obviously the leader of the pack.

"No." Marty stood his ground, his right hand clenched over his left wrist, protecting his watch. Darrin stood behind him, obviously terrified but not running. Pride

76

rushed through Adam. Good kid, sticking up for his friend—Darrin didn't have a clue Marty was his brother.

The leader backed off half a step as his three bigger friends closed the circle around the two six-year-olds. "Tell you what. I'm gonna give you a choice. Give me the watch—"

"You can't," Darrin spoke up in a voice made squeaky by fear. "It's his dad's. You can't take it."

The leader jerked his chin at Darrin. Two of the other boys grabbed him and shoved him against the wall. "Like I said. You have a choice. The watch. Or we see how much it takes to get your buddy here to wet his pants."

Before Adam could move, the leader sucker punched Darrin. Kid didn't even have a chance to defend himself. Marty threw himself at the leader, only to be grabbed by the fourth bully, a guy almost as big as Adam. He easily plucked Marty off the ground and held him so his feet kicked at the air.

"Four against two," Adam said, coming out from behind the car. He stepped over the fence as if it wasn't worth noticing. Fear coiled in his belly and he was damn lucky he didn't trip, but the bullies wouldn't know that. Adam approached slowly, not rushing, giving them time to think. "Maybe we should even those odds. What do you say, boys?"

Darrin looked up at Adam. His face filled with hope. No one had ever looked at Adam like that before. Like Adam was a hero.

Adam didn't focus on Darrin. Or Marty. Instead he focused on the leader of the pack. Scare him off and the others would follow. Just like the wild dogs trying to steal food from his dumpster back in Cleveland.

Adam forced a smile. It felt wrong, like his muscles were too tight with fear to turn his lips the right way. Whatever the result, it obviously startled the leader.

"This is none of your business. Get out of here," the leader said with bluster.

Now he too was outside the coverage of the security cameras, Adam slid his knife out. He flicked it open one-handed. "You got that wrong. Now listen close because you need to remember this. Everything to do with these two kids is my business. You lay a hand on them, you talk mean to them, hell, you sneeze in their direction, and I'm taking care of business."

Adam feinted with the knife then landed a solid left to the leader's groin that left him on the ground crying. A wet stain spread down his pants.

Adam turned to the others, frozen as they watched their leader's fall from grace. "Let them go." They released Darrin and Marty. "Take him and get out of here."

They hurried to obey, scrambling with their leader back to the safety of the playground. Adam closed his knife and pocketed it. Then he crouched down so he was at eye level with the two boys. "You guys okay?"

Marty eyed him suspiciously but Darrin jumped forward, hugging Adam so hard he almost tumbled them both to the ground. "You're real. You're really real!"

"Of course I am. Told you I'd keep an eye on you." Adam untangled himself from Darrin and held out a hand to Marty. "I'm Adam."

Marty looked at Adam then at Darrin. He didn't extend his hand.

"He's okay," Darrin vouched for Adam. "He's my big brother. Only no one knows he's here, so you have to keep it a secret, okay?"

Marty still stared at Adam, but finally nodded. "Okay."

Adam pointed to Marty's watch. It was huge on his skinny wrist, obviously meant for an adult. "Nice watch."

"My dad gave it to me before he left." Marty's voice quavered and he blinked fast. "Uh, thanks for not letting those guys take it."

"No problem. That's what I'm here for." Adam spotted movement from the corner of his eye. Mrs. Chesshir. He stood and waved at her. "Morning, Mrs. Chesshir."

"Adam," she came to a stop in front of them, obviously flustered. "You know you're not supposed to be here."

"I just came by to say goodbye," Adam adlibbed, marveling at how easily the lies came. Maybe because they were close to the truth? "I saw four big kids jumping these two. Thought someone should save them from getting beat up."

"Oh my." She crouched down, patting both Marty and Darrin on the arms as if inspecting them for damage. "You two okay?"

They nodded silently.

"Who did this?"

The boys said nothing. Only six, but they knew better than to rat out the older boys.

Mrs. Chesshir wiggled her mouth as she thought. "You guys go inside. Tell Mr. Mason I said it was okay."

"Yes, Mrs. Chesshir," they chorused and ran off. Darrin turned back to wave at Adam, his entire body getting into the movement. Marty tugged him back on course and they disappeared around the corner.

"Did you see who did this?" Mrs. Chesshir asked. It was weird, but suddenly it was like she and Adam were equals.

"Those four." Adam pointed to the bullies clustered at the far end of the yard, heads clustered together like they were plotting. "I kinda scared the leader a bit when I showed up. He wet his pants. Not used to anyone standing up to them, I guess."

"Craig Mathis and his gang. It's not the first time." She blew out her breath in a sigh. "I'll make sure they're disciplined. It was good you came when you did. We're just spread too thin…" Her hands fluttered out like butterflies, the pale November light making her wedding rings glitter.

"Glad to help. I'd better be off."

She thrust out her hand. "Thank you, Adam. I wish you the best of luck. You've turned into a remarkable young man."

Her words left him tongue-tied. All his life he'd strived to be unremarkable. The silent boy watching from the back of the class, unheard and unseen. Unnoticed by trouble. He didn't mind that the rest of the world never saw him—the only attention he wanted was his father's.

Finally he took her hand and shook it. "Bye, Mrs. Chesshir."

He left the way he came. Sweat itched between his shoulder blades as he felt her stare follow him. Being the center of attention wasn't a good thing, he decided. Far better to stick to his old ways. Hiding in the shadows, watching and waiting.

Then he glanced back and saw Darrin leaning over the fence, still waving at him. Like he never wanted to see Adam go. Like Adam was his last and only hope.

Adam knew that feeling. One he'd had too many times. Hopes that had been crushed too many times. Like back in Cleveland when Morgan and Dad drove away, leaving him to the cops.

He wouldn't let that happen to Darrin. Wouldn't let his brother down.

Now he just had to figure out how.

–

Eight months since they ditched Adam in Cleveland, and finally, for the first time ever, Clint let Morgan choose their next fish and reel her in.

But, oh boy, what a fish she was. Morgan was determined to prove to Clint the value of patience. Of reconnaissance and research. Hell, maybe he'd even start using the Internet. Well, maybe not. That's okay, that's what he had Morgan for.

No matter what, he'd see how much more valuable Morgan was than stupid Adam. Even if Adam was older, had lived with Clint all his life, he just didn't have the natural born instincts Morgan had. Didn't have the heart for the family business like Morgan did.

The fish pulled out of her driveway at a little past five in the morning. She was an ER doctor at Akron General but she had all next week off. Told her co-workers she'd booked a cabin in the Cuyahoga Valley National Park where she planned to cross country ski, sit by the fire and get over the fiancé she'd just broken up with, and finally start work on the novel she'd been talking about writing for years.

She wasn't going to get to do any of that.

Morgan lowered the binoculars as Clint put the van in gear and followed the fish. And a cabin, out there in the wilderness, no one near enough to hear her screams… that was the best part of all.

Clint was gonna love it.

They'd taken their last few fish inside their homes. Single women, living alone, in houses far enough away from their neighbors to muffle any sounds. Clint and Morgan brought along their own chains with an assortment of other toys, but now that Clint no longer cared about keeping the fish alive, he enjoyed improvising with items on hand. The last fish had been a rock climber, lived down near Seneca Rocks. What fun they'd had with all those ropes and carabineers and pitons.

But this one? A doctor? Morgan knew she carried an emergency kit in her trunk. Complete with scalpels. Morgan loved a good cutting blade. So bright and shiny… especially when the blood was wet.

Chapter 9

Jenna had more patience than Lucy would have given her credit for. She waited until they were past the snarl of morning rush-hour traffic and headed north on Route 22 before asking her first question. "I was only able to skim the case summary from four years ago—"

"Not your usual Postal Service kind of report?" Lucy didn't want to talk about four years ago but knew it was inevitable.

"Definitely not. Maybe you could fill me in." Jenna waited.

Lucy said nothing.

"So this Unsub, he kidnapped victims from all over the eastern seaboard and Midwest? No one ever saw him take his victims, they'd just *poof!* Vanish. All young. Different races, different appearances, some prostitutes, some just walking the wrong street at the wrong time. How'd you put it together?"

Listening to Jenna was like riding a roller coaster. All up and down inflections until Lucy couldn't tell which sentences ended with a question mark. "We didn't. There was no pattern, no bodies. It wasn't until my supervisor at the time, Chad Hamilton, was talking to the press afterwards that anyone even labeled him a serial killer."

Lucy remembered the grief Hamilton had given her about "traipsing off on a wild goose chase" when she first approached him with her suspicions and requested to pursue her theory. He'd refused. But Lucy's curiosity itched at her. Since one of the witnesses lived close to her hometown and another lived near DC, she used her vacation time to pursue an unsanctioned investigation. A fact buried by the official report.

"Why did you join the SAFE task force?" she asked Jenna.

"Are you kidding? Do you have any idea the career opportunities you've opened up for agents like me?" Jenna ticked her fingers as if keeping score. "First, you worked with ICE to bust that sex trafficking ring. Then you and the High Tech Crimes guys uncovered a huge online pedophile community—Taylor told me all about that one. September you saved that girl abducted by a serial killer. And now Operation Roundup, using Postal Service mail forwarding records and IRS tax files to pickup some of the US Marshals' most wanted sexual predators?"

Her voice became high pitched, excited. She hauled in a breath. "This multi-agency sexual assault task force may have begun as an experiment, more about public opinion than anything else, but let's face it, Lucy, you put the sexy back in sex crimes."

Lucy pretended to concentrate on the road in order to ignore the smile Jenna beamed at her. Like the postal inspector expected a Hollywood director to jump in front of them and yell "Action!" or something.

"It's not all big headlines. Most of what we do is just good old-fashioned talking to people. You'd probably call it boring and routine."

Jenna shook her head, her ponytail whipping back and forth. "Compared to the cases I've worked for the Postal Service? Talk about tedious. Do you have any idea how many variations on the Nigerian letter scam there are? Don't get me wrong. I like my work. But, wow, this stuff you do…"

Great. Another adrenalin junkie mired in adolescence. Just like the Pittsburgh cop Lucy worked with in September. Last thing she needed was to end up playing mother hen. Again.

Jenna bounced in her seat, pulling her legs up Indian-style. "So, what tipped you? That the New Hope cases were linked."

"I was assigned to CIRG, the Critical Incident Response Group."

"The profilers and hostage negotiation guys, right?"

"Yes. But behavioral analysis isn't like what you see on TV."

"No Gulfstream flying you all over the country?"

"Try a windowless basement office filled with file cabinets and computers. And phones. Lots of phones. Most of the work is done that way. You rarely meet the local officers who call and ask for help."

"Sounds worse than life in the dead letter office."

"With the Bureau turning more toward counter-terrorism, a lot of the profiling is done by civilian consultants. I actually worked hostage negotiation with the HRT guys."

Nick had hated that assignment. She'd leave with no notice. Fly out in the back of a C-130 with the Hostage Rescue Team and their assault gear, spend days holed up in an office or trailer or whatever location had been commandeered as a command center, talk to prisoners barricaded behind concertina wire or fanatics ready to start the second war of independence to protect their perceived constitutional rights or desperate fugitives with federal warrants.

"CIRG members also teach and do research during their downtime," Lucy continued. "So I began a project using geographical information surveys to uncover hidden violent crime trends."

"Sounds boring as hell." Jenna flounced back in her seat, obviously disappointed.

"Once I figured out I didn't have to do the actual computer stuff, that I only needed to focus on the human patterns they exposed, it was kind of fun. That's when I found our first four victims."

"Living victims?"

"I eventually unearthed seven. Well, seven cases reported to the National Center for Violent Crime," she amended. She was certain there were more victims who'd never reported the details of their abduction.

Rape-kidnappings, especially with prolonged captivity, either went all major headlines like Jaycee Dugard or they slid quietly under the radar like John Jamelske's and David Ray Parker's first victims had. After her interviews with the few victims willing to talk, she understood these women all had damn good reasons to stay quiet and move on with their lives. Something the Unsub counted on.

"Still, that's seven witnesses—"

Jenna obviously hadn't spent a lot of time interviewing witnesses, especially ones shattered by violent crime. Plus, Lucy had found them years after their ordeal. Years to forget and bury and warp memories.

"Seven women whose stories differed vastly—at least according to the raw data entered. Scattered all over the eastern half of the country. Some thought they were kept in a cellar, two said they thought it was the basement of a church because of the noises they heard. Singing and organ music. Another thought a cargo container. Only one reported a cave as the possible location. None knew how far from the site of the initial attack they'd been transported. And none saw their abductor's face."

Lucy steered up the passing lane as they rounded the switchbacks over Blairfield Mountain, passing two trucks and a dawdling station wagon. "This Unsub, he liked playing games. He kept four of the victims alone their entire captivity, the others with one or two other women. Women never heard from again. Even the way he tortured them varied, as if each victim or group of victims was a new experiment in depravity. And they all had huge gaps in their memories."

"Drugged?"

"Yes. Although I realized later it had to be more than that. Think of the sensory deprivation—it changes the way you perceive everything. These women were kept in total darkness for weeks to months. The only light came when he brought it and then it was so blinding they couldn't see anything. Any food or drink they had, he provided. He controlled every moment of their existence, even when he wasn't there."

"But you put the pieces together. You figured out the one thing they all had in common," Jenna prompted. "The ones he released."

"I got lucky. Because the link had nothing to do with geography." Lucy's gaze drifted, searching the gray-brown landscape for something she couldn't see. "The survivors were all pregnant."

"But why?" Jenna persisted. "I mean, I'm glad those women lived, but why did he let them go? It's so damn risky. Was he trying to populate a cult?" She shook her head and answered her own question. "No. Then he'd keep the kids and their moms with him. Like Warren Jeffs or David Koresh."

The postal inspector was silent as she thought, her lips puckered together like she'd swallowed something sour and couldn't get rid of the bad taste. "When we're profiling serial bombers or stalkers using the postal system, we look for tells. These guys like attention, so they keep offending. Each time we learn more about them. Not your guy. Your guy stayed in hiding. If he wanted attention all he needed to do was dump the bodies. How many victims did you find in New Hope?"

"We found DNA matches to three women reported missing. Plus DNA too degraded to definitely identify at least six others."

Who knew how many DNA traces that time, the acid in the limestone caves, and the killer's liberal use of bleach had eliminated? Not to mention how many other crime scenes were scattered up and down the entire East Coast.

"Nine presumed dead and seven living witnesses and no one even realized this guy was out there." Jenna blew her breath out. "They should've given you a medal."

Hamilton traded her a promotion and the chance to keep her job instead of the official reprimand she should have gotten. In return for his taking the glory. Small price to pay.

"You still didn't answer my question," Jenna continued. "Why let the pregnant women go?"

Lucy hesitated. Her answer was nowhere in the official report—not even in her unofficial notes. No one outside the Bureau knew about her linking the pregnant victims. Without DNA from the rapist and the children, there was no proof that they actually *were* linked.

But she had a theory. The only person she'd ever told was Nick and then as a vague theoretical abstract with no mention of New Hope. Nick agreed with her, though. That said a lot.

"I think he followed the kids. Monitored them and the moms."

"Monitor? Like a stalker maintaining control over his victim?"

"No." Lucy steered them around a hairpin curve. A vista of snow covered fields rippled out before them, framed by evergreens climbing up mountains on both sides. "I don't think it was about controlling the victims. I think he wanted the kids alive. I think the kids were his trophies."

"Trophies?" Jenna's voice trailed off as she caught the full implication of Lucy's words. "Like a serial killer reliving the crime by keeping souvenirs from their victims?"

Lucy took advantage of a straightaway to meet the postal inspector's gaze. "Exactly like that."

"Why? To see if they'd grow up as twisted and perverse as he was?" Jenna sucked in her breath with a shudder. "But wait. Do the kids know? Who their father was, what he was? Do they even know they have half-brothers and sisters out there?"

Finally the truth was out. Four years ago she'd threatened to go to the press, but Hamilton had stopped her. Now she was regretting that. "No. It was a multi-jurisdiction nightmare and with the Unsub dead, the case was closed. No one ever followed up with DNA testing on the children, much less opening the field to see if there were more kids out there. No budget, no manpower, and no one wanted to be responsible for ruining those kids' lives."

"But still." Jenna shook her head with a tiny jerk that sent her ponytail bobbing. "If your dad was a serial killer, wouldn't you want to know?"

Lucy had no answer for her.

—

Jenna had already paved the way with the Huntingdon County Sheriff's office and arranged to talk with one of the deputies who worked the original case at the New Hope substation. Lucy dropped her off there, glad the postal inspector's curiosity eclipsed her desire to find Adam.

"Shouldn't be hard," Jenna said as she swung out of the passenger seat. "Not in a town too small to have its own zip code."

Post office humor. Not helpful. Not when there were dozens of unmarked logging roads winding through miles of forest, secluded fishing camps along the streams, and all those hidey-hole caves inside the mountains themselves. Lucy hoped it didn't come to that. She could live her entire life without venturing inside another cave.

Her side burned as if in warning.

"Call me if anything comes up," Lucy said. "If you can. Cell reception is pretty spotty out here." They hadn't seen a tower since Alexandria. "I'll be back as soon as I can."

Lucy tried Adam's home first. It had once been a tidy two story brick house sitting on the outskirts of town, its backyard an open meadow with a large gnarled maple in the center—what Lucy's dad had called a "fairy tree"—and a barn converted into a garage on one side. At the edge of the meadow thick trees extended up the side of the mountain, framing the homestead with a Norman Rockwell promise of a simpler life.

Having grown up in a small, rural community not much bigger than New Hope, Lucy knew the lie behind the promise. A lot of hard work went into supporting a family out here where jobs were scarce. Even more work if you were trying to carve a living out of one of the small farms hemmed in by agri-business behemoths. But still, Clinton Caine had managed, juggling long-distance hauling with his wife's cancer treatments, trying to be home for his family when he could.

Crushed by the weight of that day four years ago when he'd arrived home too late to save his wife.

As soon as Lucy parked in the driveway, the blacktop cracked with weeds, she realized no one lived here anymore. Like so many properties they passed on the way to New Hope, a foreclosure sign sat out front skirted by unmown grass and faded with weather—maybe a few years' worth.

Just because no one lived here didn't mean no one had come here. Adam was on his own; he might return to the only home he'd known.

Lucy left the Taurus and walked to the front door. Locked. The windows were dingy with grime, revealing empty walls and naked wood floors beyond. A few scraps of newspaper and a cardboard box tipped on its side. No signs of vandalism or squatters. Or Adam.

She trudged around to the rear of the house. The wind off the mountain forced her to bow her head as she passed a cement slab porch and the back door to the storm cellar. It had metal doors designed to be weather-tight, but there a slight gap showed between them. She tugged on one side, throwing her weight into it. Unlocked. The hinges protested with sharp squeals, but finally relented, allowing her to open the door two-thirds of the way. Enough for her to get through.

Grabbing her Maglite, she looked down the cellar steps. No footprints she could see, but the steps were rough concrete and might not have held an impression. No movement except for her light. The air was thick, musty with age. A strange mix of coal dust and old paper.

She pushed her weight against the door again, forcing it open farther so gravity would prevent it from snapping shut and trapping her inside. After what happened the last time she was in New Hope, dark, dingy places were not her forte.

Shuddering against errant memories, she placed her hand on her weapon and sidled through the gap in the door. The Maglite's beam was helpful for the small area it illuminated but didn't protect against shadows lunging from either side of her. She was surprised to find herself short of breath. Not from lack of oxygen but from hyperventilating.

Focus. Stay calm. Not as easy as it sounded—even the voice in her head sounded panicked.

She stopped six steps down, stooped to clear the top of the slanted doorway, and swung the light around, confronting those shadow demons.

An old coal-burning furnace was the culprit behind most of the shadows. A short refrigerator, curved on top with a single door, also contributed. As did a washer and dryer both piled high with stacks of books. More cartons of books perched precariously on sagging wooden shelves, balanced on a Ping-Pong table faded to gray, and nested among the floor joists overhead.

The faint skitter of mice accompanied every movement of the light. Lucy dusted a cobweb away from her face and searched for a light switch. None near the steps but a string hung just a few feet beyond the bottom. She grabbed it and pulled. No luck. Electricity long since shut off.

A clear path between the boxes ran from the outside stairs to the inside ones and branched off to a door beside the furnace. Great hiding place for an ambush, so she started there. The door was metal, an exterior door, heavy duty, hinged onto the basement's outer wall.

She pulled it open, light and gun both at hand, then laughed at herself when she saw the bookcase with rows of Mason jars covered in dust and cobwebs. Root cellar. Her gram's house had one as well, dug into the hard packed dirt of the foundation, a tiny cave that stayed the same temperature all year round.

As she wove her way through the stacks of books, Lucy realized there was a design to their placement. The cartons formed walls between imaginary rooms.

A small area near the refrigerator and tub sink had a short stack of magazines in the center as if it was a table to eat on. Another area beside it was littered with comic books and pulp fiction novels alongside a deflated and dusty air mattress centered below a second light bulb. Bedroom?

And back in the farthest corner an old toilet sitting behind a shower curtain streaked with black mold and spider webs.

Had someone lived down here?

Maybe Adam?

She bent low and examined the floor. The only disturbance was visible tracks left by tiny mouse feet. Swiping a finger along the stack of magazines created a thick furrow of dust. No one had moved any of this stuff in years.

Not where Adam hid now. But the area had the feel of kid about it. The need to add structure to the empty space, as if nesting. Or hiding. Maybe things hadn't been as happy in the Caine household as she thought.

She wished she'd been to the house four years ago, interviewed Adam and his father on their own turf. But Mr. Caine had been out of town on a long distance haul, so it was Adam running breathless along the road who flagged her down after his mother's carjacking.

The scene of the crime was just outside of town, past the school. The attacker had taken Marion Caine's beat up Pontiac and forced Adam out of the car. Lucy and a Huntingdon County deputy were first on scene and the deputy asked her to help out, "seeing as this could be connected to your case and all."

At the time, Lucy doubted any connection. Her Unsub had been active for at least ten years without raising a blip on the radar. Not the type for a spontaneous daytime snatch and grab.

But the kid's story broke her heart. And Huntingdon County needed all the help they could get to stop the carjacker before he harmed Marion Caine.

Everyone's hopes for a successful outcome were dashed when they found Caine's car abandoned near the Stolfultz farm. The county deputies immediately mobilized a search, but from the looks on their faces, it was clear they were thinking recovery rather than rescue.

Lucy agreed. The statistics did as well. But no one could bring themselves to give up on Marion. Not while her ten-year-old son was right there with them, begging for them to save his mom.

Adam ended up with Lucy as they began the search. She worried about him, tried to send him back, but it would be hours before either his father or child services made it to the scene. Besides, he knew the terrain, he boasted. Had walked every inch of these mountains, hunting with his dad.

Lucy spotted the van but it was Adam who heard the screams. He rushed inside Echo Cavern before she could stop him or call for backup.

Absolute black. That's what she remembered best. She grabbed a flashlight before chasing after Adam, but given the immense weight of darkness, it was useless. Made her more of a target than it helped her spot any potential danger, but she couldn't bring herself to turn it off.

"Adam!" Her calls echoed back and forth, swirling around her, playing blind man's bluff.

Then the screams came. Women. She followed the sound and found two young women, naked, chained by iron collars around their necks. The old-fashioned collars were secured by handcuffs to the thick chains bolted to the cave wall. A lucky break—although Lucy realized later it was simply a convenient way for the Unsub to reposition his victims as his fancy led him.

She released the first girl who refused to leave without the second girl. Knelt beside her, stroking her hair, calling her name. "Rachel, it's okay. Rachel, we're saved."

The second girl, in addition to the chain around her neck, lay on her stomach, each wrist handcuffed to the opposite ankle, her limbs contorted behind her in a way that must have been excruciating. Yet she never made a sound.

Lucy led them to the car, told them to wait for the backup she'd called. Was tempted to do the same. But she had no idea how long it would take the deputy. And Adam was in there, alone in the dark.

She nearly didn't make it past the threshold. The weight of the darkness almost pushed her back outside. Megan's face kept filling her vision. Megan was around the same age as Adam. If she'd been lost in the dark... The thought gave her the courage to plunge back into the black.

Crossing the chamber where she found the girls, shadows crushing her, that's when he knifed her. He moved through the shadows so fast she never saw him. Just the shove and the burn of the blade slicing her flesh.

She lunged after him, but he was gone before she could aim the light at him, much less her weapon. Then her light caught sight of Adam on the opposite side of the cavern.

"Hurry. He's got my mom. Hurry. You have to save her."

Lucy tried. Tried to hurry. Tried to save Marion.

But the rest of what happened in that cave, well, the last thing she needed was to keep reliving the rest. Not when she should be concentrating on finding Adam and helping him.

Least she could do after getting his mom killed.

Chapter 10

Jenna paused at the substation's doorway, reading the plaque dedicating the renovated Dairy Treat to Marion Caine. If Adam Caine had come home, would the locals protect him? Maybe even the local law enforcement?

She swung the door open and stepped inside, ready to trust no one. Hard to do with the scent of french fries and chilidogs perfuming the air.

The place was pretty much empty. They'd left the plastic booths and turned the counter area into a receptionist's desk. An elderly man wearing a volunteer badge looked up from his Sudoku to greet her with enthusiasm as if she was the most excitement this place had seen in a decade.

Well, not a decade. More like four years.

She flipped open her jacket, a Black Halo leather car coat she'd bought in Century City. The clerk who assured her it would be warm enough for the Pennsylvania winters had been sorely mistaken. Resting a hand on her gun, she said, "Inspector Galloway to see Deputy Bob. He's expecting me."

The volunteer jumped up to personally escort her through the security door to the rear work area.

It also was empty except for one tall man bent over a coffeemaker at the far counter. They'd removed the appliances but left the stainless steel counters along both walls. In the cramped space in the center they'd shoved three desks together, one barren of everything except a phone, the other with a keyboard and old monitor that looked as if it weighed fifty pounds. The third desk held a matching ancient computer, fax machine, and all-in-one printer/scanner.

Jenna decided to let the locals know she was here on serious Postal Service business and sat at the desk Deputy Bob was obviously using.

"Good morning," he said, still bent over the coffee maker. Not very good situational awareness, she thought. Until she realized he could see everything behind him reflected in the polished steel backsplash. Just as she could see his amused smile.

"Morning," she replied in a neutral tone. His face in the mirrored surface was kinda cute. Boyish yet rugged with an interesting cleft in his chin and crinkles at the corners of his eyes as if he spent a lot of time staring into the sun.

Hollywood would eat him up. He turned, holding two mugs of coffee in his hands and the view got even better. Six foot, trim, real muscles, not gym-rat ones, warm brown eyes and medium brown hair that she bet got light in the summer.

What was even better was he seemed oblivious to his looks. Now that never would happen back in L.A.

"Am I in your seat?" she asked innocently.

"No problem." He gave her a mug. "Black okay? If not, we've got milk but no sugar."

"Black's fine, thanks." She noticed he gave her the mug with the sheriff's department logo on it, probably his own, while he kept the plain brown one that looked left over from the days this place was a Dairy Treat. Gotta love small town hospitality.

He leaned against the counter on her side of the small space and sipped his coffee. "How can I help you, Agent Galloway?"

"Actually, it's Inspector Galloway. I'm with the United States Postal Service."

"Postal Service? I thought you were interested in Adam Caine?" he paused, covering his scrutiny with another sip of coffee. "Didn't you say you were coming here with Lucy Guardino?"

"Special Agent Guardino dropped me off." He looked down at the tan linoleum, shifted his weight. Disappointed with a lowly postal inspector instead of a big time, world famous FBI agent, no doubt. "But this is my case. We suspect Adam Caine of violating US Code, Title 18, Section 876."

"And what's that when it's at home?"

"Using the US mail to send threatening communications."

He frowned. "And the penalty?"

"Ten years."

"But he's just a kid. Fifteen—"

"Fourteen years old." She shrugged. "All the more reason to find him, isn't it?"

"You drove all the way from Pittsburgh to see if Adam was mailing letters from here? Hate to disappoint, Inspector Galloway, but we don't even have a post office. Alexandria is the nearest."

"I know that. The letter in question was postmarked Cleveland—the last place Caine was seen."

"So you and Lucy came here—"

"The letter mentioned New Hope. We thought he might return home."

"He's alone? Where's Clint?"

"Apparently Adam ran away from his father ten months ago. Was picked up for petty theft, and when they couldn't locate the dad, they put him in the foster care system. Eight months ago he assaulted a group home worker and fled. He's been on the streets ever since."

"Doesn't sound like Clint. He loves that boy. You sure he's okay? He's a long-haul trucker. Maybe something happened to him on one of his runs and the poor kid doesn't even know."

Jenna bristled. She still had no clue where Clinton Caine was and didn't care. Adam was her case. Her fugitive.

"Inspector Galloway, seems to me—"

She felt like an old school marm, the way he kept using her title. When she did the math, she knew he had to be around her age, though he seemed so much younger. Innocent? Naive? It was appealing yet annoying at the same time. "Jenna. Call me Jenna."

"Yes, ma'am. So, Jenna, I'm guessing you think Adam coming home has something to do with what went on around here four years ago."

"So, Deputy Bob." She stopped. "Is that really your name? Or are you like the school cop who works with kids and that's what they call you?"

"No, ma'am. My full name is William Bob, but that's my grandad and my dad's Billy Bob—"

"Your dad's name is Billy Bob?" Good God, she'd driven over the mountain and into an episode of *Hee-Haw*.

"And proud of it. There's been a William Bob in our family since before the Revolution. We were one of the first settlers here."

She held up a hand in truce. "You didn't want to be Willy Bob?"

"Ah no, ma'am. Not in my line of work. Didn't seem fitting. So everyone calls me Bob."

"Deputy Bob."

"Just Bob is fine, ma'am."

"Then I'm just Jenna."

He smiled, dipped his head. "Yes, ma'am. I mean Jenna."

"You worked the original New Hope case four years ago."

He looked away, swept a finger across his brow as if expecting to find a hat there, glanced across the room to the hooks beside the door where a lonely tan Stetson hung. "I'd just started with the sheriff's. But I wouldn't say I 'worked' the case. More like accidentally fell into it."

"What happened?"

"Well, ma'am, I'd only been patrolling on my own without a training officer for a few weeks. Which is why they assigned me this side of the county. Nothing much happens except the occasional traffic incident. Except that day the sheriff himself—this is the old sheriff, Sheriff Dobbs, you understand—gave me a special assignment."

"What was that?"

"Seems a woman was trespassing on the Harding's property. Got Mrs. Harding all upset. And her husband, well, he's a bigwig down in Washington, and about the richest guy around these parts. When he's upset, the sheriff and county commissioners, they get upset. So now it was my job to escort this woman to the county line and make sure she didn't return."

"And the woman was?" Jenna asked, although she had a good idea.

"Luc—er—Special Agent Guardino. Ma'am."

"So you all had no idea there might be something going on here in New Hope?"

"No, ma'am. See, all we knew was something bad happened to Mrs. Harding when they still lived in DC. Felt bad for her. But it was years ago and far away. You think Kurt Harding would have gone to all that trouble to build her that fancy house up on the mountain? Bring her here if he knew those terrible things started right here in their hometown? Talk about bad luck."

Jenna didn't believe in luck. Good or bad. She made a note to check out the Hardings' history growing up in New Hope.

"There's no way Kurt Harding could have been involved? The killer could have had an accomplice." Maybe that was who had sent the letter. Angry with Lucy for not giving him due credit for the New Hope case.

"Lucy thought of that. Checked him out even after everyone else said the killer died. Well, asked me to, since she was officially off the case by then. But he had alibis."

"So Harding was the only victim with any ties to New Hope?"

"That we knew of at the time. Until we found Rachel Strohmeyer. See, the Strohmeyers are Mennonites from down the valley and Rachel had met an English boy—that's what they call us—while working at her folks' produce stand. College kid from Penn State. Liked to come up here and go spelunking. Real smart boy, knew everything about rocks and geology and prehistoric times. But her parents didn't approve. Anyway, when she vanished, they just assumed she'd run off with him. We looked for her, but she'd just turned eighteen, so…"

"You didn't look very hard."

"Wasn't anywhere to look. No clues at all." He shifted his duty belt, redistributing the pressure points from the various equipment. "Wasn't until Lucy got Kurt Harding all riled up. Folks talking again about what happened to Mrs. Harding back when she lived in DC. The FBI being here and all, that got folks really excited. Then someone overheard Lucy talking to the sheriff—the old sheriff, not the new one—about her theory there were more women all taken by the same man. Rumors began spreading… Well, that's when I escorted her out of the county. Except we didn't actually make it."

"Because you found Adam Caine and learned his mom had been taken."

"Right. At first no one thought they could be connected. Something that happened in DC three years before and Mrs. Caine being carjacked? Sounded crazy. Leaving the boy as a witness, taking her in daylight, it seemed so desperate. Not very smart. And Lucy said this guy was real smart. But anyway, you know the rest. How Lucy and Adam found the cavern entrance and saved those girls and Mrs. Caine, God bless her, died along with the killer."

Way too pat, Jenna thought. And the Caine abduction—desperate was an understatement. It felt different. Melodramatic. Like a magician's patter diverting your attention away from what was really happening. "The killer. You've no idea who he was?"

"No match to the fingerprints we found in the van. Lucy was the only one who could describe him at all, and she didn't get a very good look. The boy was about in hysterics. We couldn't find any missing person reports that matched and no one ever came forward saying they recognized him. Not around here, at any rate. The press flashed the composite drawing all over, but nothing ever came of it."

"What's your theory?"

"Me? I don't know. Sheriff—the new sheriff, old one was voted out not long after—says same as the FBI. Someone found the caves but wasn't local, just smart enough to come here when he needed to use them. I heard they searched other areas with natural cave systems. Down in Virginia and Tennessee. Thought he might have a few hideaways scattered all over."

Possible. Not caves though. He'd make each location special, she imagined. Or maybe Lucy was influencing her imagination. But the living victims had described different locations where they'd been kept prisoner. So if he was smart enough to have several lairs, why not just flee when Lucy began asking questions?

There was something about New Hope. Something that made it different. Important to him. She could almost hear Lucy's voice in her head. Wasn't at all sure she liked it there.

"Hey, Bob. Think I could take a look at the file myself?" She flashed him one of her best smiles, the one that got guys to buy her drinks wherever she went.

"Of course. Let me set you up with the computer. You just make yourself at home, Jenna."

An hour later, fueled by Bob's coffee and snicker doodle cookies he insisted she try, she realized just how messed up a case can get when the press and brass got involved. There was a ton of data and evidence—everything documented in triplicate. But most of it meaningless. Especially when you looked at the big picture and took into account Lucy's original profile. Which no one had bothered to do.

Too busy reassuring the public a heinous killer had been removed from this earth.

She was certain there were other agendas at work as well. Kurt Harding was a high-powered lobbyist and did his best to keep the story, and his wife's part in it, quiet.

Plus, she had to admit, the official story that the New Hope Killer—the *only* New Hope Killer—died in that cave four years ago, could very well be the truth. They had no idea.

No proof. No body. No way to identify the killer other than Lucy's description—which could have fit half the male Caucasian population—and a few smudged fingerprints in a van stolen from a Hagerstown shopping mall. Victim statements vague and contradictory. And reluctant.

Several of the living victims identified through DNA found at the crime scene had never reported their ordeal to the police. Out of fear, a desire to protect their children, and just plain old denial.

Two women who had reported their abduction and imprisonment to their local law enforcement never even had their rape kits tested or their cases adequately investigated. An officer in Virginia made a notation that one victim's story was so outlandish and unbelievable, he considered her emotionally disturbed and advised her to seek psychiatric help.

The killer had been taking women for at least a decade. And they had nothing concrete to identify him.

No wonder the brass had been so eager to brush over the fact they had no idea who he was and focus on the fact that he was dead.

Or so they hoped.

After reading the final victims' statements, Jenna wondered if Lucy was wrong. Maybe the New Hope Killer did have a partner. It just seemed too much for one man to accomplish on his own.

From the other survivors' statements, the Unsub had also used abandoned houses, packing containers, even an old church to hold his victims. Maybe he created a dramatic ending to his New Hope operation to keep authorities from looking further—maybe he, Jenna's living Unsub, killed his partner down there in the dark? Then the Unsub simply moved on, changed his MO enough that he didn't twing their radar.

Which probably translated to no more surviving victims. Not if he wanted to completely cover his tracks this time. So no more trophies.

The hairs at the back of her neck stood as she remembered what Lucy said about the killer using his own children as trophies.

She dismissed the feeling. Just the draft as Bob opened the door and entered, checking on her.

"So, what do you think?" he asked as if assuming she'd take one look at the case file and be able to answer all the unresolved questions. She held up her coffee cup—well, actually it was his coffee cup—and he hustled to refresh it.

Jenna leaned back. Technically, Lucy's old case had nothing to do with Jenna's current one. Except... How totally awesome would it be if she could answer all those questions? Put to rest the speculations once and for all? Her supervisor would love it. The USPS riding to the rescue, succeeding where the FBI failed.

It all hinged on the partner, her guy, being able to kill the man Lucy saw without revealing himself. Could someone have been down there in the cave with the killer and Marion Caine without Lucy knowing it?

"Bob, how'd you like to go for a drive? Maybe show me this Echo Cavern, so I can see for myself?"

He leaned back on his heels, scrutinizing her. "Suppose I could walk you through what little we found there." He pulled a small MP3 player from his pocket. "I downloaded the victim's statement. The college girl found with Rachel. Wasn't sure if you wanted to hear it."

"Thanks. We can listen on the way." Again with the hackles on the back of her neck, warning her this was so not a good idea. But maybe she'd find something Lucy missed. The chance was too good to resist.

Chapter 11

Marion Caine's grave was as neglected as her house. Weeds and straggly long grass grew between the memorial stone and the trimmed grass along the footpath as if the caretaker couldn't be bothered to do more than swipe the lawn-mower's blade across it. Dead leaves and pine needles clung to the stone, caught in the crevices in the granite marker.

It wasn't anything fancy. A cube shaped block of local granite. Her name. Date of birth. Date of death. That was all. Nothing to indicate how she died or even the fact that her body wasn't anywhere near this plot of dirt. Instead it was somewhere below the mountain, stolen by the underground river that cut through the limestone. Maybe someday bits and pieces of her skeleton would be washed up along a stream's bank or fished from a reservoir fed by underground springs.

Four years ago, Lucy would have wished for that. If only to give Adam and Clinton Caine something to bury, to center their grief on. But now, kneeling in the damp earth, tugging weeds, and brushing away the detritus covering Marion's stone, she doubted retrieving any piece of Marion would help.

From the police reports on Adam, it seemed as if Adam and Clint hadn't moved on so much as fallen apart.

The thought made her regret last night's argument with Nick. Crouched on her heels so the wet wouldn't seep through her slacks, she called Nick on her cell. The reception was weak, enough so his voice faded in and out, drowned by waves of static.

"Did you find him?" Nick's words fought through the crackle. "If you did, can you tell your people to go away? They're making my patients edgy."

Given that some of Nick's patients were former special ops and they all suffered from PTSD, that probably wasn't a good thing. "Sorry. Not yet."

"What? I can barely hear you."

She stood and paced between the graves, trying to find better reception. "I said, I haven't found him yet."

Nick's reply was a blur of static. "Megan wants to—party—Danny's—team—"

"You mean the soccer party tomorrow night? I already told her no. She'll be the youngest there and I don't—"

"I can't hear you—Lucy, you still there?"

The line went dead. Lucy glanced at her phone. No bars. Which also explained the nine missed calls. John Greally wondering why she hadn't shown for her psych eval. She pocketed the phone, reminding herself to call Nick from a landline when she had the chance.

John and the shrink could wait. She already knew what they'd say. Words like accountability, inappropriate attitude, career suicide.

She spotted movement at the far side of the cemetery. A tall man, skinny, sandy colored hair, jeans, black leather coat. He walked as if instead of growing up being told to stand up straight, he'd learned to hunch over, curling his spine to make himself look small, unnoticeable.

Adam. She moved forward to meet him, then stopped. Best to give him time alone with his mom first.

He didn't act like he noticed her, yet she thought he did. His gait quickened a bit, and when he reached Marion's stone, he knelt in the mud and snow with his back to her. Even kneeling, he seemed taller than she remembered. Certainly taller than his father, Clint. Clint was maybe five-ten, brown hair, brown eyes, one of those average looking guys you'd never notice in a crowd.

At fourteen, Adam was already beyond average. Not handsome, he was too lean and hungry looking for that. But he was almost Nick's height, six-one. Gave off the same kind of vibe she'd seen in prisoners doing hard time: as if their bodies were frozen in a never-ending state of apprehension, shying away from the danger surrounding them. Hard to believe this was the same boy she'd known four years ago.

His hands were naked in the cold. He pressed both palms flat against Marion's stone. Lucy was glad she'd cleared it off. His shoulders hunched even farther, head bowed so low she thought he might hit the top of the grave marker.

The wind rolled down off the mountain and swept through the cemetery, taking aim at Lucy's open parka, making her shiver and shove her hands deep into her pockets. She was tempted to zip it shut, there was no threat here, but she didn't want to risk disturbing Adam with the movement.

Finally, just as her toes went numb with cold, he turned to her.

"Agent Guardino?"

Lucy looked up, surprised at his use of her title and surname. She'd always been Lucy to him. He stood, weight unevenly balanced as if torn between running away and staying put, hands clasped in front of his belly, holding something in. Scared. The kid looked scared.

She covered the distance between them in a few steps. As she moved, so did he, edging sideways to place Marion's stone between them.

"Hello, Adam."

"You here alone?"

"Yes." His expression filled with despair and she knew it wasn't the answer he wanted.

"Can I ask you a question?" His voice as tight as his hands were knotted. He didn't meet her eyes.

"Of course." No, *Hey, how ya been? Last time I saw you a monster killed my mom and we both almost died.* Lucy waited to see where he led.

"You told me once you have a little girl about my age?"

"Megan. She just turned thirteen." If he was the letter writer—and Lucy was now more convinced than ever he was—he already knew that.

The air between them stuttered with the force of his inhalation as he gathered his breath. "Go home, Agent Guardino. Be with her. Don't let anything bad happen to her. To you."

The last came out in a snuffling half-sob. Lucy couldn't help herself. Stepping around the stone, she gathered the almost-man into her arms and hugged him as fiercely as she would Megan. "It's okay, Adam. Everything is going to be okay."

Lucy never made promises she couldn't keep. Hell, she wasn't even sure what she was promising him. The words just flowed and she couldn't stop them.

III

It was the wrong thing to say. Adam pulled away, knuckles swiping at his cheeks, gaze chiseling the memorial stone. "Please, leave. I need to find my dad. Go home, Lucy."

She wasn't family, couldn't take the place of a father. Still, it gnawed at her that she couldn't comfort or help him. Poor kid had been through so much.

He stood there braced against the stone, fists clenched at his sides—still holding in whatever fourteen year old boys kept to themselves. Lucy wondered if Megan would be like that in a year. She hoped not.

"Goodbye, Lucy."

He said the words but didn't turn away. As if testing her. Daring her to leave—or stay. She removed the letter from her pocket. Extended it to him. He shook his head, shoving his hands in his pockets.

"I know you wrote it, Adam. Want to tell me why?"

–

"One minute I was puking my guts out behind a frat house and the next I woke up in the dark…" The girl's voice trailed off. The recorder picked up a small, desperate snuffling sound. "Dark. It was so dark. I thought I'd gone blind."

The UNC student's voice wove its way into Jenna's mind as she listened while Bob drove them to the original crime scene.

"I was naked. It was cold. Hard stone, floor I guess you'd call it. Too rough to be manmade. And the echoes. Every little sound ambushed you from twenty directions at once. He—he handcuffed my hands. Behind me, at first. Later he didn't bother. But when I first woke up, they were behind me and the collar… God, I hated that collar. More than the chains or the handcuffs. It was so heavy. Cold. Dead. Made me feel like I wasn't human. But I was. I kept trying to tell him that. Told him about my parents and my brother and sisters and what I dreamed of doing with my life."

A pause accompanied by the rustling of tissues and a few sobs.

"He didn't say a word. Not at first. But I knew he was there. Felt him breathing, watching. I cried and screamed and pleaded. Until finally I just… stopped. Couldn't make another sound. I lay there on the cold stone and waited for what would happen next."

They turned off the paved road and bumped onto a narrow gravel one.

"That's when he threw water on me. He'd been behind me all that time. It was cold, so cold. Not as cold as his hands sliding over me, making sure I was wet all over. I begged—God, I don't even remember what I said— anything I thought might make him think twice. Nothing worked."

The murmur of a man's voice asking a question.

"What happened next? He—he laughed. Not a word to me. Just laughter that echoed and roared and hurt more than if he'd hit me. But then it got quiet. Except for this humming noise. God, how I hated that noise. But the first time, that first time, I didn't know what it was. But I knew it was bad. I tried to run. Ran as far as I could until the chain jerked me short and I slipped. He rolled me over, face up. Then he straddled me. I felt him getting hard. He kept rubbing himself against me. But all I could see was this tiny light. Buzz. It turned from red to green. Then it touched my breast and the world turned to fire."

The girl's voice shredded with pain. Jenna pulled the earbuds out, unable—unwilling—to listen further. She curled her arms around herself, pretending she was cold. Bob cranked up the heat and adjusted the vents to blow in her direction. Didn't help the real reason why her insides trembled.

"You okay?" he asked.

"Yeah. Fine."

The gravel road wound into the woods, ending in a snow-covered clearing. Not much snow, not yet, but enough to create a pristine carpet of white over the fallen leaves. That, along with the flurries swooshing through the crisp midday air and the hushed noise, made Jenna feel as if they'd been magically transported inside one of the snow globes her grandmother collected.

As they sat in the car, the engine humming, she half expected a girl's palm to crash down on top of them and shake them, turning everything upside down.

"Where's the entrance?" she asked.

"Sealed off with concrete and stone." He pointed to the bare rock at the base of the mountain. If she squinted through the snowflakes melting against the windshield, she could make out a difference in color. As if someone sealed a crack with putty and tried to make it blend in. "Didn't want anyone to wander in. Not again."

She swallowed hard. Stared at the unnatural pale rock. The girl's voice echoed inside her head. "I need to see inside. Is there another way in?"

He turned to give her a long, hard look. "After hearing that, you still want to go inside?"

Jenna nodded despite the shiver that shook her.

Without a word, Bob put the cruiser in drive, did a neat three point turn, and they left. Jenna had the sudden urge to cross herself like she would when leaving Mass. Been a long time since she'd been, not since her grandfather died. But her fingers lifted in the familiar movement with a primal reflex.

She watched Bob as they drove. He handled the cruiser easily, attending to the radio and computer terminal sitting between them as much as to the road. A single line creased his forehead and she wondered why he'd interrupt his day to take her on a tour of a crime scene four years old.

Sure, he smiled like he was attracted to her. Jenna expected that of men. But he had his own agenda.

"You think Adam might be there? Inside Echo Cavern?" she asked.

More trees, more dirt roads, then a two lane paved road—she wasn't sure if it was the same one they left town on, there were no signs—then another dirt road. This one was flat, gently curving behind a single story red brick school, into a forest, and coming out the other side with cornfields spreading out to the left and the foot of the mountain on their right.

Finally he answered. "Doubt it. Not after what happened inside there. But if you're looking, I'd like to be the one to find him. Make sure he's okay."

She shrugged. What was with this Caine kid that both Lucy and Bob felt the need to protect him? Kid was a fugitive from the law, plain and simple. "Fine with me. But if he's my guy, he's federal property."

He focused on the road, not answering.

A well-maintained wooden fence marked the property line until the road dead-ended at a stone barn. The barn backed up to the mountain, evergreens as tall as its hayloft on both sides, a paddock fenced in beyond the main doors. A small frame house, not dilapidated but obviously not occupied, stood a hundred feet away.

"Stolfultz used to keep his dairy cows here. Even used the caverns for storage—have for generations. Better than a refrigerator since the temperature is constant and you never worry about power running out. But now." Bob shrugged. "No one comes out here now. Not even the cows."

"How far are we from the first entrance?"

"By road, around three miles. But only about half a mile by way of a crow flying." He unfolded a map across the computer console between them.

"See how the river forces the mountain to twist and fold in on itself? The cavern beneath the mountain makes for a short cut. Folks said the Shamokin Indians actually used Echo Cavern that way—could go from one side of the mountain to the other no matter the weather and in a quarter of the time. Sneak up on their enemies. Or escape them, I guess. Just vanish into the mountain and no one could follow."

Jenna glanced out the window. Looked like something out of a fairytale. Rounded hay bales dusted with snow. Whitewashed barn and house against the dark green of the forest and mountain beyond. Nothing to be frightened of.

Bob folded his map neatly, grabbed his Stetson, and got out of the car. He opened the trunk, removed two heavy-duty flashlights then returned to her door. "Sure about this?"

She'd never been inside a cave before. Never even been inside a barn. Chiding herself for her sudden anxiety—she was a kickass federal agent, dammit!—she got out of the car and took one of the lights. "Aren't any cows in there, are there?"

"No ma'am. They're out in the pasture or inside the new barn across the way." He nodded with his chin.

Jenna scoured the landscape. Hay bales and empty fields with the occasional recalcitrant dead cornstalk as far as she could see. Then she made out movement on the horizon. A few black dots milling on a cleared hill, the mountain looming up above them. The mountains and trees made one feel penned in. Kind of like the canyons around L.A. Except less civilized.

Bob slid the barn door open along its rails. The sweet scent of hay and clover made Jenna sniff twice. Then she caught the sour smell of cow dung.

"Watch where you step," he cautioned, his footsteps stirring stray pieces of hay on the wood plank flooring. Stalls lined the walls. Lonely and gloomy in the shadows cast by their lights. Bob led her down the center aisle then turned past a room filled with steel milk cans and other equipment. They came to a large padlocked wrought iron gate. Beyond the gate was a black silence that made the dim light of the barn feel as cheerful as walking on the moon.

Lanterns hung on pegs outside the gates. Bob handed her his flashlight as he removed two, lit them, and then hung them from hooks dangling down from the rafters above. The oily sharp scent of kerosene mingled with the other smells.

"Aren't they worried about fire?" she asked.

"Amish," he said with a shrug. As if the word explained everything.

He removed a key chain from his equipment belt and unlocked the large padlock securing the gate. "Never used to lock anything around here," he muttered. He swung the gate open on well-oiled hinges bolted into a wall Jenna realized was solid rock. He lit two more lanterns. "Wait here."

He vanished into the shadows. The entrance to the cavern was lined with shelves, a few still holding milk cans, others smaller, designed for cheese and other perishables. The air was cool, like opening a refrigerator door on a hot summer day, and drier than she'd imagined.

Which didn't explain the trickle of sweat shivering down her spine as she stepped past the gate. Dim light revealed the path Bob had taken. Her grip on the two large flashlights grew slippery but she continued into the cavern, stopping at the place where he'd vanished, face to face with a wall of solid rock. She craned her head up. The ceiling was ten feet high here, also solid rock.

The weight of the mountain pressed down on her, making her work for each breath. She transferred one light into the crook of her arm and slid her fingers down the rough rock face. They came away damp even though the rock looked dry.

"Limestone," Bob came up behind her, making her jump. He took his flashlight back. "That's why you get those stalactites and stalagmites—can't ever remember which is which—but the ones hanging down will drip stuff that looks like milk but it's really rock eaten up by acid in the water."

He was so damn comfortable in here. As if there weren't tons of rock overhead ready to bury them forever. "Didn't come for a science lesson," she snapped. "Where's the crime scene?"

He pushed his hat up with the tip of his finger, then gestured down the way he had come. "Right this way."

She followed him a few steps. He'd hung the two lanterns about twenty feet apart but after that was total darkness. Hurrying to catch up with him, she touched his elbow. "Sorry about that. Never been inside a cave before. Do we need to worry about bats? They carry rabies, right?"

He made a clucking noise but she couldn't see his face in the dark. "No bats anymore. The white nose got most of them. But, yep, they do carry rabies. My kid brother had to get shots when he found one in his bedroom. Woke up and the damn thing was perched on his nightstand eyeing him like he was a piece of leftover pizza. Mom freaked out for sure."

His voice echoed. Jenna swung her flashlight up and could no longer make out the ceiling, just blackness spiraling over head, broken by the occasional glint from a stalactite hanging down. She searched the darkness in awe. Bob added his light to hers.

"Pretty neat, isn't it? And all created without the aid of man, science, or any of our gadgets." His voice hushed as if in church. He took her hand. "Stay close. There are drop offs and you'd never see them until too late."

They'd never found any of the bodies, she remembered with a shudder. Hadn't quite believed it until now, looking up into the belly of the mountain. She let him keep her hand. Just wished it wasn't so clammy with sweat.

Bob guided them through the darkness. Jenna was glad he was there. Even with the powerful flashlights designed for search and rescue operations, she'd never find her way in or out again.

Suddenly he stopped. "Okay. This is the other side of the first entrance. The way Lucy and the Caine boy came."

They'd only come a half a mile? Felt like ten times as far.

He led her through a narrow, high-ceilinged passage that opened into a larger cavern. She flashed her light about. Metal rings had been bolted into the walls and floors at various places. The dark stain that was Lucy's blood still marred the pale limestone rock only a few feet to the right of where Jenna stood. The ceiling sloped up from knee level to soaring out of sight. The opposite side of the cavern was wide-open, sheer blackness her high intensity light couldn't penetrate.

"This is it." Bob's voice was barely a sigh, telling her what she already knew. The temperature hadn't changed but goose bumps shivered across her flesh.

Jenna didn't answer. Instead she clicked off her light, keeping her thumb on the switch. She wandered into the center of the cavern, knowing there was nothing to trip her, but even with Bob's light still on, she felt disoriented, her stomach spinning as if she was falling. "Turn yours off."

"That's not a good—"

"Turn it off."

"Okay. But don't move. There's a sheer drop on the other side of the cavern."

Jenna nodded, hands out to her side as if bracing herself against the nothingness that surrounded her.

Bob's light went out.

The darkness was suffocating. Worse than being blind because she couldn't even try to imprint her memories on the black canvas of nothingness.

Her head pounded as the vertigo worsened. The sound of her heartbeat, of Bob's boots scraping against the limestone, of her gasps, of the girl's voice describing her torture. They spiraled and echoed, ricocheting from the rocks to ambush her from unexpected directions. Each sound was a body blow.

Each breath was swallowing thick, sticky cobwebs. They swelled up inside her, squeezing her heart and lungs, even as the blackness tightened around her from the outside, wrapping itself around her entire body, strangling her.

She dropped her light, clawed her neck, fought for air.

With one last cry of panic, she fell to the ground. But even with her palms pressed against the earth, she couldn't tell which way was up. The darkness just kept pressing down on her from every direction, crushing her.

Bob's light clicked on. Blinding. She blinked against the harsh light. He gathered her into his arms, helping her to sit up. Then he added her light to his. Twin beams of hope in the darkness.

"How long?" she gasped.

"Thirty, forty seconds, give or take," he said, his voice filled with concern. "You okay? Should've said you were claustrophobic. Never would've brought you in here."

She pushed to her feet. Red spots danced in her vision, but the panic banished. "I'm not. Claustrophobic." She held her light with both hands, unwilling to chance losing it. "Thirty seconds?"

"Yes'm." He stood beside her, his light glinting against one of the steel rings.

"And they were held here for weeks—"

"A few for months. Best we can tell." He cleared his throat. "Lucy said he liked the control the darkness gave him. He had night vision goggles, so he could see. Could surprise them, do whatever he wanted and they were powerless."

Jenna nodded. Powerless. Good word for it.

"Show me where the bastard died."

Chapter 12

Adam took the paper from Lucy. Stared at his own words in black and white. He barely remembered writing them. Idiot. So much for his brilliant plan.

Dad was right. Adam should leave the planning to him. A snowflake fell, blotting the paper and smearing the ink. He would if he could. He'd leave everything to Dad, follow him anywhere, do anything. But first he had to find him.

Lucy hugged him again. She pressed her palm between his shoulder blades, rubbing his back. The place his mother used to rub when he was a baby.

He didn't want to push her away, but after a moment spent with his eyes shut, imagining she was his mom, he did.

She hadn't changed at all. Still the dark hair that glinted red when the light caught it a certain way, worn tucked simply behind her ears. Still the expression that said she'd listen to anything he had to say. She wouldn't judge, because she cared, she really cared.

But if she cared so much, then, "Why did you come alone?" His voice deteriorated to snuffles but he felt no shame. Not with Lucy. "Now he'll never find me. I need him. I don't know what to do without him."

She gave him another hug, this time with one arm, pulling him so they stood side by side facing the memorial stone. "What happened, Adam? Why did you leave your father?"

He sank down to sit on the granite marker. Mom wouldn't mind and he wasn't sure his legs could keep holding him up.

Suddenly he realized the burden he'd taken on when he took Sally. He had to find Dad. He thought of Marty and Darrin facing those bullies—the ones in the playground and the ones in their own homes. Dad would know how to keep Sally and the boys safe. How to keep them all safe.

But Dad wasn't here.

"It was all my fault," he told Lucy. "I screwed up."

"Everyone makes mistakes, Adam. Did your father kick you out? Are you frightened to go home?"

He shook his head. "Of course not. I just can't find him. I've been looking and looking and I thought if I came back here and if you came with all the reporters and fuss and all, well, he'd know where I was. I thought he'd come and get me. Take me back."

It sounded stupid. He glanced at her, surprised she wasn't laughing at him. Instead she looked worried.

"Adam, sending a threatening letter wasn't the way to get your dad's attention. It's against the law."

"But—" For the first time ever, Lucy frightened him. Was she going to arrest him? She couldn't. Then who would take care of Sally? "I didn't hurt anyone. I just—" He swallowed hard. "I just wanted my dad back."

"I know. I know. Don't worry, we'll figure it out. And I'll find your dad for you." She brushed her palms against the back of her pants as if ready to get to work. "First, where are you staying? We need to get you hooked up with social services while we look for your dad."

"No." He stood, for the first time realizing how much taller he was than her. Not just taller. Bigger.

But she didn't look frightened at all. Not like the fish had. But Lucy was no fish.

"No social services. No foster home. No more creeps. I want my real family. A real home." Even if it was the bunk in the back of Dad's truck. Even if it was the floor of a dingy motel room. He didn't care. Anything was better than another Rick the Prick.

Lucy held her hands up but she didn't surrender. "Adam. You can't live on the street. It's not safe."

Wind gusted between them, a swirl of snow. Nothing serious, not yet. Just a promise. As if Mother Nature sided with Lucy.

Adam didn't care. "I have somewhere safe. I don't need social services." He backed up a few steps, his mom's stone between them. "I don't need you."

Before she could say anything, he sprinted for the trees. "Adam, wait!"

He didn't stop. He didn't look back. There was nothing left for him there anyway. Lucy couldn't help him. Not anymore.

Only Dad could.

Branches snapped against his arms and face but he didn't slow down until he was certain he'd lost her. He circled back through the trees, angling along the side of the mountain and came to a vantage point where he could spy on her. She'd returned to her car and was talking into her phone, walking in a circle, seeking him out. He held his breath as her gaze brushed over the spot below him.

He waited until she got in the car and drove away. Then he waited some more. The snow fell for real now, dusting his shoulders, helping him blend in. His cave was on the other side of the mountain. If he walked along the logging roads, it would be dark by the time he got there. What if they brought dogs to chase him?

But no one came. He climbed down and returned to where he'd hidden the truck behind the cemetery's barn. He glanced at the dashboard clock. Just enough time to go shopping before school let out.

He knew what he needed to do. Protect his family. Exactly like Dad would.

—

Lucy let Adam go. She cursed herself as he bounded from the cemetery and up into the trees on the mountain. He was a fugitive who'd crossed state lines. He'd confessed to a federal felony, using the mail to threaten her.

Jenna was going to be so pissed off. Lucy's first attempt at a phone call when she found one brave bar appearing on her cell wasn't to the postal inspector whose suspect she just allowed to escape. It was to Nick.

"My next patient is here," he answered. Not to be rude but to let her know he didn't have much time.

"Adam sent the letter. He just wanted to get me here. There's no threat to you or Megan."

"What about to you? Why did he want you there?"

Lucy wished she had all the answers. "He thought if I came it would be like last time, press and all. He's trying to find his father and thought the media attention would bring his dad here."

"That's one mixed up kid. You sure he's no danger?"

Her gaze scoured the mountainside, trying to spot movement between the barren tree trunks. Too far away, too many trees, too many hiding places. "He's no danger. Just in a world of pain. I wish I could help him."

"Come home, Lucy. There's nothing you can do for him."

Her breath shimmered silver in the cold. The flurries thickened, halfway serious. "I know. But—"

"You can't save the world. Although I love you for always trying." There was the sound of a knock. "Gotta go. See you tonight. Love you."

She pocketed her phone, but didn't get into the car, reluctant to give up on Adam so easily. The snow spiraled around her, quickly turning the world to gray. No movement on the mountain.

Maybe she couldn't ease Adam's pain. But she could keep her word and find his father for him. She hoped he knew that.

Finally she got into the car and drove away.

–

Once Adam was five, old enough to be left on his own, Adam's mom used to go fishing with Dad. For a while Dad was happy, so Mom and Adam were as well. Adam wanted to go with them but they'd leave him home, locked up safe and tight. When they came back a few days later, they'd be laughing and smiling and touching and kissing and he felt as if he had missed something special.

Then his mom got sick. One night Dad dragged him out of bed, said Mom was too tired and he was taking Adam instead of her. Adam had to put his shoes on twice—the first time he got them mixed up and on the wrong feet, he was so excited. He said goodbye to Mom. She seemed sad she wasn't going. Told him to do everything Dad said and not to ask any questions. Told him to make Dad proud.

Adam wondered why there were no fishing poles in the van. The back had been covered in plastic and the tackle box held duct tape, rope, box cutters, a bottle of adhesive remover, and handcuffs. He wanted to ask Dad what was going on, but as soon as they left the driveway, Dad hunched forward over the steering wheel, eyes wide with excitement, talking to himself as if Adam wasn't even there.

They didn't drive out to the lake like Adam expected. They drove over the mountain and into Altoona. Dad sat up straighter. He pulled a ball cap down over his eyes and adjusted the mirrors so he could see anyone coming as he slowly drove up and down the streets.

"There's a good one," he'd mutter. "What do you think of that one?"

It took Adam awhile to figure out he was talking about the women on the street. Adam had only been to the city once when Dad took him to visit Mom in the hospital the first time she got sick.

The city had its own melody. A bass line of car horns, women laughing in counterpoint, the click-clack of footsteps keeping rhythm. Adam loved the dense harmony but its strangeness terrified him. Nothing at all like the birds and crickets and farm machines that colored his world back in New Hope.

Years later when Dad told Morgan about Adam's first time fishing, laughing at what a rube Adam was, thinking that hick town was a real city—they were now in Atlanta, so he had a good point—Adam still remembered that symphony of city sounds, the way his pulse raced hearing it for the first time.

"That's the one," Dad finally said, pulling the van to the curb. "Jump out and reel her in."

Adam shifted in his seat, using the mirror to watch the girl. She looked a lot like Mom, except much younger. Dark hair, skinny waist, she wore a black halter-top and really short denim cutoffs. Her heels must have hurt because while the other girls turned the corner, this one lagged behind, leaning against the brick wall of a warehouse.

"What do I do?" Adam asked. He didn't like talking to strangers—heck, he didn't even like talking to people he knew. Far better to stay out of sight, keep quiet. That way he didn't get into trouble.

"Hop out. Tell her you're lost and ask to use her cell phone."

"What if she doesn't have one?"

"It doesn't matter. But if she does, you get it in your hand and don't let it go, hear me? And make sure she's facing you, not the road."

Dad had his own phone, so Adam didn't understand why he wanted a stranger's. But he got that look on his face, the one that made him look dark and mean and usually came before he took his belt off and Adam got a whipping. So Adam hopped out of the van and ran the half block to where the girl stood.

"Excuse me, Miss?" he said, out of breath and flushed with terror—what if he messed up? "Miss, could I use your phone?"

"Go away, kid," she said. "I'm busy." She adjusted the strap on her platform sandals.

"Er—I can't. Don't you have a phone?" Adam fidgeted. He had the sudden urge to pee. "Please?"

"What's wrong with you?" Then the girl looked more closely at him. "How old are you anyway? Whatcha doing out here so late?"

"I'm lost—"

Before Adam could say anything more, the van glided up behind the girl and Dad hopped out. She was still looking at Adam, fumbling in her purse, when Dad caught her in a bear hug with one arm and zapped her with a stun gun with the other. Adam had barely picked up the purse she dropped, and she was in the van with the door closed.

Adam stood there, holding the purse, not knowing what to do. No one else was watching them or even seemed to notice. Dad climbed from the back of the van into the driver's seat.

"You want me to leave you here, numbskull?" He started to pull away from the curb.

Adam ran, yanked the passenger door open, and jumped in.

"You really are an idiot," Dad muttered as he drove them out of the city. "You can't stand there forever jabbering with them. Just get the damn phone so they can't call no one and keep their attention off the road. Jeezit, a monkey could do a better job. I wish your mom was here. You should see her. Smooth as silk, bing-bang-boom, they're in the van, barely a hair out of place. You? Can't believe you're any son of mine."

"I'm sorry. I didn't know—" Adam shrank into his seat. His father's words hurt more than if Dad had used the belt. He'd been so happy to come along tonight, but obviously Dad expected him to know how to do this.

A muffled thud came from the back of the van. The big cooler on wheels shook and Adam realized Dad had shoved the girl into it. He hoped she was getting enough air, but didn't dare ask. Dad already thought he was an idiot for not knowing how to talk to the girl.

What were they going to do with her? Where were they going? Adam's mouth went dry as he considered the answers to those questions.

That's when he wet his pants. Dad didn't get angry. Instead he laughed and laughed and laughed.

Adam promised himself he'd do better next time. Make Dad proud of him. Mom, too.

Chapter 13

Bob kept Jenna behind him as they walked to the far edge of the cavern. "Step where I step."

The path wove between three large stalagmites jutting up from the floor, surrounded by deep pits. Jenna stopped and aimed her light down one. Slip and fall and a broken leg would be the least of your worries.

But the greater danger came from the sheer drop about fifteen feet from the cavern. Bob led her along a narrow ledge, their backs pressed to the rock face, shining his light across the crevasse. It sputtered out before hitting the other side. Then he directed it down. Again the high-powered stream of light died in darkness.

"Bottomless."

"Not really. But just as good for disposing bodies. Can you hear the river?"

She listened. It didn't sound like a river—at least not any she was used to hearing. More like a faint sigh that occasionally crested into a wail.

"Keep going this way," he pointed with the light along the narrow path, "and you come to two more chambers. Just like the first, only smaller."

"He kept multiple women here at once?"

Bob nodded, the light making the shadow from his hat brim dance across his face like a shroud. "Nancy Townsend, the UNC student you were listening to on the tape, she said she was originally held back here. Wasn't sure which cavern, but she heard another woman screaming not far away. Then he moved both women to the large cavern. Had a pulley system set up so he could manipulate them by the way he chained them. Made the other woman stand upright, on her tippy toes, while Nancy was secured to the floor, unable to do more than kneel or sit. When the chain around the other woman's neck began choking her and she didn't have the strength to keep standing, Nancy put her body under her feet to support her."

He paused. The light in his hand trembled, golden-white beams crashing on the rocks in ripples. "Guess he didn't like that much. Nancy interfering. Killed the other woman, gutted her, chained Nancy to the corpse and left it to rot for a few days."

Jenna fought to keep her shudder out of her voice. "Did we ID her? The other victim?"

"Nancy said her name was Adrian Goings. From Cincinnati. CSU found one of her teeth. DNA matched." He cleared his throat. "After that Nancy was alone for awhile. She's not sure how long before he brought her Rachel. She said he seemed very angry with Rachel. Was determined to break her—his words. Told Nancy it was her job to keep Rachel alive, no matter what."

"Jesus." Jenna pressed back against the wall, glad that the darkness shielded her face. She'd read the files, but hearing it here, it all suddenly seemed real.

"Rachel held out for a long time. Fought back. Never made a sound while he was there except to cite Bible verses. But in the end, he broke her. After that, she tried to hang herself with her chain. Nancy said she almost let her, was

133

ashamed that part of the reason she saved Rachel was fear. She was afraid of what he'd do to her if Rachel died. When he found out, he hogtied Rachel's arms and legs so Nancy had to feed her, get her to drink. Then he left them. They were rescued a few days later."

Jenna hugged herself. The leather coat no match for the chill that crept into her bones. "Rachel never said a word?"

"Refused to make a statement. Refused treatment at the hospital. Refused to see her family. Thought she'd kill herself for real, but she didn't. Guess maybe the baby helped get her through."

"Baby?"

"She was either pregnant before he got her or the baby was his, no one can say except Rachel and she isn't talking. She had a little girl. Sally—Sarah, she named her. Sweet thing. I thought for a while there Rachel might make it, but then she began using meth and heroin and hooked up with Roy Collins and his lot, and well, seems like hard luck just keeps knocking on her door. Can't tell you how many times I've been called out there on domestic disputes. She never says a word, just shows me Sally's well cared for and sends me on my way again."

He sighed. Jenna was glad she didn't have to deal with that kind of bullshit in her line of work. Shit like that would drive her nuts. Probably end up shooting someone just to make them see sense.

"Anyway," he stepped across her and towards the edge of the abyss. "Here's where it happened. I'm standing about where Marion and the killer were." He moved carefully to the edge of the crevasse. "Can you get a good look at me?"

"No. That rock outcropping is in the way."

"Exactly. He used it as cover. And Marion as a shield on the other side." He rejoined her. "All Lucy had was a tiny Maglite she held in her left hand, the same hand she struggled to hold Adam with. She had her gun in her right, plus she was bleeding and in pain. All either of them would've been able to see was Marion being pulled over and maybe the briefest glimpse of the killer."

"Miracle she saw anything." Which meant there could have been a partner. A killer who was still alive. Jenna's pulse revved into overdrive.

Bob began leading the way back through the cave system.

"No one ever had any ideas about the killer's identity?" Jenna asked.

Bob hesitated, finger pushing his hat up, casting a shadow on the wall that looked like some kind of goblin chomping down a nasty meal. "No. There's only one man unaccounted for who was seen in this area."

"Who's that?" she asked after they navigated the narrow slope leading away from the cavern where the women had been imprisoned.

"The Penn State student Rachel Strohmeyer supposedly ran off with. He was reported missing a few days before she was abducted."

"Do his prints match the ones on the van?" If so, they could find DNA, see if it matched any of the rape kits... Except all this would have occurred to Lucy and the other investigators four years ago. "They don't, do they?"

"No. His camping gear was found down in Georgia, near the Appalachian Trail. He told his friends he wanted to hike it that spring. They figured after he and Rachel broke up, he decided to get an early start. Even got a postcard from him."

"Before or after Rachel went missing?"

"Two weeks after. Three days before she was found. His prints on it, verified."

Seemed awfully damned convenient. But also very possible. College kids did stupid ~~shit~~ things like that. "He hasn't been heard from since?"

"No. But in all the fuss with what happened up here, I don't think anyone other than his family has done much searching. Appalachian Trail, that's one helluva big crime scene to cover."

Jenna stopped, trying to read Bob's expression in the dim light. "You don't think he's there, do you? You think the killer had a partner."

"Or maybe he's not dead. I'm not sure. FBI sure wouldn't agree. But I can't help but wonder why Rachel Strohmeyer never gave us a statement. If the killer was dead, why wouldn't she? But if he was alive and threatening her…"

"You think her missing boyfriend might be the killer?" No, he'd be much too young to have begun a decade or more ago. "No. You think he might be a hostage? After all this time? Or a partner?"

He shrugged. "I don't know what to think anymore. Until you showed up, I thought I was the only person still asking questions. Wondering if I'd screwed up."

"How is that?"

There was a long silence. He took her hand once more as he led her over the narrow ledge with the drop off on the other side. He didn't let go once they were back on safe ground.

"Guess I can't stop thinking that if I'd gone with Lucy, if I'd been in that cave with her, maybe she wouldn't have gotten hurt and we could have saved Marion Caine."

—

Taking the fish at the cabin in the middle of the Cuyahoga National Forest was ridiculously easy. Everyone let their guard down when they left the city.

Morgan liked the forest. Sounds were muffled. You could hear someone approach, but you also didn't need to worry about anyone hearing you until they were close. The thick foliage, hemlocks and rhododendrons, provided cover even now in the middle of winter.

Plus, it was peaceful. All the better to focus on the job at hand.

Clint let Morgan handle it all: from first approach to entry to subduing the fish with the stun gun. Then they were both inside the cabin with the fish on the floor between them. After that, everything happened just the way they planned.

Morgan skinned the fish of her clothing, then stood back to guard the only exit while Clint took his time getting to know her. The fish kept staring at Morgan, reaching a hand out. Idiot. Big mistake, thinking because Morgan was so young that was where salvation lay.

It always made Morgan laugh when they did that. It was so much fun to see their faces when Morgan knelt beside them, brushed their hair back oh so tenderly, then pressed cold steel to their cheeks, the point resting just below their eye.

Power. Sheer intoxicating power. Delightful the way it rushed through the veins.

Morgan first discovered the rush playing with a stray cat back in Kansas. Then playing mind games with the fish who called themselves parents. But the games Clint taught Morgan? They opened a whole new world.

A world Morgan never tired of. Not as long as there were fish in the sea.

Chapter 14

When Lucy got to the sheriff's substation in the old Dairy Treat, she found the front counter where people used to order soft serve now served as a reception desk manned by a civilian aide. She identified herself and was buzzed through the door to the former kitchen area.

The sheriff's department had made only the bare minimum of changes. Budget constraints no doubt. After all, this entire substation existed only to assuage voter anxiety after finding a monster in their midst. Wasn't like New Hope was a high crime area. And with a staff of only seven deputies, no way the sheriff could maintain a presence here. Probably more like a quick stop once a day as they patrolled this side of the county.

The original white tile walls remained, along with stainless steel counters running the length of the room. The walk-in freezer's door had been replaced with a metal mesh security door to create a makeshift holding facility. The pantry door now had a window in its top half. Interview room, Lucy surmised.

Jenna had made herself at home. The postal inspector had commandeered a desk, computer, a sheriff's deputy, and what looked to be the only coffee pot. Not to mention someone's coffee mug. She and the deputy, William Bob, were head to head, deep in conversation. When they caught sight of Lucy, they broke away abruptly.

"Hey, Lucy," Jenna called out as if she hadn't just seen Lucy a few hours ago. "You know Deputy Bob, right?"

Bob hadn't changed in four years: still clean-shaven, with teeth so white they'd squeak if you ran your finger across them. But his smile wasn't for Lucy, it was aimed at Jenna, even as he straightened and shook Lucy's hand. "Nice to see you again, ma'am. Let me know if there's anything I can get you."

Jenna shooed him away with a gesture. He turned, took a few steps, grabbed a second coffee mug from the counter, rushed back to press it into Lucy's hands, then left through the security door to the reception area.

"Did he just ma'am me?" Lucy asked, holding her cup out for Jenna to fill. Reminding the postal inspector who was boss.

"Don't be upset. He did it to me, too. While I fought the urge to card him. But damn, these Pennsylvania country boys are fine specimens of humanity. Now I see the attraction."

Lucy shook her head. Bob was the same age as Jenna and, living out here where he had daily contact with the people he worked to protect and serve, probably had seen more of reality than the postal inspector, despite her big city upbringing. "Glad you've had a good morning, because I'm about to ruin your afternoon."

"What happened? Did you find Caine?"

"I did. Actually he found me. Turns out that's what all this fuss was about. A misguided attempt to reach out to me." She didn't go into all the details. No need to unveil Adam's personal troubles.

"Great. So where is he? In the car?" Lucy said nothing. Jenna lowered her feet to the floor with a loud thump. "Don't tell me you let my fugitive go?"

"He's just a kid."

"He's *my* kid. It's my jurisdiction. My case. Officially you're not even here."

"It was a judgment call."

Jenna's expression mirrored one Lucy usually saw on Megan. "Next time at least do me the courtesy of asking my opinion about my case. If you don't mind, Supervisory Special Agent Guardino."

Lucy didn't take the bait. She'd had enough of adolescents for one day. "Let me call into Walden and we'll head home."

Jenna frowned, looked disappointed. "I thought you wanted to re-open the New Hope killer case."

"I wanted to make sure there was no threat to my family. We've done that."

"Maybe you've done that. Maybe. But I spent the morning going over the New Hope case. A lot happened after you were removed from it." Jenna's polite way of saying after Lucy became a victim instead of an investigator. No longer privy to the after-action reports, forensic analysis, or witness statements. "Did you know one of the victims you saved that day was an Amish girl named Rachel Strohmeyer?"

"Mennonite. And the other an undergrad from University of North Carolina. Why?"

"Strohmeyer's family lives just down the valley. But after you saved her, she didn't go back home."

"Where is she?" Lucy cursed her curiosity. If they left now, she'd be home in time for Megan's soccer practice.

"Here in New Hope. Lives in a trailer with a suspected meth dealer. I have directions if you want to pay her a visit. From what Bob says, she might need our help more than the Caine kid."

"Why the sudden concern? Strohmeyer didn't send any threatening letters via the United States Mail."

"Never met an Amish chick before. Plus, Bob said he was worried about her. Said he's certain the boyfriend's abusive but she'd never talk to him after neighbors called in complaints. Thought maybe a woman's touch would help."

So Jenna had a soft touch for victims of domestic violence? Lucy wondered how long that would last. The things they saw working felony sexual assaults and crimes against children—some people, no matter how well trained or motivated, just couldn't handle it.

"Okay. We'll stop on our way out of town." Lucy pulled the car keys from her pocket. Jenna promptly snagged them.

"I'll drive."

—

Having the truck turned out to be a blessing. Instead of going to Thomson's Hardware and risk being spotted by Lucy or one of her cop friends, Adam drove over the mountain and into Huntingdon where there was a Walmart.

Everything he needed. One stop shopping. With the cash from Sally's freezer, he didn't have to limit himself to what he could steal. It was a strange feeling, pulling items off the shelf without worrying about security alarms or armed guards chasing him.

Somehow not as much fun—but also no knot bouncing in his stomach with each step. No need to constantly be on the lookout for security cameras, RFID inventory labels, or nosy sales clerks. For the first time ever, he felt, well, normal as he walked through the aisles with their shiny displays calling out to him: *buy me, buy me.*

Maybe it was the boots. They made him walk tall, no slouching. And they rang out each step, making it impossible to hide. His heels stung with new blisters so he wouldn't be able to run again, not like he had from Lucy.

He added three down sleeping bags to his cart. Scooped in more flashlights. A porta-toilet with a seat—Sally would like that. Moving in jerky movements like the maniacs he used to avoid on the streets, he filled the cart. Duct tape. Rope. Socks. First aid kit. Dehydrated food rations.

Clatter, thud, ker-plump, he threw them all in. Not even reading labels. Too focused on not hitting anything. His anger at Lucy mounted. Should have never counted on her to make things right. Had to take care of this himself. There was only him. No one else. No one he could trust. No one who could save the kids.

He stopped. Knives. An entire wall filled with knives. Hanging in bright plastic sleeves that glistened in the overhead fluorescent lights like tinsel hanging from a Christmas tree. Short blades, long blades, multi-function, fixed, folded, serrated, straight, double-edged.

He didn't need another knife. He had his dad's. Razor sharp. Perfect for cutting what needed cutting.

But... His gaze fastened onto a Gerber Covert FAST. Titanium coated blade. One handed opening. If he had it, he could save Dad's knife. Use this one for workaday stuff like getting all this shit out of the plastic boxes they came in. It was so shiny.

He examined the knife; the overhead light reflected from the plastic wrappings at a strange angle, making the blade look red. Or maybe that was just his memory.

Either way, by the time he turned down the aisle with toys and coloring books, the knife was safely tucked away in his pocket, its wrappings kicked beneath the bottom shelf. You didn't pay cash. Not for a knife you were planning on using. A knife like that deserved the risk and thrills and effort that came from stealing it.

Suddenly he felt like himself again.

He had a plan—or the beginnings of one. After loading up on games and crayons and sketch pads, he realized he needed one more thing. Marty. He couldn't be sure about Marty. Darrin would be fine, but Marty... He hated the thought of treating family like fish.

It was all Lucy's fault. If only—never mind. He'd just have to risk Marty. Like Dad always said, sometimes you just had to go all in. That's where the fun was. The rush that told you you were alive.

He pushed the cart around a corner too fast and almost ran down two middle-aged women. Something about his face must have scared them because they scurried off faster than jackrabbits. He ignored them. Chain. Heavy as it rattled to the bottom of the cart. And locks, strong locks. Just in case.

No stun guns here in Walmart, although there were plenty of shoot-you-dead pistols and rifles and shotguns. Dad never relied on any one tool. If the stun gun didn't do the job, he'd use his bare hands or a cloth smothered in an adhesive remover made of chloroform. Adam turned away from the gun aisle and rolled his cart down the cleaning supply aisle.

Better safe than sorry.

Chapter 15

"Deputy Bob seemed upset he wasn't the one coming with you," Lucy observed as Jenna spun the Taurus out of the sheriff's station with a yank of the steering wheel. The postal inspector drove like a mailman, all jerks and stops and lurching leaps forward. Or maybe that was how people drove in L.A.

"Oh him. He's just a fetch and carry flirt."

"A what?"

"You know. A guy you flirt with to get him to fetch and carry. Doesn't mean anything."

"I'm not sure Bob would agree." Jenna's callous attitude surprised Lucy. She couldn't get a handle on the postal inspector. Had a feeling it was because she hadn't actually met the real Jenna Galloway yet. Just one mask after another. "Not very PC of you."

Jenna snorted. "Oh please. Sexual equality is bullshit and you know it. Don't tell me you never used your womanly charms to get what you wanted."

"Undercover, maybe. If it went with the role. But otherwise, no."

"Let me guess. Married your childhood sweetheart, haven't looked at another guy since." Jenna's voice dripped with disdain. And something more. An undercurrent of envy?

Lucy didn't answer. Mainly because Jenna was right. She and Nick were college sweethearts; she'd never met another man who made her feel like he did. "Guess I'm just lucky," she answered. "Found the right guy early."

"You mean you settled for a guy. Humans aren't meant to be monogamous. Mate for life like wolves. Which is one of the reasons they're going extinct."

"Does poor old fetch and carry Bob know what you think of him?"

"He's not an idiot. I'm sure he knows the score without me telling him." Jenna glanced over at Lucy. "I'm not a slut. I'm just a healthy woman who enjoys men—plural—any way I can get them."

Implying Lucy was some old biddy who couldn't get with the times. Maybe she was. She grew up not so far from here and even though she'd lived in Atlanta and DC, she never really left those small town sensibilities behind. Or maybe it was the security Nick offered after spending her days immersed in the extremes of human sexuality and witnessing firsthand the damage it could do.

Lucy answered, "And I'm a healthy woman who enjoys her man—singular—any way I can get him."

"Whatever floats your boat," Jenna said dismissively. But again the undercurrent of envy tinged with something else. Pain?

"Why did you volunteer for the SAFE team, Jenna?" Lucy had read Jenna's personnel file, knew her official answer, but she wanted the truth that would never make it into the files.

Jenna pretended to concentrate on the empty road. "Haven't these rednecks ever heard of street signs?"

"You mean like the one to the Twin Oak Trailer Park you just drove past?"

Jenna swore and hit the brakes, sending the Taurus into a controlled skid as she made a U-turn, sliding into the gravel drive of the park. "Couldn't see it from the snow. Which number?"

It was barely spitting flurries. "Forty-three."

"Have you seen Strohmeyer, I mean, since—" Jenna fumbled, obviously not liking her word choices. Lucy understood. Easier talking about Unsubs and crime scenes than real people with real names.

"Since Adam and I saved her? No." She tried to visit Rachel in the hospital after the docs finished stitching Lucy's own wound, but the girl had already left.

"The after-action report is pretty sketchy. She received medical care and a forensics eval but refused to sign the releases, so we never got access to any results. Never made a statement either. Refused."

"There's no body to compare the evidence to anyway."

"I guess. So, I thought she was Amish—"

"Mennonite."

"What's the diff?"

"They have cars and phones." Not that their connection to technology helped Rachel's family. Lucy remembered their initial interview when they realized their little girl hadn't just run off with an "English" boy. They'd held tight to each other, swallowing their emotions, leaving the station with a stiff gait, clutching hands and their Bibles.

The day after the rescue, she spotted two deputies escorting the Strohmeyers into the station., coming back from trying to see their daughter. They looked more haunted than ever. Worse than if she had died.

Jenna navigated through the twists and turns of the trailer park. "I'll circle the location first," she said, steering them around another curve. Procedure dictated scouting a residence, then parking a short distance away before approaching.

"Should be up on the left."

Jenna turned the corner too fast, gravel spitting behind them and a dead end in front of them. Not exactly a stealth approach—not that Lucy was anticipating the need for one. Still, she watched the windows and mirrors as Jenna made a three point turn. Hands inching back curtains in the trailer opposite and the one beside Rachel's. Hands no doubt also connected to cell phones.

"Sorry about that," Jenna muttered. They had no choice but to park in front of Rachel's trailer.

The good news was the only vehicle in the yard had a flat tire. The bad news was it was the last trailer on the street, backing on scrub bushes and a neglected meadow bordering the forest. Their car was the only cover and there were plenty of escape routes out the back.

Maybe the meth-head boyfriend was gone. That would make life easier for everyone.

Lucy checked her cell. One tiny bar, barely hanging on. "You got reception?"

She shook her head. Lucy handed Jenna her phone. "Call Bob. Ask him to send backup. If he can't, we'll come back later."

Before Jenna could complete the call, the door to the trailer slammed open. It bounced off the outside wall. A large man, shirtless, wearing saggy jeans below his hips, dragged a woman to the doorway. He held a pistol to her head. The woman—girl, really—was barely conscious. She slumped in his arms. Her shirt unbuttoned and hanging open, her hair stringy and matted. Rachel Strohmeyer.

"Come on in, five-oh," the man shouted. He swung the girl back and forth, using her shoulder to brace his gun arm. "Why the hell not? You're the least of my worries."

–

Adam parked the pickup beneath the overhang behind Stolfultz's hay barn. It was snowing harder now. With the cows in the main milking barn, no one would spot the truck all the way out here. It took him three trips to haul all of the supplies to the cave.

He set everything up in the main room, laying the sleeping bags out around the rock he used as a bed. A tight fit, but slumber parties were like that. At least the only one he'd ever went to was. A bunch of boys bumping and crowded and giggling when they were meant to be sleeping. He was six then. With his mom in the hospital, Mrs. Leary made her son invite Adam to his birthday sleep-over.

She hadn't realized she was inviting Adam to be a sheep in a den of wolves. She just thought he was a shy kid. A little strange. Too quiet for his own good.

He stayed quiet that night. Silently suffering as the other boys threw all his clothes out the window, leaving him shivering in his underwear. They played games where the winner got to pick the next torture: shoving Adam's face in the toilet and flushing it, giving him an Indian rub, squirting soda up his nose, locking him in the cedar closet and ignoring his tears because he was afraid of the dark.

But the dark turned out to be his protector. Left in the closet for the night, he made a nest for himself of old coats that smelled of Christmas and slept. In the morning when Mrs. Leary found him curled up in now-dirty underwear, she yelled at the boys and apologized to Adam, making him French toast while the boys ate plain old cereal.

Tonight would be nothing like that slumber party. Adam stepped outside to fill the Coleman lanterns, lit one and brought it back into the cave so he could assess his arrangements in brighter light. Perfect. The boys would love it.

He checked on Sally in the pit, anxious to see her joy at the new art supplies he'd gotten her. She was curled up, sound asleep, sucking her thumb. He didn't have the heart to wake her. Besides, it was nearly time for school to let out and he needed to pick up the boys.

He left the light at the top of the pit so she wouldn't wake to darkness, grabbed his new knife, duct tape, and plastic baggie with the washcloth he soaked in chloroform, and went to collect his brothers.

Chapter 16

Rachel's head lolled to one side. Then she raised her lips to kiss the hostage taker's cheek.

Being caught in the middle of a hostage negotiation with a suspected meth-user was bad enough: they tended towards the paranoid and unpredictable end of the crazy spectrum.

But a hostage situation where the hostage was too stoned to realize she was a hostage? Talk about a nightmare.

Lucy made a snap judgment call. Defuse the situation before things escalated. "Cover me."

"Where the hell you going?" Jenna asked, drawing her service weapon.

Lucy didn't answer. She left the car and stood with the engine block between her and the hostage taker's shaky aim. She raised her arms, palms up. No threat here. Just your ordinary Pittsburgh soccer mom.

"What's your name?" she called, feeling the weight of stares on her from all sides. As if the trailer park had sprung to life in a heartbeat. "How can I help you out of this mess?"

The hostage taker scratched at his beard with the barrel of his pistol. Unfortunately the weapon didn't discharge and he never gave Jenna a clear shot. The postal inspector qualified as expert on the range but had no real life experience.

Lucy hoped she wouldn't get any here—at least not if Lucy did her job right.

"It's cold out here, Roy. Take me back inside, baby. Light me up again. I'm crashing hard," Rachel murmured, her eyes fluttering open. Rachel slumped in Roy's arms once more. "Why're we out here? What's going on?"

"What's going on?" Roy shouted as if Rachel were in the next county. Or as if this was somehow her fault. "Someone's stolen my boots, my truck, my jacket, and Leon's money. He's on his way here now to settle up and I ain't got squat to give him except your sorry ass."

Lucy wished Roy's conversation with Rachel involved more body language. He relaxed into a pose holding Rachel tight as a shield against his body, his weapon aimed at her head, finger on the trigger. Lucy glanced into the car at Jenna who gripped her Sig Sauer with both hands, steadying her aim on the open window ledge. It was a shot Lucy wouldn't trust to a trained sniper, not the way Roy kept moving his head up and down behind Rachel's, so she shook Jenna off.

"Sounds like hard times, Roy. My name's Lucy. Maybe I can help."

He jerked as if he'd forgotten she was there. "How the hell you gonna do that? Got three thousand dollars in your purse there, Lucy?"

Lucy didn't even have a purse. Much less three thousand cash. "I could invite you down to the sheriff's station. If you're safe and sound in custody, might give Leon time to cool off." The throbbing sound of a motorcycle missing its muffler rumbled through the snow-laden air. "You can even tell him we confiscated it. No one the wiser and you'd be clear."

Except for the attempted murder and assault charges he'd be facing. But no need to tell him that.

Roy seemed to consider her offer until Rachel began squirming in his arms. "Hit me again, baby. Please. I'll do anything you want." The girl didn't even bother opening her eyes as she shimmied her hips against Roy's pelvis and reached between his legs with her hand.

The roar of the motorcycle grew louder and Lucy realized there was more than one of them. Shit. Hopefully Bob and his fellow deputies were on their way. Fast.

"What do you say, Roy?" she called out before Rachel could distract the man further. "Leave here safe in my custody or face Leon and his buddies on your own?"

"I'm good as dead either way," he said with a sigh. He lowered his gun and Lucy thought he was about to surrender when the first cycle spun through the gravel, rounding the corner, a second bike close behind.

The first rider, a bald man with biceps bigger than Lucy's thighs, quickly sized up the situation—tipped off by one of Roy's friendly neighbors, no doubt—and raised a Mac-10 semi-auto machine pistol. He aimed towards the trailer, rolling his wrist sideways like he'd seen too many gangsta movies.

"You pissant little snitch!" the biker hollered.

Roy raised his gun at the bikers, who now numbered four, and bullets flew.

With Lucy in the crossfire.

—

Jenna leaned out the window, weapon still in hand, not sure who to aim at, Roy or the bikers. Roy spun towards the trailer door. To give the man credit, he shoved Strohmeyer inside before reaching behind the door and pulling out a Remington pump action shotgun. From the fist-sized hole his first shot punched into the second biker, Jenna figured it was loaded with slugs.

Jenna gunned the engine, thinking the middle of a firefight was not the best place to be right here and now. "Lucy, get in!"

Too late. Lucy had already dove beneath the Taurus.

Jenna took aim and dropped the first biker, but now the other two were firing at Roy, the trailer, and Jenna.

Bullets pinged against the Taurus. Roy took at least one round, stumbling as he pumped another shell into the Remington. Jenna juggled her weapon and the cell phone, calling for backup. Was assured it was on the way. "Faster, damn it!"

She fired two more shots but missed both times. Blamed it on the side view mirror she was using to aim with as she wormed her way beneath the window and as close to the front of the car as possible.

Another biker went down—not because he was hit but because Roy blew out the guy's front tire to hell and back. That pissed the bikers off more than it scared them and they fired a fresh volley at Roy.

The aim of their illegally modified Mac-10s wasn't very accurate and they only hit the trailer, shattering the kitchen window. There was a low roar, almost subliminal, like a cougar clearing its throat before it pounced. Roy glanced behind him, fear in his eyes.

"Sonofabitch—" His shout cut short by the fireball that blew the roof off the trailer.

The Taurus rocked with the blast, the sound deafening. Jenna peered above the dash, hoping Lucy was okay. Roy dove and rolled. He lost his weapon in the process but miraculously avoided any of the flying debris.

The last two bikers weren't as lucky, both flattened by the front wall of the trailer. One scrambled to his feet with blood running down his leg, but his escape was blocked by a patrol car. Deputy Bob to the rescue.

No more gunfire. Jenna hauled herself up and out of the car. She rushed to help Bob secure the bikers before they could recover.

Lucy rolled out from her cover and grabbed Roy, pulling him clear of the flames now dancing across the lawn. One of the propane tanks blew. It flew into the air and bounced off the Taurus' roof, leaving a dent that was going to be hard to explain when Jenna signed it back into the pool.

Not to mention the fact it was directly over where she'd been sitting just moments before. Adrenalin sang through Jenna as she jerked a biker's arm back to cuff him. He cried out in pain, but she barely heard it through the ringing in her ears.

"Rachel," Roy sobbed, lunging back towards the trailer. It was way beyond too late for Strohlmeyer. Not with the blaze so hot it bubbled paint into ugly black blisters and the entire structure engulfed in the inferno.

"We're gonna need hazmat," Bob spoke into his radio, rallying reinforcements. "Whatcha cooking with, phosphorus or ammonium nitrate?" he asked Roy.

Roy's face twisted into something ugly as he stared at the fire, not fighting Lucy as she marched him past Jenna and his biker friends. "I'm not saying shit without my lawyer."

Bob shrugged as if he'd expected as much. "Oh, and call the coroner. Tell him he's got a crispy critter, so be prepared for a bit of a mess."

Roy turned green at the words, bent double, his wrists cuffed behind his back, and vomited into the rhododendrons on the side of the road. Jenna dodged the splash back just in time.

She surveyed the scene with the biker prone and cuffed at her feet. So much for the quiet of country living. Laughter bubbled through her but she choked it back and forced her focus back on her prisoners.

Helluva lot more fun than chasing down a kid sending anonymous letters.

The strange feeling of being disconnected, everything moving in slow motion, wouldn't leave her. Each breath filled her mouth with the taste of cat piss and burnt plastic; she couldn't stop trying to swallow it away.

Finally, she bent to the second biker, the one she'd shot. He wasn't moving, was face down as she searched him for weapons. Safety first. After removing a knife and two pistols, she rolled him over to begin first aid.

His face was pale but she could swear his lips were moving. Fighting to breathe or trying to tell her something, Jenna wasn't sure. She pulled open his leather jacket and vest. Blood gushed up as she opened the vest, like water caught behind a dam that burst. She wadded his tee into her fist and pressed her weight against it.

Blood kept welling, covering her hands, at first bright red, then darker and darker.

"I need some help here!" she shouted. "Don't you die on me, you bastard," she told him as she fought to stop the bleeding. "Don't you dare."

His lips kept moving even after his eyes went dead. Why wouldn't they stop moving? Was he cursing her or forgiving her? She needed to know. She had no idea how long she knelt there, trying to force life back inside him, but finally Lucy pulled her away.

"He's gone," Lucy whispered.

The sounds of the scene: the roar of the fire, the snap of plastic exploding, the ambulance wailing and the fire truck's horn blaring, rushed back as if a bubble surrounding Jenna had popped. The noise cursed and clanged and clamored for her attention but she couldn't tear her gaze away from the man she'd killed.

Still the taste of cat piss and ash caught in her throat. Sagging, only Lucy's grip around her waist keeping her on her feet, she bent double and vomited, staining the freshly fallen snow with bile.

Chapter 17

When Adam was in fourth grade, during his last year at school, and the bullies chased him, he'd devised a few plans of escape. The first was to remain inside his classroom, hoping they'd forget about him. Big mistake since as soon as the teachers left for bus duty, he became an easy target in an enclosed space.

Next he tried being the first out the door, even if it meant leaving his coat and books behind in his locker. He'd stand right in front of everyone, teachers especially, on the curb, waiting for his bus. But the big kids would simply follow him on board and push him into the back while the bus driver talked to the teachers. Or worse, they'd drag him behind the bus and keep him there until his bus left without him and he'd be forced not only to suffer whatever torture they had in mind that day but also walk home alone in the cold, without his coat.

His third stratagem had a fifty percent success rate. Better than the first two, it quickly became his preferred option. He'd jump the fence near the teacher's parking lot, hide behind a car—usually Mrs. Chesshir's Beetle, just because it was so cool he loved being near it and always had the secret hope she'd find him and offer him a ride home— and then make a run for the bus just as it was pulling out of the drive. If the driver saw him and was in a good mood, he got a ride home and an excuse to sit in the front of the bus. If not, he had a head start on anyone chasing him.

One January day during his final year at school, he slipped going over the playground fence and fell into a cinder and salt covered snow bank at the edge of the parking lot. The big boys spotted him and pelted him with ice-balls as he fought to regain his feet. The biggest, meanest bully of all, Fat Ollie, was heaving his weight over the fence, ready to pounce on Adam, when a miracle occurred.

Mrs. Chesshir came out, looking regal in her long puffy down coat and jaunty red beret, and caught Fat Ollie and his friends just as Ollie stomped Adam's face into the snow bank.

Ollie and goons got detention while Mrs. Chesshir clucked over Adam's sorry state. She wiped snow and ice and cinders and salt from his face and hair and front, finally pronouncing him much too wet and cold to risk a ride home in a drafty old school bus, and offered to drive him home herself.

So there he was, perched high in the front passenger seat of Mrs. Chesshir's bright yellow bug, toasty warm with the heat howling from the vents, waving goodbye to Ollie and company. One of the best days of his life.

Still was.

He wasn't too surprised to see Marty and Darrin had adopted the same survival skills. Marty was already over the fence, trying his best to help Darrin make it to the other side, but Darrin kept falling, his weight pulling him back to the playground side.

"Go without me," he told Marty as Craig Mathis and his comrades in arms rounded the corner.

"No. You can do it."

"Hang on," Adam said, striding up from behind the corner where he was blocked from everyone's view except the two boys. "Darrin, swing your leg up. That's right. Now push your hip over, shove your weight behind it."

Gravity helped, dumping Darrin onto the ground—but on the right side of the fence. The boys gave a whoop of delight and raced to join Adam.

"Darrin says you're his big brother," Marty said. "They told us about you guys in Sunday School. Said you do cool things with younger kids like teach them stuff?"

Wrong kind of big brother, but Adam didn't correct him. "That's right. I thought today it would be fun to go exploring a cave. It's very safe," he quickly added when Darrin showed alarm. "There are tons of cool Indian artifacts and stalagmites and even a room that glows in the dark. What do you think?"

At the mention of Indian artifacts, Darrin bobbed his entire body from his nose to his toes in eagerness. "Cool. Can Marty come, too?"

Adam hesitated. Pretended like it was a big deal. "Okay. But I need you guys to run over to the woods. See where that path starts? Wait for me there while I go tell your bus driver not to worry, that you're with me. Make sure no one sees you because there's not room for anyone else, okay?"

The boys nodded and took off for the woods. Anyone who saw them from the school windows—although the classrooms were empty so it was low risk—would simply see two boys playing. Adam walked around to the far side of the school, towards town, then as soon as he hit the road, he turned into the trees and doubled back, out of sight.

Easy as pie, Dad would say.

The first person Lucy called as she and Jenna followed Officer Bob over the mountain to Huntingdon was Nick. Just in case this cluster-fuck made the evening news. After letting him know she'd be stuck in Huntingdon for the foreseeable future, she hung up and called John Greally, her Assistant Special Agent in Charge.

"So now you call? Where've you been for the past eight hours?"

"You know where. New Hope. Galloway and I got caught in a firefight." She quickly explained.

"Anyone hurt?" he asked.

"No," she answered, knowing he meant law enforcement. "But one shooter DOA and two more injured. A woman presumed dead in the fire. Our witness."

"Cut the crap. You had no reason to be there and that girl had nothing to do with Galloway's case. If the locals make a stink, this could have serious ramifications."

"Technically, it's a Postal Inspector Involved Shooting. Maybe let them handle it, keep the Bureau out of things?"

"Were you involved?"

"Only as a witness. I took cover, didn't fire a shot. Never had a chance it was over so fast."

"Maybe that would work. Who the hell do I call? Not like there's been many US Postal Inspector Service involved shootings. How's Galloway doing?"

"Stunned. But okay. She handled herself well." She didn't tell him about Jenna puking over the dead biker's body. It was a perfectly normal reaction to that kind of stress but no reason to give the desk jockeys any reason to Monday morning quarterback.

"Locals giving her a hard time?"

"No, not at all." The sheriff's dispatcher recorded the entire incident since Jenna had been on the phone to Deputy Bob at the time. Plus he'd seen most of the action and corroborated her story. "She's in the clear."

"You're certain this has nothing to do with any case we have jurisdiction over?"

"No sir. Just wrong place, wrong time."

"Okay. Let me talk to someone over at the post office and I'll get back to you. In the meantime, Galloway needs to be on restricted duty."

"The locals already took her gun into evidence."

"She doesn't carry a backup?"

"No."

He made a noise that sounded like a swallowed chuckle. "By the time she's finished hanging out with you, she will. Keep me posted." He paused. "And don't think I've forgotten about your psych eval. You're walking a fine line, Lucy. Don't do anything I'm going to regret."

He hung up. Lucy handed Jenna the phone. "Anyone you want to call? It's okay if you need to talk to someone. Just use my phone so you won't have to worry about the record."

Jenna said nothing. She stared straight ahead at the snow swirling in the headlights. Then she looked at her hands, frowning at them as if she still had blood on her, despite the paramedics cleaning her up at the scene. Then at Lucy. Back to the snow.

"You killed a man, didn't you?" Jenna asked.

Lucy knew Jenna knew the answer—anyone not living on the moon heard about what happened in September, given the national headlines and media coverage. "It gets better. I promise."

"I don't even know his name. Do you?" Jenna swiveled towards Lucy, stretching her seat belt. "Know his name?"

"No. We'll find it out soon enough." Lucy hated to tell the postal inspector, but knowing the name only made things worse. It gave the ghost a voice. And Jenna would be haunted no matter how righteous the shoot.

"His lips kept moving. Like he was trying to say something. They just kept moving."

"Probably pressure from you leaning on his chest."

"Oh." Jenna hauled in a breath. "But they just kept moving."

Lucy steered into the sheriff's parking lot. The snow had accumulated enough to skid the Taurus' rear wheels as she turned into a space and hit the brakes.

"This is it?" Jenna asked, leaning forward to peer up at the two-and-a-half story fieldstone building. "Are you serious? This place belongs in a museum."

"Built almost two hundred years ago." Lucy kept the car running but turned the windshield wipers off so they could have some privacy. "You okay with this?"

Jenna shook her head, her gaze aimed up at the top floor. "Is that a turret? Like on a castle?"

"Yes." Lucy didn't care about the sheriff's department's antiquated design. "If you need to wait until tomorrow, it's no problem. You have twenty-four hours."

"I feel like I'm Robin Hood visiting the freaking Sheriff of Nottingham."

"Jenna—"

The postal inspector turned to face Lucy. "I'm a fully trained and qualified federal law enforcement officer who shot and killed a man who was shooting at me and my partner. There's nothing more to say. I'm fine. Honest."

She opened the car door and marched up the steps and inside the double doors before Lucy could say anything more.

The interior of the department was like local law enforcement offices all over the country: cramped, under-manned by overworked officers and civilian staff, gray industrial carpeting, acoustic ceiling tiles once white now grayed by age, and the background vibration of people talking, walking, and ready for action.

The receptionist passed them off to a deputy who escorted them into the bullpen. The noise level suddenly decreased as all eyes focused on them. First at Jenna, but the older staff turned their attention to Lucy, recognizing her from four years ago. The deputy fled, leaving them standing beside an empty secretary's desk.

"You know how much a meth lab cleanup is going to cost me now that the federal money's dried up?" barked a man in a brown suit through the open office door behind the secretary's area. The uniformed officers ignored him, knew he wasn't talking to them. He remained at his desk, beckoning Lucy and Jenna inside like an old-time king seated on his throne.

"Jack Zeller. That's Sheriff Zeller to you," he introduced himself with a flick of his bolo tie. "Don't suppose we could work a deal? I'll trade you one hazmat clean up for a walk on the OIS."

Lucy's smile was diplomatic. They both knew he had no say in the officer involved shooting investigation's outcome. "Sorry, Sheriff. No can do."

"What was his name?" Jenna asked, her voice with a hint of a quaver.

"Who? Oh, Leroy Lamont. That's the one you nailed. For the next few weeks, maybe even a month, our crime rate will be cut in half thanks to you, Agent Galloway."

Jenna swallowed hard and nodded, saying nothing, not even correcting her title. But her color was pale.

"Sit, sit," Zeller instructed.

Jenna sank into the chair in front of his desk, just tall enough to make eye contact with him over the stack of brown cardboard folders. Lucy remained standing, her adrenalin still pumping too fast to let her sit still.

Zeller narrowed his gaze at Lucy. "I remember you. Why do you always bring trouble with you?"

Then he gave Jenna a grandfatherly smile, even though he was only in his late forties. "I never been where you are, young lady. Most of us around here haven't. But you need anything, need someone to talk to, you just let me know."

"We appreciate that, Sheriff," Lucy answered for Jenna. She felt protective of the younger woman. "How long do you think you'll need Inspector Galloway here for the investigation? It'd be nice to get her back home."

Jenna planted both feet on the ground. "No. I still have a fugitive to catch."

"Who's that, then?" the sheriff asked. "I thought you were following up on Rachel and the New Hope Killer. Is there something else going on in my jurisdiction I should know about?"

"No," Lucy said in a firm tone.

"Yes," Jenna argued. "I'm on the trail of a kid who sent a federal agent a threatening letter. In violation of US Code 18-876."

"What kid?"

"Adam Caine. And we'd already be long out of your jurisdiction if my partner here hadn't—"

Lucy spun to face Jenna. "I'm sure the sheriff has more important things—"

"The Caine boy's back?"

Before Lucy could answer, Deputy Bob poked his head inside the office. "Docs cleared Roy. Once we're done processing, I'll take him upstairs to interview number three."

Jenna stood. "Can I listen in?"

The sheriff glanced at Lucy who nodded. "After you give your statement. Roy can stew awhile, think on what's happened today." The sheriff motioned for Bob to take her. Then he scrutinized Lucy. "You remember me from before?"

"You were Chief Deputy then."

"Sheriff Dobbs was running unopposed that June. But after you and—" He raised his hands wide. "Everything, he lost. So I became Sheriff by default. Oh, it's official. Ratified by the County Commissioners and all, but still. Not how any of us wanted things. I'm sure you understand if the last thing I need on my watch is you barging into my jurisdiction and stirring up ancient history."

"Not my intention. I just came to see if I could help Adam Caine. Figured I owed him that much." She made a mental note to call her office and get the ball rolling on tracking down Clinton Caine's whereabouts as soon as she was finished here.

He scowled. "Reckon you do. Owe him. You see the New Hope substation? They dedicated it to Marion Caine. Only place Bob will work out of."

"He's a good man. Saved our butts today, that's for sure."

"Yeah, he's okay. Gets a bit moody at times. Mainly come spring."

"On the anniversary?"

He nodded. "Has it in his head that if he went into that cave with you, things would have worked out differently."

"He's wrong."

"Hear you're working sexual predators and crimes against kids. You like that stuff?"

"I don't like the crimes. But," she shrugged, "I'm good at it."

"Not many can stomach it." He jerked his chin as if in approval. Like she'd redeemed herself somehow. "But it needs to be done. Imagine it must be hard to keep that kind of work at work, not bring it home with you?"

Before Lucy could answer, a female deputy ran in. "Sorry to disturb, Sheriff, but I've got a mom out here says her six-year-old never came home from school. I think you should talk to her. Sounds for real."

Zeller got to his feet—not appearing rushed but definitely moving faster than Lucy would have otherwise given him credit for.

"Can I help?" Lucy asked.

"This what you do in the city?"

"High risk missing juveniles? Yes."

"Come along with me," he commanded her, jurisdiction be damned. "If this is for real, we're going to need all the help we can get."

As Lucy followed him from the office, he glanced over his shoulder at her and shook his head. "Trouble. Always trouble."

Morgan's fun was over much too fast. Not the fish's fault. Not this time.

Clint had gotten upset. Grabbed the poker he'd been heating in the fire and plunged it into the fish, spearing it, gutting it, batting it until bits and pieces sprayed the cabin like a piñata bursting.

It would have been a great climax to the week, especially if Morgan had a chance to play as well. But coming so early, before the fun even got started, before Morgan had a chance to try any of the bright and shiny tools in the doctor's kit, well, that was disappointing.

Morgan really was to blame. And the Google alerts Morgan set up for each of Clint's children. When Clint saw them come across the phone, he went ballistic. No one messed with his kids. No one.

The fish paid the price.

They both knew it had to be Adam. Sending a message to Daddy.

How could Adam be so stupid? He could ruin everything. Should've killed him when they had the chance in Cleveland, instead of leaving him for the cops to grab.

Morgan shrugged and turned to the dirty work of moving the fish onto the chair beside the fire. A quick dousing with the doctor's favorite scotch, a tumbler overturned on the hearth, and voila! Instant inferno destroying all evidence they were ever here.

They watched from the van, making sure the entire cabin was demolished, then left. Once they hit the highway Morgan used a burner cell to call 911. Didn't want the entire forest to burn. Much too lovely a place.

But a fire could be a good thing. Cleared out the weeds and brush, leaving healthy trees more room to survive.

Sometimes Morgan wondered if Clint's attachment to his other kids was like that. Clearing them away would give Morgan space to breathe. Might be a chance to get rid of the weeds.

Starting with big brother Adam.

Chapter 18

Bob escorted Jenna up a set of creaky wooden stairs to an interview room on the second floor. She was glad she kept her coat: The room boasted no central heat and a draft around the window AC unit. The radiator along the wall hissed and creaked but when she touched the ancient cast iron housing, it was cold.

"I'll be right next door," Bob said, hesitating as if worried about leaving her alone. "Watching over Roy."

"Don't let them start without me. I want to hear what the hell that was all about out there."

He gave a little shake of his head and his finger reached for his hat even though it hung on the pegboard downstairs. "Doubt anything he says will answer the questions you have."

A few minutes later the detective arrived. To Jenna's surprise he was African American. The first black face she'd seen since leaving the city this morning. He was in his late fifties, older than the sheriff, even, and she wondered how he wound up here—a drafty room that smelled of wet socks in a building so old it should have had a moat dug around it. Helluva way to end a career.

"Let me guess," she said by way of breaking the ice as he arranged his recording equipment. "Your family's been here milking cows for the past two hundred years, right? Isn't that everyone's story around here?"

He chuckled. A deep rumble so genuine it made her smile. She loved men who knew how to really laugh. No pretense at politeness, just letting it all hang out. "Not my family. Far back as I know they've been boosting cars and rolling drunks in Newark." He put out his hand. "Ed O'Hara."

"O'Hara?"

"Stepdad adopted me. Now his family, potato farmers back two hundred years—until they got conscripted into the English army and sent over here. Fell in love with this area. Said it had almost as many shades of green as back home in Kerry, so they stayed."

"Haven't seen much of that green today."

He gave her a knowing smile. "Come back in the spring. June. When the mountain laurel starts blooming and the wheat smells so sweet." He sighed, then flipped his notebook open. "You ready, Inspector Galloway?"

He made all the official noises for the recorder: her rights, the time and date and circumstances of the interview, his credentials. She almost lost track of why they were there until he paused and nodded to her.

The statement took less than four minutes. It came out smoothly, just as she'd rehearsed in the car. Sounded like any other witness statement she ever reported. No hint of the shock that ambushed her after, no tremble to betray the roiling in her gut now. Amazing. A man's life ended just that quick. A few sentences and it was over.

He asked a few questions for the record, but given that the entire incident had been recorded by dispatch and Bob's dash cam, there really wasn't a whole lot more to add. He shook her hand again. "Thank you, Inspector Galloway. Please let me know if there's anything you need."

She sat there for a moment, one side chilled by the draft, the other sweating from the radiator which had finally kicked on. Leroy Lamont's body would be in some morgue somewhere by now, the routine of evidence collection underway. That's all he was anymore. Not a man, just a case number.

At least his family had a body. Knew how and why he died. More than those women in the cave. Women like Rachel Strohmeyer. Jenna wished to hell she'd been able to talk to her before she died. She wasn't sure why, especially after how freaked out she'd gotten in the caverns that morning, but it felt like something she needed.

And she wasn't going to get. She stood and left the room.

"You need anything?" Bob asked, concern in his eyes as she slipped into the dark observation room.

Everyone kept asking her that. What she needed was a shot of tequila and some mind-blowing, head-banging sex to wipe the memory of Leroy's mouth moving, the warmth of his blood, the stink of the fire from her mind.

Not that she was going to get either. Although...

She sat down, edging her chair close to Bob's, and covered his hand with hers. "Thanks. And thanks for not telling Lucy how I lost it down in the cave this morning."

"Nothing to tell." He flipped his hand palm up, intertwining their fingers. "Can I ask something? You don't have to answer if you don't want to, but—"

"Go ahead."

"What was it like?"

She hesitated. Not because she didn't have an answer but because she knew he wouldn't like it. And right now she very much wanted him to like her. More than like her.

She glanced through the one way mirror separating them from Roy. The meth dealer sat with his head on his folded arms. His shoulders moved like he was either crying or snoring. She wasn't sure which.

"It was just like training. A man shot at me and my partner, my weapon was in my hand aimed at him, so I pulled the trigger. It didn't feel like anything. No thought, no angst. Just: clear shot, center mass, double-tap."

He was silent. She didn't dare look at him for fear she'd ruined everything. But his fingers tightened around hers. "I wish it had been me."

"No. You don't." She swung around in her chair so she faced his profile instead of his reflection in the glass. "I'm glad you're here with me. I really need a friend right now."

"A friend?" he turned to her. His gaze settled on her lips, his body angled towards her, closing the distance. "Is that all you need?"

To hell with the small talk. She grabbed both sides of his face and pulled him to her in a kiss that rocked her chair off its legs. Within minutes they had each other's shirts off, lips pressed together, hips rocking in synch, pausing only long enough to lock the door.

"He can't hear?" she gasped as Bob undid her slacks.

He shook his head.

She wove her fingers through his hair, not caring if it was sweaty from wearing his hat all day. She wished he had the hat now, had some ideas for that Stetson. Maybe later…

–

The boys loved the cave. They'd been a bit surprised when Adam took them to the pit where Sally was just waking up, but then they raced down the ladder with him and all three of them opened the new toys he bought, laughing like it was Christmas morning.

Adam watched them and smiled. Warmth filled him from the inside out and it had nothing to do with the kerosene heater he brought to the pit. This was what family felt like. How could he have forgotten this?

Memory twinged, a tiny kick at the base of his skull. A stray voice inside his head wondered if he'd ever had this feeling before. Sally laughed as Darrin pretended to make Miss Priss talk in a falsetto and Adam shoved his inner voice aside.

Just after dark, which came early this late in the year, he let them use their new flashlights to go outside and collect wood for a fire. Sally was in charge of pinecones and the older boys in charge of tinder. He taught them how to look under the hemlock boughs to find wood not wet from the snow that now fell at a steady rate, like a lace curtain they parted with every movement. Already a few inches covered the ground with more to come. They bundled back inside and he showed them how to build a fire, although he cheated by using one of the pre-fab logs he'd gotten at the store.

They moved the sleeping bags down to the pit where they made grilled cheese mountain pies for dinner followed by s'mores. He thought for sure they'd all be so exhausted they'd fall right asleep. Lord knew he was about ready to drop. Family was exhausting. But they wanted stories.

Holding Sally in his lap, he told all the stories he could think of. Fairy tales he'd read, short versions of his favorite books, ending with the cave scene from Tom Sawyer, figuring that was only fitting. Soon Sally was asleep, curled around Miss Priss, her thumb in her mouth, so he snuggled her into her new sleeping bag. The boys were fighting exhaustion, their eyelids drooping.

"You sure my mom knows where I'm at?" Marty asked, stifling a yawn. "She gets worried sometimes."

Adam remembered how angry Marty's mom had been when he spied on them through the window. "Then why was she yelling at you last night?"

The kid was so tired he didn't even wonder how Adam knew. "I had a bad dream and got scared. Wanted my dad."

"She ever tell you about your dad?"

"All the time. He's a hero. See. US Army." He extended his watch proudly. Darrin, sitting silently beside him, reached a reverent finger to touch it. "Flies helicopters. Kiowas. Then he got shot down and died." Marty stuttered the last word out and pulled his arm back, clutching his watch. Darrin gave him a one-armed hug.

Maybe Marty's mom hadn't been angry, just upset, Adam thought. Still, she had no right to take it out on a little kid. Or to hide the kid's real father from him.

"I want to go home now," Marty announced in a loud voice that echoed up through the cavern. "I miss my mom."

"I want my mommy, too," Darrin chimed in. "And my sister. Can we go home now?"

Adam was surprised. Hadn't he given them everything they wanted? How could they want to leave? Family was supposed to stay together and like it. "Didn't you guys have a good time?"

Darrin nodded but sniffed back tears. Marty was more direct, standing up and kicking his sleeping bag aside. "I want to go home. Now."

"You can't. Not in the middle of the night." Adam tried reason. "I can't leave Sally," he lied. "Just go to sleep."

"No. You can't make me. I want my mommy!" Marty screamed the last. Adam was surprised Sally didn't wake, but she merely gave a twitch and kept right on sleeping. Darrin began blubbering, clutching Marty's hand.

They were far enough away and deep enough inside the cavern that no one would be able to hear Marty's screams unless they stood right outside the entrance. Even then, they'd probably just be distorted echoes.

Adam did what Dad would do: give the boys time to think about their actions and the consequences. He scrambled up the wooden ladder then pulled it up behind him. The fire below was almost out, but he'd keep an eye on the kids, make sure they didn't burn themselves. They had the red glow from the kerosene heater, plenty of food and water, and if they were good, he'd leave one of the lanterns he'd set on the upper edge of the pit going.

Now both Marty and Darrin choked out shouts as they ran to where the ladder had been. As their noise escalated, Adam regretted not using the chloroform soaked rag in his pocket, but he'd been too scared it might be too much for them. They were so much tinier than the fish Dad used it on.

The noise echoed, bouncing back and forth from the cavern walls until it was like a Ping-Pong ricocheting through Adam's brain. He fled. Raced out into the fresh air, stood in the cold, stared up at the snow-filled sky, and wondered what he'd done wrong.

Chapter 19

It didn't take long. Bob seemed to understand this had nothing to do with him. Or even sex.

It was all about Jenna regaining control. Feeling powerful. In charge of at least one small piece of her life.

As they fumbled their clothes back into place, Jenna enjoying the way Bob looked down every time she made eye contact then looked up again with a flush, O'Hara entered the interview room and sat down across from Roy.

Bob snapped the intercom on and waited for Jenna to take her seat first. Seemed he didn't mind letting ladies go first in most things, she thought with a smile, re-buttoning her shirt. Sex without a condom—she'd never done that. Not even in the back seat of Ricky Jimenez's dad's car during her first time as a kid. But damn, the risk was exhilarating. And it felt so natural. As natural as holding a pistol, taking aim, pulling the trigger.

She should reassure Bob. She'd been tested. Was on the pill. But he didn't ask. Either he trusted her or he was embarrassed. He sat down beside her, his leg pressed against her thigh. Then his hand was there. Resting, as if it belonged there, yet not possessive. All she had to do was shift her weight and it would be gone.

Her choice. She liked that. Liked that he didn't ask all the awkward questions that usually spoiled the mood. Liked the feeling of being wild and doing what she wanted. She let his hand stay where it was.

Was about to do some exploring with her own hand below the table when Roy burst out crying. Not just tears and sobs but hair-pulling, shirt-renting cries of grief.

"What did O'Hara say?"

"Told him they found Rachel's body in the fire," Bob whispered back. "Poor girl."

O'Hara leaned forward. He faced away from them, but he seemed to be trying to comfort Roy by patting his wrist.

Roy sniffed hard, head hung low. "Sally? Did you find her?"

"Not yet. They're still searching the debris," O'Hara said.

Roy gave another cry of anguish.

"Who's Sally?" Jenna asked.

"Rachel's little girl. Just turned four."

"She was in the trailer?" The memory of that blast, the heat, the fireball, seared her vision. No way anyone survived inside that trailer. If she hadn't been killed before-hand when the automatic weapons the bikers used ripped the thin walls to shreds. "Christ, who would raise a kid in a place like that?"

Bob looked away.

"It wasn't your fault," Jenna said. "You tried to help her, help them."

"It wasn't my fault," Roy shouted at O'Hara. "I was trying to save her! You can't hang this on me. It's not my fucking fault! If those bitch cops hadn't of shown up, none of this would have happened!"

Suddenly everything became crystal sharp for Jenna. Sitting in the dark, watching a man fall to pieces.

Roy was right. This wasn't his fault.

If Lucy hadn't let Adam go, they would have never stopped to see Rachel. They would have headed back to the city and Jenna would never have killed another human being. Rachel and her little girl would still be alive, and this awful taste of cat piss that kept filling Jenna's mouth, making it hard to swallow or breathe, would never have come, and she would never have pulled the trigger and…

She scraped her chair back and stood so fast the table rocked. "I have to go."

"I thought you wanted to hear—" Bob opened the outside door for her. "Jenna, are you all right?"

There was a restroom across the hall. Jenna plunged through the door and fell to the floor in front of the toilet, dry heaving. No, she wasn't all right. She wasn't sure if she'd ever be all right again.

Bob followed her inside. Held her hair, mopped her face with a wet paper towel, then helped her to her feet when it was clear nothing was coming up. It was all too deep inside her. Living there, festering, ready to ambush.

How could she have imagined she was in control? Jenna splashed water on her face and gave a weak laugh. Bob pressed his palm against the small of her back, supporting her.

Funny thing was, she didn't feel embarrassed that he witnessed her weakness. As if it didn't matter. Or he didn't matter.

All she felt was relief that it wasn't Lucy, the super hero, all-star FBI agent who probably never felt out of control in her entire life. Damn her to hell. Who'd she think she was, letting Jenna's fugitive escape?

"Can I get you anything?" Bob asked.

Jenna shook her head. Bob didn't have what she needed.

She needed to find the person really responsible for all this mess. Adam Caine.

–

The deputy led Lucy and Zeller next door to a conference room. A blonde in her mid thirties paced behind the table, her L.L. Bean parka unzipped to reveal maroon hospital scrubs.

"Colleen Brady," the deputy made introductions.

Zeller strode forward, hand stretched out, and took the woman's palm. "Sheriff Zeller, ma'am. So sorry to meet you under these circumstances. Why don't you sit and tell us what happened?"

The woman nodded, wiped her nose with the back of her hand, and dropped into a chair. "My mother, she watches Marty when I'm at work and I was on eight to four, but she's had a real nasty cold and took some cough medicine and fell asleep, and as I was leaving work she called and when she woke, Marty wasn't there, so you were on the way and I just, I just…" She ran out of steam, tears choking any further words.

"So you haven't been home yet yourself?" Zeller asked.

She shook her head.

"Let's start there." He nodded to the deputy who excused herself to dispatch a unit over to the house. "You and Marty live with your mom?"

"We moved in with her when Martin was deployed."

"Your husband, he's overseas?"

Another shake of her head. "Killed. In action. Four months ago."

"Sorry for your loss." He pulled the phone between them and put it on speaker. "What's your mother's name?"

"Cathy. Cathy Silvetti." She dialed the phone, her finger trembled. "Mom? Did you find him? I'm with the sheriff."

"Colleen." The older woman's voice was pitched with panic. "I can't find him anywhere. I looked all over."

"Mrs. Silvetti," the sheriff put in, "we're sending a car out there, so you just sit tight. What time were you expecting Marty home from school?"

As he began to work the particulars, Lucy slid her notebook from her pocket and made notes of questions that would be helpful and slid the page to Zeller.

"And what was Marty wearing today?"

"I'm not—I can't—" Panic flooded the grandmother's voice.

"Green fleece top over a Spiderman tee," the mom supplied. "Blue jeans, gray—no, black—sneakers. Navy blue jacket and a red and blue backpack with a glow in the dark Spiderman decal."

"Are any of those in the house, Mrs. Silvetti?"

There was the sound of the grandmother walking. "No. They're all gone."

Zeller read from Lucy's notes. "And do we know for certain he went to school this morning?"

Colleen jerked at that. "You mean, maybe he—oh no, this is all my fault." New tears shook her. Lucy scooted her chair closer and handed her a box of tissues.

"What happened?"

"I got called in to work an extra shift last night, didn't get home until after midnight." Colleen gasped for air as if trying to stop her words and failing. "I woke Marty. He came running out, so excited and happy—thought I was his father home at last. When Marty saw I wasn't his father, he threw a tantrum, screaming, crying for his daddy, demanding him. He wouldn't even let me hug him or anything. And I, I just miss Martin so much, I lost it."

She paused, looked up in regret. "I yelled at him. Told him his dad was never coming home. Then I sent him back to bed."

"Was there any physical contact?" Lucy asked gently.

"No—no, nothing like that. When he was flailing about, so upset, I gave him a bear hug, held him until I knew he wouldn't hurt himself. He kept hitting me, screaming for his dad, and when I said he wasn't coming home, he just stopped. Looked at me like I was a monster. And ran back to bed."

"How was he this morning?"

"Seemed fine. Like it had all been a bad dream. He was prone to night terrors and sleep walking when he was a toddler, I kinda hoped he really had slept through it."

"But now?"

"Now I can't help wondering if he ran away. Maybe to look for his dad? Because of me."

–

Dad made it seem so easy. So typical of Adam to screw up. Who'd he think he was, thinking he could be as good as Dad?

Fear and worry forced him into a rapid pace. He stomped down the snow until he saw the tracks he left behind. Not good. Leave no trace, Dad always said.

He tore free a hemlock branch and erased all traces of himself and the kids, backing into the secret entrance to the cave. He left the branch against the boulder in the foyer—he'd use it to cover his tracks when he left again.

He snuck through to the rear cavern and peered over the edge of the pit, keeping to the shadows on the opposite side from the lantern. The fire appeared totally out now. Marty and Darrin sat with their heads together, their voices low murmurs. Conspiring against him. He was family. They were supposed to love him, not defy him.

He remembered all the times he'd questioned Dad. Even though he never voiced his doubts out loud, Dad always knew when he wavered.

He'd sit Adam down and grill him, not letting him move until Dad was satisfied with his answers. The sessions went on hours, long enough that once or twice when Adam was just a kid, he'd soil himself. Why couldn't Adam be a good son? Hadn't Dad earned his trust? What would Adam do to regain Dad's trust? Would he follow Dad's instructions no matter how painful they were?

Eventually Adam saw the light and repented any doubts. Then Dad would test Adam. Sometimes it was something gross like eating a bug. Other times it was something painful like holding his hand over a candle until Dad said he could move it.

The worst times involved a fish. Pick one out and reel them in without Dad's help. Or deciding what Dad would use on them first: the cattle prod or the knife.

Their fate in Adam's hands, Dad would say. That's how it felt to be a parent. That was the responsibility Dad faced every day with every choice he made. Was Adam really ready to take all that on himself?

No, he whispered. But Dad forced him to make the choice, pass the test, before he'd give Adam what Adam craved: the faintest hint of a nod and smile, Dad's hand surfing through Adam's hair, letting him know all was forgiven.

"I'm not ready," Adam whispered as he crept over to the lantern. He took it, leaving the kids in darkness except for the light of the heater. Darrin's shrill cry spiraled up, but Adam steeled himself to ignore it. Being the grownup was tough, but he had to do the right thing and keep the family safe.

Even if that meant letting the kids learn the hard way to listen to him. Obey him. Like he had obeyed Dad.

If only Dad were here. Adam curled up on his sleeping bag, toasty warm and unable to hear the kids now that he was in the front chamber of the cave. Usually he wasn't afraid of the dark, not here in his sanctuary. But tonight he left the lantern burning.

Just in case the kids needed anything, he lied to himself, hugging his knees to his chest. His heart ached like it hadn't since that first night when Rick the Prick tiptoed into his room.

A tear stung his eye. He wanted his Dad. Now. He didn't want to be the adult anymore. It was too damn hard. Someone was going to get hurt and he wouldn't be able to stop it.

"Please God," he prayed. "Please let him find me. Soon. Please send my dad."

The prayer still echoed through his mind as he drifted to sleep, more comforting than any lullaby.

Chapter 20

So this was what limited duty meant, Jenna thought as she stomped her feet and hugged her body against the night wind and waited for the school janitor to open up.

The entire sheriff's department searched for little Marty Brady. Both shifts of deputies canvassed his neighbors, called his classmates, alerted the media. And they sent Jenna to search his school. The vice principal was supposed to meet her here and check the attendance records as well as footage from the security cameras. See if they could pinpoint a time and place when Marty was last seen.

If the kid even made it to school. They had no proof he'd made it out of the house alive. Not that Jenna was cynical or anything. But after seeing the stuff folks put on film and sent through the mail, doing unimaginable things to their own kids, she wasn't taking anything for granted.

Neither was Lucy. When she called Jenna in, she'd been gently interrogating the mother, asking about grandma's drinking habits and health issues, and getting a feel for the family dynamics. Said she had a good vibe about mom and so was sending Jenna to the school instead of the house.

Yeah. To stand out here in the cold and dark, hungry since she missed lunch and now was about to miss dinner, while Lucy was nice and warm inside the sheriff's station where no doubt some local merchant would spring for pizza to curry good will with the local law enforcement.

She kicked at the door, her hands too cold to rap on it with bare knuckles again. She'd spotted a Walmart in Huntingdon, was half tempted to run over and grab gloves and a warmer coat. Especially as neither the janitor nor the principal were anywhere in sight.

Just as she was trudging back to her car, she spotted someone peering through the windows of the school. From their height, a teenager or short adult. She couldn't tell if they were male or female, not at this distance.

One way to find out. Jenna approached them from the side, staying in the shadows cast by the spotlights arranged around the roof. A girl. Moving from one classroom to the next, shining a flashlight inside as if looking for something.

Or someone.

Jenna got close enough to grab her. "Mind if I ask what you're looking for?"

The girl yanked her arm free but didn't bolt, although her feet were turned away from Jenna as if she wanted to. "My brother. I thought he might be hiding in there."

"Your brother?"

"He didn't come home from school today. But after what my dad did last night… Well, he loves school, is always saying he wished he could live here…" She trailed off, her gaze locked onto Jenna's badge. "Oh my God! Has something happened to Darrin? Do you know where he is? Please tell me he's okay."

"Come with me." Jenna led the girl back to the Taurus. "What's your brother's name?"

"Darrin. Darrin Harding."

Harding? She knew that name. From the case files. "How old's your brother?"

"Six. He's in second grade."

"Does he know Marty Brady?"

"Yeah. Marty's his best friend." She hesitated as if caught telling a fib. "Actually, Marty's his only friend. Why?"

"Get in the car and give me a minute." Jenna pulled out her phone. Seemed like this end of the valley had the only cell reception. Two bars. Which was good because she sure as hell didn't want to drive around searching for a signal and delay things even more. "Lucy? It's me. I'm at the school. No, haven't had a chance to search it yet. But there's a girl here. Looking for her brother who never came home from school. Marty Brady's best friend. We have two kids missing, not one."

"Who's the other boy?" Lucy asked.

"Wasn't the whole reason you came to New Hope four years ago was to interview Karen Harding? And her asshole husband threw you out of town? It's her kid. Darrin Harding."

Jenna smiled at Lucy's silence. Nice to know even the superstar FBI agent could be caught by surprise.

"Sonofabitch," Lucy finally said. "I'm on my way."

–

Shadows danced around Darrin down in the pit. Worse than being the target in dodge ball. The light from the little round heater only made them worse. He held his breath and pulled his knees in, not sure which direction the attack would come from.

Marty sat down on Darrin's sleeping bag. "Here. My dad's watch." He pressed his treasure into Darrin's hands. "Look. It glows in the dark."

"Thanks." But that didn't help stop the shadows. "I'm sorry."

"I don't like your big brother," Marty said. "He's mean." He stood and shouted once more into the black, "I want my mommy!"

The echoes rang back down on them like a rain shower, distorting Marty's words into "Iowa salami."

Darrin laughed. "Let me try." He stood beside Marty. "Daffy Duck stinks!"

"Taffy yuck ink," the cave answered back.

Darrin sat back down on top of something hard and plastic. He grabbed it. The cool crank-it-up flashlight Adam gave him. Soon the pit filled with light. And they saw the other flashlights Adam bought them. The colored LED ones they played tag with earlier, a pink one with a tiny grip that fit Sally's hand, and big ones for Darrin and Marty.

"Maybe he wanted us to figure out we don't need to be afraid of the dark," Darrin said. He handed Marty back his watch.

"I think he's just mean. We need to find a way out of here." Marty explored the pit even though they'd already run around the entire area when they were playing.

Darrin experimented with his light. A shadow lunged from the other side of the ring of stones they'd built the fire in. A bear or a monster? His breath caught. He aimed both lights at it.

Then he laughed. Just Sally rolling over in her sleep. No monsters here.

Sheriff Zeller was walking a tightrope that just caught on fire. Lucy felt bad for him, but that was the lot of politicians. He wanted her help—although truth be told, he was doing a fine job with the limited resources he had—but also he needed to keep her name quiet for now, keep the press and public focused on today's situation, not the one that happened four years ago.

If things went well, he'd be a hero. If they went wrong, he'd let Lucy take the blame.

Lucy understood all of this. It was the way of the world. The path an elected official needed to tread.

She told Zeller about Darrin Harding, knowing she'd just made his already complicated job worse.

"I'll go to the school, review the video tapes and interview the sister," she offered. "But sooner or later, Kurt Harding is going to know I'm here. You remember what happened last time."

Harding had gone over the local officials and used his Washington connections to reach Lucy's boss. He ordered her immediate return to Quantico, despite the fact she used personal leave to pursue her theory in New Hope. Harding kicked up such a fuss, the previous sheriff sent a deputy to escort her out of the county.

Until they stumbled upon Adam Caine.

"I remember," Zeller said with a sigh. "Doesn't change the fact that two boys' lives are at stake and we can use all the help we can get. Besides, Karen is going to be devastated and she's a fragile lady to start with. I seem to recall you were the only person able to calm her down last time—Lord knows Kurt can't. We'll just tell him his son's disappearance is so important we called the big guns in right away."

"Good idea. Make it all about him and how important he is. He'll probably enjoy the chance to order me around again."

"I'd like to see him try." Zeller glanced through the window where the snow fell heavier than ever. She knew he was thinking the same thing she was: what were the odds of two six-year-olds surviving a night in the cold?

"I'll send a deputy with you to the school. Get started there while I head to Harding's and pave the way. Meet you there when you're ready."

"Thanks, Sheriff."

"I'm the one who should be thanking you. If this goes wrong, Harding will have your badge."

—

When Lucy and the deputy arrived at New Hope Elementary, the single-story building was ablaze with lights. The janitor and principal bustled about inside, obviously upset by the sudden turn of events.

"We've never had anything like this happen," the principal kept repeating.

Lucy sent the deputy and janitor to search the premises while she had the principal check attendance records and gather the security footage.

"My assistant usually takes care of all this," the principal, a forty-ish man named Culpepper, muttered as he leafed through sheets of attendance records. "It will take me a minute."

Lucy resisted the urge to dive into the records herself. "Call your assistant in to help. There are two boys' lives at risk here."

He reached for the phone, grumbling about budget and overtime. Lucy left him to check on Jenna and the girl.

She'd only met Olivia Harding briefly during her last visit to New Hope. Even then the girl's delicate beauty had struck her. Like her mother she had pale skin, dark hair, and large eyes that ranged from blue to violet, depending on the light. Now at sixteen, Olivia hid her good looks beneath layers of black leather, flannel, a bulky hoodie, and clumps of dark eye shadow and mascara. All she accomplished was making herself stand out even more.

Lucy had a sudden sense of *deja vu*. Ashley, the girl she'd saved in September, also tried to hide in plain sight. And failed. Instead attracting the attention of a predator.

Who was Olivia trying so desperately to hide from?

"Do you remember me?" Lucy asked. Jenna sat on a teacher's desk, feet propped up on the desk chair, while Olivia paced.

"Did you find him? Is Darrin okay?"

Lucy shook her head. "We're looking. Searching the school. The security tapes—" She nodded at Jenna, who took the hint and left to cover that angle. "But," Lucy wheeled the teacher's chair for Olivia to sit in before taking a seat beside her in a student's chair, "I'd really like to hear what happened. Tell me everything."

Olivia plopped into the chair, an exhalation escaping from her, and Lucy thought of Megan. Hoped she was still awake by the time Lucy got a moment to call home again. While Olivia adjusted her quilted leather jacket, then twisted the silver rings on each of her ten fingers, she assessed Lucy with a sidelong glance.

"I remember you. You made my mother cry."

"I'm sorry."

"No. It's a good thing. First time I'd ever seen her cry. She hasn't since." Another sigh. "Kinda sleepwalks through life. Pops the pills the shrinks give her and she's gone. I mean, she's there, she's just not there. Know what I mean?"

"I have an idea. Not uncommon after the kind of trauma your mother suffered." Although Karen Harding seemed to be taking it to the extreme. Lucy wondered what else was going on to prevent Karen from healing. "It must be hard on you kids. Especially with your dad away so much of the time."

Now a resentful sniff. "He's gone even when he's here. Sleeping with a girl over in Juniata. A college freshman who was an intern in his office last summer. Gives him an excuse to come home more often, otherwise he'd just stay in DC. Except when he wants to torment us. You'd think a guy who controls millions of dollars and thousands of votes and all those powerful politicians in DC wouldn't need to bully his wife and kids to feel good about himself, wouldn't you?"

"When you say bully—"

"I mean nothing you or the law can do anything about." Disdain colored her tone black. "No marks left for you to photograph or enter into your precious evidence. Nothing you could prove in a court of law."

"I'm not talking about proof. I'm talking about your little brother. What happened that made you think he ran away from home?" Lucy had a thousand more questions—

like why had no adult reported Darrin's absence?—but she let Olivia set the pace.

Olivia shifted in her seat and stared at the far corner of the room where the exit sign glowed bright red. "Sometimes Darrin wets the bed. Only happens when Dad's home. I think he just gets so nervous; he can't stop it. Doesn't help that Dad checks on him before he goes to bed. Says it's to get Darrin up to pee so he won't wet the bed, but I think he wants to find Darrin's already had an accident. Usually I try to sneak in before Dad gets there, just in case, but last night I fell asleep." Her gaze shifted down to her feet. She knocked the heel of one boot against the toe of the other.

"So your dad found Darrin had an accident?"

Olivia nodded, a tight jerk of her chin all the way down to her collar and back again. "Made him get up, take the sheets off the bed, then marched him downstairs. Yelled at him, sent him to the basement. Darrin hates the basement. Scares the crap out of him, all dark and spooky. Then locked him in."

It felt like Olivia had more to say. But before she could, Jenna ran into the room. "Got them!"

"You found him?" Olivia bounded to her feet.

"No. But I know when they left and where they were headed." Jenna led them back to the office where she had the security footage up on a computer monitor. "He and Marty. They left together, see here." She pointed to two small boys on the screen. They were out at the bus pickup point, then both turned together and ran off the screen.

"That's 2:47. Then you can see them again here at 2:52." Now the camera caught the backs of the two boys on the edge of the screen as they ran through a snow-covered field.

"Where's that second camera?" Lucy asked the principal who'd joined them.

"The teacher's parking lot. They're headed across the playing field."

"And where does that lead?"

"Into the woods," Olivia said. She collapsed into a kneeling position, hands clutching the corner of the desk, as she stared at the last sighting of her little brother. "Those woods go on for miles. There's no way we'll ever find them. Not in this weather. Not alive."

Chapter 21

Lucy left Jenna coordinating search and rescue efforts at the school while she drove Olivia home. Now that they knew the two boys left of their own accord, their high-risk missing persons response moved into a whole new direction. One that required boots on the ground as fast as possible.

They still needed to interview the boys' teacher and classmates, see if they gave any hint of their destination. Lucy would start with Darrin's family, then work her way down the list the principal provided. It was going to be a long night, but hopefully the boys left enough of a trail.

Lucy was relieved. Usually her job meant racing to expose a predator, her wits deciding a child's fate. This time she was just a grunt doing legwork while the local SAR experts battled the weather, and time, their constant enemy.

"You think he'll be okay, right?" Olivia asked as they navigated the long, winding drive up to the Harding house. "I mean, he's with Marty. Marty's real smart. His dad was in the Army, took him camping and stuff."

"We're doing everything we can. Sounds like Darrin and Marty make a good team."

"Yeah. They watch out for each other. Darrin's kinda quiet and shy, but he's a good kid. Doesn't say a lot, but pays attention to everything. And reads. He'll read anything he can get his hands on. But sometimes he lives too much in a fantasy world. Like he's trying to escape reality." She blew out her breath. "Like Mom. He even made up a new imaginary friend. A big brother to take care of him. Guess that doesn't say too much about me. I should've stuck up for him more."

"You did the best you could." Lucy wanted to say that it was the adults who should have protected Darrin, but since it sounded like they were the problem, she kept quiet. "After this is over, is there anyone you could stay with? Maybe give your mom and dad some time?"

Olivia turned to face Lucy. "I'm not going anywhere without Darrin. I've been reading about being emancipated, seeing if I could get custody of him. But I don't have a job or anything."

"Maybe we could get your mom some help? So you don't have to take care of everything by yourself?"

"Maybe." Olivia sounded skeptical. "You know what I worry about the most? What happens to Darrin once I leave for college and he's alone with them? Part of me wonders if maybe he was smart to run away now before it's too late."

Lucy pulled the car over and stopped. "Olivia. If there's some reason why your brother shouldn't be living with your parents, you need to tell me. If either of you are being hurt, I can stop it. Trust me."

Silence except for the engine idling and the wet *shoosh* of snow being cleared by the windshield wipers. "There's nothing you could prove. They never touch us." She sniffed, a lonely sound in the dark car. "Maybe that's part of the problem. I don't know."

They sat there for a moment longer, then Lucy put the car in drive. Minutes later they reached the house. The lights were all on, making it look like a cruise ship had grown out of the side of the mountain. Dark shadows loomed beneath the cantilevered first floor they parked beneath. Olivia led her inside the basement entrance and up the steps to the kitchen.

"I'm back," she called out, her voice rattling around the large, empty glass and chrome kitchen.

Lucy kept her coat on. The house was warm enough but she couldn't stop shivering. The kitchen faced the rear of the house with large windows and sliding glass doors backing onto a small deck. The only thing between them and the mountainside. It was a bit claustrophobic and unnerving. She had the urge to grab the countertop for balance as if the entire house might slide off the mountain.

"You get used to it after awhile," Olivia said. She led the way through the hall into the front of the house, which had Frank Lloyd Wright styling combined with a post-modern industrial decor. At least that's what Olivia said, her inflection that of a bored tour guide. "I call it Edward Scissorhands chic. Sharp and sterile."

They emerged into a wide-open living room/dining room with a staircase splitting the two areas. The space was empty.

"Mom!"

No answer. Olivia shrugged and began up the steps. "Sometimes I wonder if this house isn't half her problem."

Lucy couldn't help but agree.

Sheriff Zeller greeted them at the landing at the top of the steps. He looked relieved. "She isn't taking it very well."

Olivia rushed into the master bedroom to tend to her mother. Zeller walked Lucy back down the stairs and over to the front door which stood on a side wall to make room for the two walls of windows. "I finally reached the husband. Out hunting. He's on his way back."

"Did you search this house?"

"Nothing. No signs of any advance planning or anything worrisome." He dropped his voice, glanced back up the stairs. "Nothing comforting either. Sooner we find these boys the better."

"Jenna and your team are coordinating the search and rescue. Marty's mom has her church doing a phone tree getting volunteers and the Civil Air Patrol will come in at first light if we need them."

"Good." He put his hat on and reached for the door. "You need me, I'll be at the school for the duration. Oh, when Harding gets here, try to stay on his good side. Apparently one of the guys he was out hunting with is the Lieutenant Governor."

Lucy shut the door behind him and turned around. The wide-open space angled out on either side, the windows floor to ceiling. In the daytime they would have revealed only sky across the valley below. The vista should have given the room a sense of grandeur, but all that black emptiness felt bleak. Wind rattled the massive walls of glass and clouds scudded black on black across the darkness, adding to a feeling of impending doom.

No wonder Karen never got over her trauma. Trapped in this house would leave anyone unbalanced.

She climbed the stairs again but instead of going to Karen's room she opened the doors to the other bedrooms down the hall from the master suite. Olivia's made her smile. A mirror image to Megan's, all chaos and color and trying hard to make a statement without having any idea what that statement was.

The next room was a bathroom shared by the kids. Nothing out of the ordinary, not much cleaner than her own although the Hardings had the resources to hire a cleaning woman if they wanted.

Then came Darrin's room.

The scent of disinfectant hit her nostrils as she opened the door. Darrin's mattress sat on the floor in the corner. Covered with plastic, no sheets, a single pillow. As if no one expected him back.

On the opposite side of the room was a dirty clothes hamper with a lid. Beside it, a white dresser, no mirror, nothing but a small black comb, the kind they gave out at picture day at school, sitting on top. White walls. No posters, no toys, no music, no games, no electronics.

Prison cells held more warmth and comfort than this room. The room faced the mountain, so no need for curtains, the large window stood naked, exposed. A few small handprints and what had to be nose prints marred the surface.

"Dad took everything." Olivia's voice came from the door. "Told him as soon as he made it a month without wetting the bed, he could earn some of it back."

Lucy hauled in her breath, trying not to show her anger. Not the time or place. Or the right audience. "How's your mom?"

"She wants to talk with you. In private." She looked hesitant as if that might not be a good idea.

"It'll be all right. I'll call you if we need you."

Olivia gave a reluctant nod and led Lucy to the master suite. There were two large bedrooms with an adjoining bath. That surprised her. That Kurt Harding would make such a concession to his wife—or put her needs above his own.

Karen's room had two walls of floor to ceiling windows, giving it the same paradoxical claustrophobic feeling as the living room downstairs. As if the wide open space beyond the windows was a thin disguise for a prison cell with no escape.

The rest of the room mirrored the white on white decor of the kitchen. Bare walls, minimalistic bed and dresser, two white chairs that looked more uncomfortable than sitting on than the pale wood floor. Perched on one of them was a woman, also dressed all in white: white silk pajamas, white silk robe, pale white skin down to her bare feet. Even her lips were blanched white.

She sat in darkness, staring out the window. Her vacant gaze not registering Lucy's arrival.

"Mom," Olivia said, arranging a white wool shawl around her thin body. "I'll be in my room if you need me."

Karen Harding nodded, not looking at her daughter. Lucy sat across from her and waited. Sometimes it was best not to rush. Especially with someone as fragile as Karen.

If it wasn't for Karen and the notoriety surrounding her release, Lucy never would have begun her investigation. But once she heard about what happened to Karen, she knew there had to be more victims. No Unsub could have perfected his methods of abduction and protecting his identity so well on the first try.

Karen hadn't been kept in a cave. She described her prison as a hole dug into the dirt, narrow like a grave, not quite long enough to lie flat or tall enough to stand in. But with a door on one wall and a ceiling made of wood. The type of structure that could have been hidden anywhere outside of a city. All you needed was a vacant field with no foot traffic and some camouflage.

The Unsub made a mistake with Karen. He let it get personal. His need to degrade her and her family with as much public humiliation as possible outweighed his need for secrecy.

He'd taken Karen in the middle of a political fundraiser where her husband was to introduce the guest of honor. An immediate search had been mounted. Her face in every newspaper and on every TV station, first in DC, then nationwide. But no sign of her.

Not until eight months later when she'd been dumped at another of her husband's public functions, naked, hair shorn, an iron collar and chain around her neck, and seven and a half months pregnant. Again the national headlines plunged the family into a media feeding frenzy.

Her husband could neither deny the child nor abandon his wife—although Lucy had the feeling he wished she'd stayed missing—so he made a huge production out of building her a new house back in their hometown, the "safest place in America." Under public scrutiny, and at the urging of the conservative politicians he worked with, he officially adopted the child.

On paper at least. Obviously never in his heart.

The investigation pried relentlessly into his background, trying to find someone with a grudge strong enough to go to such lengths to humiliate Harding. They found plenty of people with grudges and some rather shady though legal business dealings, but no one they could link to the kidnapping.

If Kurt Harding was the real target, then the Unsub failed. Harding's business skyrocketed with the public sympathy he received. He'd even been approached about running for office himself, although he declined, saying he didn't want to put his family through the scrutiny. Lucy bet it had more to do with the financial disclosures public office would require.

But she was a cynic.

Hard to believe another Harding family member had gone missing. Even if Darrin had run away.

"I'm sure you must be imagining the worst," Lucy finally broke the silence.

Karen flinched but said nothing.

"Did Sheriff Zeller explain that Darrin left school of his own volition? With Marty? No indication he was coerced or taken by force."

She nodded. Her fingers kept tugging the robe's belt tighter and tighter until Lucy wondered how she could breathe. Despite everything that had happened to her, she was still a beautiful woman. But it was a brittle beauty. Lucy hoped she hadn't reached her breaking point.

"How about if you come down to the school? Marty's mom is there and the sheriff is organizing the search parties from there. You can help people understand Darrin. How he'd think. Would he panic, is he the kind of boy who would keep going if he was lost or would he stay and wait for help?"

"I can't." Karen's voice was raspy.

Lucy had almost forgotten. Eight months wearing the iron collar, screaming and crying, not to mention having a cattle prod rammed down her throat, had permanently damaged her vocal cords.

"Sure you can. I'll take you. Olivia will be right beside you. We'll have someone here waiting just in case Darrin calls or comes home."

"You don't understand." Karen shrugged so hard, the shawl slipped to the floor. "I don't leave. I can't leave. This house—it's all I know anymore. I haven't left it in six years."

Lucy suspected as much, but was still shocked to hear Karen admit it. That even with her son's life in danger, she couldn't leave the house her husband built to keep her locked safe away from the world.

"I understand," Lucy finally said, holding Karen's hands in hers.

"Do you? Do you really?" Karen sounded like she was crying but her eyes were dry and unblinking as they searched Lucy's.

"Two months ago a man almost killed my daughter. Almost killed me when I tried to save her. I would have done anything he asked to keep her alive. I killed him. But after…" Lucy blew out her breath. She hadn't told anyone this, not even Nick. Although she was sure Nick suspected. He was too smart not to—and too wise to say anything when it wouldn't help.

"After, I had a hard time leaving the house or letting her go anywhere. I'd take her to school, sit there in my car, watch the building. All day if I had to. My husband made me stop. It was hard, but I did. Only then came the panic attacks. They ambushed me in places so ordinary, it was pathetic. Like the grocery store. It got to the point where I couldn't get out of my car to go inside. Too many people, too many blind corners."

Karen hands tightened on Lucy's. "The way the noise echoes and you can't tell what direction it's coming from."

"Exactly. Then at work—and I work in the most secure building in the city—I could drive there okay, but I had to go earlier and earlier so I could get the parking spot next to the elevator. But then I couldn't ride the elevator. Not alone and definitely not with anyone else."

"No room to run. What if they attacked?" Karen agreed as if it were the most sensible thing in the world.

"But taking the stairs? You're so exposed. From above and below, behind you and in front of you. Where do you look without tripping and falling down? Finally, I'd walk up sideways, my back against the wall. It took me forever, always checking the landing above and below before I committed to the next step. But still the panic wouldn't stop. No matter how hard I rearranged my life to avoid it."

"What did you do?" Karen asked breathlessly.

Lucy shrugged. "Nothing. I just kept living. Refused to let it close me in, take any more of my life. I had to. For my family. The panic still comes, but each time I survive it and the next time I remind myself of that. Maybe someday it will go away, but until then, I can't let it take my life or my family. I won't."

"You make it sound so easy." Karen sagged back in her chair, pulling her hands away from Lucy's in disappointment.

"It's not easy. It's the hardest goddamn thing I've ever done. But I just don't give myself a choice."

"You see a choice." Karen turned to face the darkness. "I don't. My choices are all gone. There's nothing left. Not for me." Despair flattened her voice, as if each word was heavier than she could bear. "Maybe for my children, though. Will you take care of them for me, Lucy? Do what I can't? I'm just so tired. So very tired." Her eyelids fluttered and then closed as her head slumped against the back of the chair.

Lucy waited but Karen didn't move. She picked up the shawl, covered Karen and left the room, making sure the door was open and the hall light on. Karen was already surrounded by darkness, she wanted her to see there was a way out, if she chose to take it.

Olivia waited out in the hall. Gone was the cocky teenager facade. She wrung her hands with worry. "I'll stay. Watch over her," she whispered. "I'm used to it."

They were maybe the saddest words Lucy had heard all day. She wished she'd never stayed, wished she'd never came. Suffering through the psych eval would have been better than this desolation. And she'd be home with her family right now.

But she owed it to Adam. And Karen. Not to mention the two boys. Even Olivia.

After all, protecting kids was what she did best. No one ever said it would be easy.

—

The knife was a SOG. Military surplus, razor sharp. A knife meant for killing, not a child's toy. Morgan slid the blade a millimeter below the apple's skin and peeled one long, unbroken ribbon away from the juicy flesh.

"I think," Morgan chomped down on the apple's exposed heart and chewed thoughtfully, "maybe Adam's become a fish."

Clint said nothing for a long while. His gaze fixed out on the two-lane highway unwinding before their headlights. Driving in the dark, in the snow, in the mountains, faster than the speed limit marked on the curves because Clint was smarter than any Penn-DOT bureaucrat who decided how fast was safe, used to excite Morgan. So very different than the flat, boring, endless wheat fields Clint had plucked Morgan from.

Morgan waited for Clint's answer because it would change everything.

Finally Clint spoke. "Maybe. We'll see. But," his large palm landed on Morgan's head, squeezing not in a loving father-child manner but in a "I'm the boss" power grip, "I'll be the judge of him. Not you."

Morgan nodded. Clint released his grip.

Using the knife to dissect the apple, Morgan chewed and smiled at the thought of Adam, the eldest, the good son, squirming like any other fish beneath the blade.

Chapter 22

Footsteps echoed up and down the halls of New Hope Elementary. Some running, some merely rushed. Boots stomping, sneakers squishing, even heels clacking. All coming to Jenna.

The principal had been worthless, but his secretary was good. They quickly sequestered the principal in his office. Set him the task of soothing parents of other kids who had no possible contact with the missing boys, while she and Jenna coordinated the search efforts and triaged the phone calls.

The secretary, her name was Gail, wheeled in a large county map pinned to a corkboard and a second white-board to keep track of responses. As volunteers and professionals from surrounding communities trickled into the school, Jenna assigned them to a search group, keeping civilians with trained first responders.

By the time Lucy arrived back from the Harding house, they had over fifty people out in the field with another two hundred promised for the next morning. The hardest part wasn't the actual search—there was only so much that could be accomplished in the dark and they didn't want too many amateurs out there compromising possible evidence or tracks—but rather the fielding of phone calls. Seemed like everyone in the county called to ask what they could do or just to ask what happened. All with an undercurrent of unvoiced anxiety: had evil returned to New Hope? Were their families at risk?

Jenna let Gail handle those. She'd run out of patience for holding hands and soothing worries. Her nerves jangled with adrenalin and something she couldn't describe. A strange, restless, building pressure. She was half tempted to track down Bob for another session of hit and run sex, but he was out searching.

"Savannah Gleason, WOLT News." A blonde in heels and a shearling coat burst into the office, waving her microphone in Jenna's face as her cameraman followed close on her heels. "I understand we may have a child predator on the loose. Any connection to the New Hope Killings four years ago? Is it true one of the missing boys is Darrin Harding, son of the New Hope Killer? What are you doing to protect the citizens?"

Jenna blinked, glad she stood behind the counter, her badge out of sight. "Sheriff's giving out interviews in the cafeteria. Down the hall to the left."

"Where are the families?" Gleason persisted. "Any chance of getting them on camera? Could make all the difference," she wheedled.

Difference in ratings, not the lives of the boys. "Ask the sheriff."

"I'll talk to you." A short man with dark hair strode into the room. Muscular in the ex-jock going to seed way, he wore camouflage from his hat to his boots and a bright orange vest. "And your lawyer if you go on air with those defamatory accusations about my son's parentage."

The blonde stumbled back. The reason why she was still in a small-town market, no doubt. No guts. "Oh, Mr.

Harding, I'm so sorry, sir. I didn't see you there. I was just trying—"

"You were trying to goad these women into making a statement that would get you ratings instead of letting them focus on finding my son and his friend." Despite his initial bluster, Harding ushered the woman and her cameraman out as if politely asking guests to leave a party. "Now, let's leave these women in peace, and we'll start coordinating interviews for everyone." He flashed a smile full of charm at the room at large. "Don't worry, sweetheart, we'll let you go first so you can scoop the rest of the boys."

And he was gone.

Jenna arched an eyebrow at Gail. "I take it that's the world-class lobbyist Kurt Harding?"

"Yep, that's Charming Harding. Friend of the voting man," Gail said, quoting a slogan. "If you've got ties to agri-business, fracking, or coal mining."

Jenna pursed her lips. Harding hadn't seemed all that charming to her. But the reporter sure seemed to fall for his patter. "He seemed more upset about their mentioning Darrin's real father than he is about Darrin being lost."

"It's the boy I feel most sorry for. Might be better off if he stays lost." Gail turned away as she mumbled the last, but Jenna caught it. For a town called New Hope, it sure seemed like there was a lot of despair. Even before the events of four years ago brought to light what was happening in the caverns below the mountains.

—

Adam slept in fits and bursts, getting up to check on the kids. They finally stopped crying and went to sleep. But still he hid in the shadows surrounding the pit and watched them.

He did the right thing rescuing them, he was sure. Dad would be so proud.

So why did he feel this knot in the middle of his chest, making it hard to breathe? Every time he swallowed it burned. And each time he closed his eyes and laid down to sleep his ears filled with screams.

Finally he gave up and went outside. A good half-foot of snow had fallen overnight, making him glad for his new boots. There were no human tracks anywhere near the cave's entrance and he used the hemlock branch to cover his, although given the depth of the snow he trudged through, he couldn't hide them completely. The snow was still falling pretty heavy, so he thought it would be good enough.

The sun wasn't up yet, but on the edge of the woods he spotted lights on at the school on the other side of Stolfultz's cornfield. He edged through the stalks of dead corn, keeping low and out of sight, until he emerged onto the road, then backtracked to the school to see what was going on.

To his delight, three news vans were parked on the front lawn of the school, one each from Huntingdon, Altoona, and State College. Their bright lights aimed at reporters huddled in down coats and fur lined gloves, trying not to look cold, as they talked about the two missing boys and the search that continued throughout the night.

They didn't know about Sally yet. He wasn't sure if that was good or bad.

Didn't matter. The news was out. Dad would be here soon. He'd know what to do.

Adam blinked and the image of Dad's smile eased the morning chill that had settled into his limbs. Dad would be so proud of him. He'd never leave Adam again. Not after today.

The overnight search teams, mainly law enforcement officers and members of the Bradys' church, straggled into the staging area at the school. They grabbed cups of coffee and cocoa and dragged their feet in defeat, gray puddles of melting snow shadowing them.

Colleen Brady stood at the doorway waiting in hope. Hope that ebbed fast with each sorrowful shake of a head.

Lucy stood beside her, wearing her parka as defense against the wicked draft from the constantly open door, and tried to offer some comfort. "This morning's search has Civil Air Patrol volunteers from three counties joining in as well as other volunteers."

The State Police were helping the sheriff supervise and coordinate the effort. They gave each group a map grid and assigned them a law enforcement officer. She didn't tell Colleen about the special team of experienced spelunkers being assembled to search the caves. Although the volunteers, mostly college kids from Penn State, were thrilled by the prospect, with the complexity of the numerous caverns, there'd be no quick answers coming from below the mountains.

Echo Cavern, the cave system the New Hope Killer used, was first on the list to search, a fact that had sent the media into near-hysteria. Colleen and her son hadn't even lived in New Hope at the time, but that wouldn't stop the press from speculating about the possibility her son might lay dead at the bottom of a crevasse. Alongside the body of a serial killer.

Deputy Bob shuffled past them, head hung low, not even bothering to take the coffee Colleen offered him. Despair clouded the corridor behind him. Colleen made snuffling noises. Silent, heavy sobs that shook the coffee from the paper cup, splattering the floor and her hand.

Lucy loosened her fingers from the cup and tossed it into the trash. She shepherded Colleen into the girl's bathroom, its bright posters full of cheerful school pride a slap in the face after the gloom outside. Colleen didn't notice. She lurched to the sinks, gripping the edge of one, her body folding as if her spine had broken in half, head resting on the cool porcelain as she finally gave into grief.

It always happened in missing children cases. No matter how strong the parents and loved ones were, when kids were involved, there was always a breaking point.

Lucy had seen God-fearing, law-abiding men attack innocent bystanders they thought might somehow be connected to their child's disappearance. An investment banker from Medina, Ohio, had even grabbed at an officer's gun to try to force more information, new information, good information from the officer. Lucky he hadn't been shot.

She knew from experience there was nothing to do but wait. Which was the hardest part. The part the parents were left with once the initial crisis passed and the investigators moved on.

The second hardest part of Lucy's job. Shutting down a search and leaving the families with little hope and a lifetime of waiting.

Colleen's breakdown was short and hard. And nowhere near over. Nurses, doctors, cops—people required to compartmentalize—snapped, vented, then shoved it all down until they became overwhelmed again. They needed to do. Something. Anything. Even if it was just stand in a drafty corridor and hand out coffee to the volunteers.

"I can't go back out there," she whispered after splashing water to dilute her tears. "Can we go outside? Some place quiet? I need air."

"Of course." Lucy handed the mother her coat, made sure she had it buttoned straight, and ushered her out of the girls' room, down the hall past the gymnasium where the next group of searchers received their briefing, and out the back doorway. They emerged in a quiet corner of the yard near the teacher's parking lot.

Colleen stood braced against the brick wall, staring in the direction her son was last seen. She held one hand over her mouth, as if swallowing a scream, her posture stiff. Lucy turned her back to give her some privacy. She watched for signs of reporters or anyone else who might intrude upon the mother's solitude.

Lucy had forgotten how much she hated Pennsylvania winters. Not so much the cold or the snow, but the absolute bleakness. The way the clouds pressed down, trying to squeeze the life out of everything that dared to live below. The wind that sliced between every stitch in every seam of clothing. The gray light that drained all energy, as if it already swallowed the sun and was hungry for more.

After a few minutes, Lucy tried to distract the mother. Sometimes too much thinking made things worse. "I don't remember winter being this gray when I was a kid.

I remember blue skies and jumping out of bed in the morning hoping for a snow day."

The winters she remembered as a child were filled with sunlight reflecting from pristine snow drifts, ready and waiting for her to leap into them and spread her wings, carving out angels.

The laughter of her dad and mom, usually accompanied by the click of a camera. On special days, they'd tumble and roll in the fresh powder alongside her, laughing so hard they'd end up flat on their backs, holding hands, their gasps filling the air with fluffy puffs of joy.

"Marty's like that," Colleen said, clutching her hands together. "Gets up even earlier than usual when it's supposed to snow. He loves school, don't get me wrong. But you know little boys. Excited by the possibilities, you know?"

"My daughter just turned thirteen and she's still that way. Me? I just want to stay in bed under the covers. Everything seems so gray when it snows. Bitter. Dark."

"Maybe it's climate change?"

For Lucy winters changed at age twelve, when her dad died. After that she was cold all the time. Probably because she refused to wear her hat or boots or mittens, and God forbid she appear in public wearing anything less I-don't-give-a-shit cool than her dad's old denim jacket. Winter seemed interminable back then. She and her mom, shut up together in their tiny house that seemed so very crowded and so very empty, both picking at the fresh scars her dad's death carved.

Winters never regained their appeal. Not after that. Certainly not this morning.

Lucy surrendered to the cold and zipped her parka tight. Not like she'd be shooting anyone, not while on a search and rescue mission. Everything they learned made it seem like the two boys had wandered into the woods on their own and gotten lost.

Colleen drifted into silence once more. Lucy slit her eyes against the wind shrieking across the fresh snow, scouring it clean of evidence, and stomped feeling into her feet. California Jenna suffered more, but she impressed Lucy by not complaining, instead throwing herself into the job of coordinating the search teams and logging their results.

Unfortunately for Marty and Darrin, the findings had been slim. A few of the experienced hunters tracked the boys a quarter of a mile from the school, into the woods that curved around at the base of the mountains, but then lost any sign of them to the snow. Another team found tracks left by an adult but they entered the woods nowhere near where the boys had, headed in the direction of a nearby dairy farm before they too vanished.

That was it. Two boys missing for fourteen hours and that was all they had. Ghosts of footprints lost in the snow.

"It's not that cold," Colleen said, despite the shivers that shook her. "They could have found shelter."

"They're smart boys. You said Marty's dad took him camping, taught him about the outdoors."

"When he was home. Before——" A tear, frozen into a diamond glint, slipped from her eye.

Lucy had the sudden urge to call home and wake up Megan. Anything to hear her voice, even if it was whining. But not in front of Colleen. The woman had already lost so much.

The briefing over, the school parking lot quickly filled with civilians milling around, sipping coffee from thermoses, checking maps, adding layers, and preparing to go out into the field. With a large swath of the mountain prime hunting grounds, the police distributed blaze orange vests—although most of the folks around here had their own. They also told the locals to leave their weapons behind. Last thing they needed was a bunch of over-excited civilians with loaded weapons pretending they were on the prowl of some TV serial killer instead of looking for two boys who were probably already scared to death.

The media played up New Hope's past history of "harboring a monster, a man only known as the New Hope Killer who used the local cave system as his killing ground." Not wanting to feed the flames, Lucy made sure her and Jenna's affiliations as federal law enforcement officers stayed quiet. This was a simple search and rescue for two lost boys. That's all.

So why did she keep unzipping her parka and resting her hand on her weapon?

Chapter 23

Jenna used the girls' locker room to wash up after the long night and add a few layers against the cold. Gail lent her a left over sweatshirt from a recent school fundraiser. It was lime green with rainbow tie-dye splatters, but beggars couldn't be choosers. Besides, Jenna was basically an over-paid volunteer here, not even carrying a weapon.

She emerged from the bathroom feeling a little less stale, but not by much. Inside the gymnasium the latest group of searchers finished their briefing and headed out. Walking against the tide, she aimed for the tables at the far side where volunteers had brought food. Doughnuts and coffee, hot cocoa, bottles of water, bagels, homemade muffins, cookies, even apple pie.

The pie looked so tantalizing with its layers of apple and caramel and cinnamon topping toasted to the perfect level of crispness, Jenna couldn't resist. She cut herself a big piece, earning a beaming nod from a woman dressed in a plain gray dress with a little bonnet holding her hair back.

"Milk?"

Jenna nodded as she scooped the pie into her mouth. Okay, maybe this place was cold and gray and lacking in any semblance of civilization, but damn, they knew how to bake a good pie. She gulped her milk, wiped her face and wondered if she could sneak another piece without looking greedy.

The rear doors opened out onto a blacktop court and then the playing fields. Jenna threw her plate and cup into the trash and leaned against the corner staring at the unbroken field of snow. White on white on white. The monotony only relieved by the brown and green of the tree line in the distance that quickly blurred into the gray haze that covered the mountain.

Give her city smog any day.

Motion caught her eye. A man, hunched over, edging along the side of the building away from the parking lot where the searchers assembled. Trying to keep his feet dry and out of the snow? Then why not come in the front door where the walk was shoveled?

Jenna repositioned herself at the other side of the door to get a better look at him. Black leather jacket, jeans, black boots. Not the hiking boots most of the searchers wore, these looked like cowboy boots. He swiveled his head and she caught a glimpse of his face.

Holy shit. Adam Caine.

Her hand went to her Sig Sauer. It wasn't there. Shit, shit, shit. She glanced around the room and spotted Bob just coming in, head bent low with defeat.

"Bob, Bob!" She restrained the urge to shout, not sure if it would carry through the door and outside. Instead she ran over and grabbed the deputy's arm, jerking him across the gym floor with her.

"What's going on?" he asked, sounding ten miles past exhaustion.

"My fugitive. Adam Caine. He's just outside."

Bob straightened at that. "Show me."

Jenna led him to the door. Caine was hunched down, back to the wall, facing out from the corner, watching and listening to the searchers. He seemed focused on the blonde reporter set up on the other side of the fence.

"Stay here," Bob said, pulling the door open quietly.

Hell she would. She was a federal agent, not some Nancy Drew he needed to protect. She held the door for him so he would have both hands free, and watched his back.

Not that it needed watching. The whole thing was over in ten seconds and was rather anticlimactic. Bob simply tapped Caine's arm, hauled him to his feet, cuffed him, then patted him down, removing a knife, a wad of cash, and some keys, which he handed to Jenna to secure.

"You're Adam Caine?" Jenna asked. Last thing she needed to do was arrest the wrong man. But he looked just like his photo from Cleveland, except his hair was longer and stragglier.

He hung his head. "Yes'm."

"It's him," Bob said, sounding more sad than satisfied. "Adam, do you have any idea the world of trouble you're in?"

Lucy came around the corner with Colleen Brady. "Adam." She pulled up short. "Jenna, you're not seriously—"

Jenna took her prisoner's arm. "Adam Caine, I'm Inspector Galloway of the United States Postal Service and I'm taking you into custody for violation of United States Code 18, Section 876." She recited the Miranda rights to him, stumbling only a few times. "Deputy Bob, please escort the prisoner to the sheriff's station and we'll meet you there."

Lucy's scowl could melt ice. She ushered Mrs. Brady inside and pulled Jenna farther away from the reporters. "You're making a mistake. Jenna, let him go."

"I'm making a mistake? I'm doing my job. If you'd done yours yesterday, I might not have killed a man." Anger sliced through Jenna and for the first time in a day she felt warm.

"You were the one who wanted to play girl detective and interview Rachel Strohmeyer."

"And you're the one who ended up under a car with me covering your ass."

Bob stepped between them, one hand on Caine's arm. "Um, ladies—"

"What?" They turned to him in unison.

"Let's take this down to the station where there aren't so many—" He jerked his chin at the people and reporters in the parking area.

"Good idea. Walk him around the far side of the school. Less people." Jenna regretted her decision as soon as they took two steps through the snow. Jeans and sneakers— even if they were Coach sneakers made in Italy, or maybe especially if they were Coach sneakers made in Italy— offered no protection. By the time they made it to Bob's cruiser parked at the front of the school, her feet burned with cold and snow sloshed between her toes.

Lucy irritated her even more than the cold, reassuring Adam that she'd find Clinton Caine and have him released. No way. Adam Caine was her prisoner, not Lucy's. About time Lucy realized that.

They watched Bob pull away in the squad car, Adam hunched down in the back seat. Jenna glared at Lucy, then marched towards the school entrance, hugging herself against the cold. "Let me get my coat."

Lucy nodded, staring after the car vanishing into the snow. Jenna shook her head; she'd heard rumors about Lucy. Good and bad. That she was brilliant; had some kind of spidey-sense that led to her having one of the highest clearance rates of anyone in the Bureau. That she was a maverick, taking crazy risks that were totally against policy.

That she was burned out and unstable after killing a man two months ago.

Jenna was starting to think they were all true. Which made for a dangerous combination.

She swung the heavy glass door to the school open and almost ran into another woman rushing out.

"Why are they arresting Adam Caine?" the woman asked, stepping back so Jenna could get inside out of the cold.

"I can't discuss an open investigation, ma'am." Jenna held to protocol.

"He couldn't—I mean, I saw him with the boys, but—"

Wait a minute. Jenna straightened and led the woman inside an empty classroom. "What's your name, ma'am?"

"Mrs. Chesshir, Amanda Chesshir. I teach fourth grade. Adam was my student. Four years ago, before—you know about his mother, right?"

Jenna nodded and forced a smile to encourage the teacher. "You saw Adam with Marty and Darrin?"

Chesshir hesitated. Struggle appeared on her face, then resolved itself. "Yes. Yesterday morning. A couple of bullies were picking on the boys and he stopped them before things could escalate."

"Who were these bullies?" They were working their way through the school, interviewing students and parents, but these kids would go to the top of the list if they had reason to harm the boys.

"Craig Mathis is their leader." Chesshir hesitated again, touching her chin with one finger. "Adam said he was leaving town. That was yesterday morning." Then she brightened. "Of course. He came back to help with the search. That explains it. See? He had nothing to do with this."

Right. She'd just see about that. Jenna smiled. "Thanks so much, Mrs. Chesshir. We'll be in touch if we need anything else from you."

Jenna left the teacher, grabbed her coat, and stopped by the school office to get contact info on their friendly neighborhood bullies. From the expression on the vice-principal's face when she asked about the boys, they were no strangers.

"Bunch of hooligans, the lot of them," she muttered as she printed out their home addresses. "But Craig Mathis, he's the worst. Forget budding sociopath, he's a full-blown psychopath. Had him in for detention once and he told me how much he loved hunting. Not for the sport or being out in the woods. No, he liked to bring a deer down without using a kill shot so he could watch it die. Said he likes to gut it while it's still alive so he can reach in and squeeze its heart and make it stop beating himself." She shuddered. "Just so you know who you're dealing with. Not sure his dad is any better. Never met his mom."

"Thanks for the warning." Jenna grabbed the addresses and left. Lucy would be pissed, kept waiting in the cold, but the hell with it. Not if Jenna just broke the case wide open. A flush of anticipation made her cheeks burn. She ran out the door, still climbing into her coat, when she saw Sheriff Zeller stomping towards her, phone in hand.

"What the hell do you think you're playing at?" he stormed. "Sending one of my men to take care of your prisoner? A kid you arrested for mailing a letter?"

"It's a federal offense. Plus—"

"I don't give a shit!" He cut her off. "In case you haven't noticed, we need every man we have here if we're going to find those boys before they freeze to death. Just because you're federal, you've no right to order my people around. Do you understand me?"

Jenna leaned forward, her adrenalin surging, ready for a fight. Then she spotted the reporters to one side and the crowd of volunteers to the other. Lucy pulled up in their car and stared as well.

Professional pride conquered her anger. She rocked back on her heels and cast her eyes down. "Yes sir. I'm sorry, Sheriff Zeller. It won't happen again."

"See that it doesn't. Now get your butt over there and relieve my deputy so he can return to duty."

Jenna nodded and fled for the safety of the car.

"What was that all about?" Lucy asked.

"He didn't like me using Deputy Bob as my boy toy."

"That makes two of us. You didn't have to go all Elliot Ness on Adam. He's no threat to anyone."

"Excuse me? Isn't that the whole reason we came here?"

"That was before I spoke to him. He's just a lost kid. He needs help, not jail time."

"He was seen with Marty and Darrin."

Lucy straightened at that. "When?"

Jenna told her about the bullying episode. They were at the stoplight on Main Street. "You know, Craig Mathis' family lives not far. We could go there first. Check him out."

"Did you tell the sheriff about this?" Lucy's voice had a definite edge to it.

"No. He said himself, he doesn't have manpower to spare. And high-risk missing minors fall under our jurisdiction."

"If we're invited to assist local law enforcement."

"Which we were." They were still stopped, despite there being no other traffic on the road. She was wearing Lucy down. "C'mon, Lucy. Isn't that why we're here? To help out, maybe save those kids?"

Lucy sighed. "I remember when I was young. All I wanted to be was a hero. Like you."

"Hey, it's why we're paid the big bucks."

Lucy flipped the turn signal on and Jenna knew she had won. A thrill of anticipation surged through her, erasing her fatigue and dampening the anger and self-doubt that dueled inside her ever since the shooting. She wasn't a bad guy, a killer. No, she was one of the good guys.

Especially if she helped to break this case and find those boys.

Damn, being a hero felt good. Almost better than sex.

Chapter 24

The heat in the squad car and the hypnotic *swish-swosh* of the wipers put Adam to sleep as he slumped against the molded plastic of the rear seat. He jerked awake when they pulled into the parking lot at the old Dairy Treat, the patrol car lurching through the pile of snow deposited by snowplows at the entrance.

"They're supposed to plow the lot," Bob said, but he didn't sound annoyed. "They always forget." They slid into what may or may not have been a space beside the sign marked for handicapped parking. "Wait here one sec."

Bob left the car, jumped through the snow like Neil Armstrong landing on the moon, then stood at the front door, shaking snow from his pant legs. He unlocked the door, moved inside and lights began to shine through the windows. Finally he returned and opened Adam's door.

"Careful, it's slippery." Bob guided Adam's head so he didn't hit it on the door frame. They tramped through the snow into the old Dairy Treat. "Sorry the heat's not up yet, but when it does, you'll be roasting. It's all or none around here."

Adam looked around. He spotted one camera above the security door aimed out over the reception space. Bob used his keycard to unlock the inner door, then took him into the rear work area.

"You need anything, kid?" he asked, not unkindly, as he sat Adam in a plain metal chair at one of the battered desks. He removed one of his handcuffs and attached it to the chair arm. "Coffee or water? Maybe a pop?"

Adam shook his head, slouching in the chair so his legs were hidden under the desk. He'd blown it. Dad would never come get him from jail. He always said anyone who couldn't outsmart a cop deserved to be locked up.

This was Adam's second time being stupid enough to get arrested. True, the first time in Cleveland, he took the fall so Morgan could escape. But still, he'd gotten caught. Just like a fish. In Dad's reckoning, that was all that counted.

Once Adam was secure, Bob set Adam's personal items out on a shelf against the front wall. "We'll inventory them for you, don't worry." Then the deputy shed his parka, hung his hat, and slid into his chair all without turning his back on Adam. "I know you've been through the system and you know I can't question you without a parent or guardian. So I'm not asking anything for the record, you understand. But you had Jenna—Inspector Galloway— pretty riled up. About a letter you sent?"

"Yes sir. I'm sorry I did it. Told that to Lucy. Agent Guardino."

"You sent the letter to Agent Guardino?"

"Yes sir. It was a big mistake. I just," Adam shrugged and swallowed back a sudden lump in his throat, "didn't know who else to go to." His arms and legs felt leaden as he realized the enormity of his mistake. Stupid, stupid, stupid. He'd lost Dad. Lost everything.

The kids would be okay. They had plenty of food and water. He wasn't sure how long the heater's fuel would last, but it never got too cold in the caves. They'd be fine. Except he wasn't sure what the hell to do about them. If he told, he'd be in big trouble. Kidnapping? That was heavy-duty time.

Worse, they'd send them all back to their no-good families. He blinked against the memories of Marty crying, Darrin suffering alone in the dark, Sally trying so hard to take care of a mother who was so out of it, she didn't even know Sally existed.

They deserved better. They deserved to be with someone who loved them like Adam did. Like Dad did.

How the hell could he make that happen if he was locked up?

Bob interrupted Adam's whirlwind thoughts. "I know what happened. To your mom. What you saw." The deputy flicked one finger across his brow as if pushing back his hat. "You probably don't remember me. We only met for a minute or two."

"I remember. You went to look for my mom."

"I left you with Lucy—Agent Guardino. If I hadn't, if I'd stayed. Well, all I can say is sorry. About your mom. About everything." He leaned back, away from Adam.

If Bob had come with them, he'd be dead.

Adam squirmed, miserable, his butt falling asleep in the hard chair. Said nothing. Finally nodded.

That seemed to be enough for Bob. He straightened his shoulders and tapped at the edge of his computer keyboard.

"Why were you at the school this morning? You know they're getting ready to search Echo Cavern, right?"

"Figured. I just wanted to talk to Lucy. Apologize again. And see if I could help. I guess that's all." He kept his face down, talking into the top button of his jacket. It was freezing cold, but the deputy didn't seem to notice. Maybe fear kept Adam shivering. Fear he'd never get another chance to find his dad.

His eyes burned and he blinked furiously and sniffed. The deputy pretended not to notice, but slid a box of tissue close to Adam's free hand as he reached for a coffee mug and stood. "Sure you don't want anything? I'm brewing a fresh pot."

Adam rubbed his face against his collar, refusing to admit defeat and take a tissue. "I'm fine."

Before Bob could reach the counter with the coffeemaker, a loud buzz jangled through the air. Adam jolted in surprise, his handcuff chain rattling against the chair arm.

"That will be Jenna." The deputy put his cup down and moved to the glass partition between the reception area and the office space. "What the hell?"

–

Morgan loved this part. The getting ready part. The part when blood pounded like rain and tasted like copper pennies. Anticipation.

Almost as fun as the actual doing.

This time was different. This time Clint trusted Morgan to fly solo.

Morgan watched the cop take Adam into the police station. A tiny building that looked surprised to still be standing as the wind knocked against it. Like the Big, Bad Wolf huffing and puffing.

From the pattern of lights, the inside would be divided in two. Made sense. Wouldn't want the public getting in the way of official business. One camera on the parking lot, probably one more inside, maybe two.

Easy peasy.

Morgan crossed the snow-covered parking lot. The public door was unlocked even though it was early, not business hours yet. Expecting someone?

The street was empty in both directions. The nearest light, on again, off again, in the pre-dawn gloom, was the blinking amber that marked the edge of town.

Savoring the taste of blood that would soon be shed, Morgan opened the door and stepped inside, knowing Clint watched.

Morgan was about to make him proud. So very proud. The one thing that mattered most in the world. Keeping Clint happy. Because when Clint was happy, Morgan was his whole, wide world.

Nothing was going to take that away from Morgan. Nothing.

Not even a big brother.

Chapter 25

If the Caine family home looked like a solid house fallen on hard times, then the Mathis residence appeared to be the opposite: a house built in hard times that survived long enough to see better times.

It was a frame house built on the eastern shoulder of the mountain, which should have given it the appearance of majesty. It looked out upon stunning vista of mountain meadow tumbling gracefully into forest and then down across the valley. But the house was two stories high with a sharply peaked roof and looked half as wide as it ought to be. As if someone had cut the original plans in half, leaving a scarecrow of a house, tall, thin, and giving the illusion of leaning, ready to slide off the side of the mountain.

Despite its awkward architecture, the road was well tended—already salted and plowed—and when they grew closer, Lucy noted a roof in good condition and wood siding recently painted. Freshly cut logs were stacked to the porch roof. A curl of smoke from the chimney made a dark smudge against the snow and the pale dawn light.

They walked up flagstone steps that had been cleared of snow so long ago, a fresh coating was already forming. They'd just reached the front door when a rifle shot rang out, echoing back from the mountain behind the house.

Lucy rolled to the porch wall, pulling her weapon. Jenna pressed up beside her. Shit. The postal inspector had relinquished her weapon because of the shooting yesterday. Lucy pulled her leg up, drew her backup Glock from its ankle holster, and handed it to Jenna. "You have nine rounds."

Jenna nodded. Lucy motioned for her to stay where she was and cover her back. Then she drew a deep breath and sidled along the wall, past the stack of logs, to the rear corner of the porch. The direction the shot came from.

Lucy craned her head around the corner ready to shoot. Then relaxed. The side of the house nearest the mountain opened onto a deck that looked out onto the meadow where snow glowed ruby-orange in the rays of the sun piercing the clouds. A man in a red and black checked wool coat lounged in a chair, sighting his rifle at a black bear ambling along the tree line at the edge of the forest.

"Federal agents, Mr. Mathis. Would you please lower your weapon?"

"Can't it wait? Damn thing must be deaf and dumb and I'm tired of him tearing through my garbage." Mathis kept sighting the bear but the bear disappeared back into the forest. With a sigh, he set his rifle at his feet and turned to Lucy. "What the hell do you want?"

"Show me your hands, please, Mr. Mathis." The man looked like he was about to argue, but the sight of Jenna also holding a weapon on him, shut him up. He raised his hands, flipped them up and down.

"Nothing up my sleeves either. You two do realize you're trespassing on private property. Got no right to pull a pistol on a man in his own home."

Lucy holstered her weapon and motioned for Jenna to do the same. "Afraid you startled us with that rifle shot. We're not from around here."

He wrinkled his nose and rubbed it red. Mathis was in his late thirties, trim but with a thick neck and thinning brown hair. He stood. Jenna jumped, but Lucy laid a hand on the postal inspector's arm. "City gals, eh? Probably should come inside where it's warm and you can tell me what brought you all the way out here."

"I'm surprised you're not out searching for those missing boys," Lucy began once they were inside, cups of steaming coffee in their hands. Another kitchen table. This one was a wide plank with benches along two sides and two chairs at either end. Mathis sat at the head of the table. Lucy had started to take the chair opposite but he gave a slight wince and she moved to sit on one of the benches instead. Jenna stood at the wood-burning stove, gripping her cup to her chest like she was a Titanic survivor fished from the North Sea.

"Would be—should be, but, I've got to take care of my boys first." He said it like a man who didn't feel sorry for himself but wasn't altogether crazy about the hand life had dealt him either.

"Your wife?"

He shook his head, glanced over his shoulder to the main part of the house where a TV playing cartoons could be heard. "Dead. Last year. Drunk driver. Just me and the boys."

"You have a son, Craig?"

"Yeah. The oldest. Having a rough time of it. I ask too much of him, I guess."

Lucy wondered at that. Jenna's description of the Mathis boy sounded like someone having a lot more problems than just a "rough time." She waited to see if Mathis had anything more to say before asking, "Does Craig know the missing boys?"

"Look here. I'm a plainspoken man. I know my son acts out, but he had nothing to do with them two boys running off. You can ask him yourself." He tilted his chair back and hollered into the other room, "Craig, get in here. Now."

A sullen looking skinny kid shuffled into the kitchen, not making eye contact with any of them—especially not his father.

"Did you talk to those boys who went missing? Marty and, what's the other one's name?"

"Darrin. Darrin Harding," Lucy supplied. She wished Mathis would let her do the questioning.

Craig shifted his weight back and forth, one finger digging into a hole in his sweater sleeve.

"Answer me, boy." Mathis' voice cracked but Craig didn't startle. Like he was used to it. Or it took a lot of stimuli to get a reaction from him. A possible early indication of sociopathy.

"Sure, I talked to them. But in the morning." Finally he looked up. Met Lucy's gaze with defiance. "Until that big kid came by. Had a knife. Bet he took those boys out to the woods and cut them up, left them with their guts hanging out to rot."

Lucy kept her face blank, not giving Craig the response he wanted. From the corner of her eye she saw Jenna take a step away from the boy, hand dropping to the pocket where she had Lucy's gun. "What boy was that, Craig?"

"Dunno. Mrs. Chesshir knew him. They talked like they were old friends."

"That was in the morning, right?"

He nodded grudgingly, unwilling to admit anything on the record.

"When did you see Marty and Darrin last?"

"They were playing chase with a few of my friends. We like to include the little kids," he added, protecting his cohorts in crime. "But Dad already picked me up. We were driving away when I saw them running across the field."

"I picked the boys up early yesterday," Mathis put in. "We had dentist appointments over in Huntingdon. All three of them."

"Do you remember what time you picked them up?"

"Had to sign them out. It was 2:40. By the time I got them all in the truck, the other kids were out, running for the first bus or playing in the yard. Not sure what time we actually left the parking lot."

"And Craig was with you from 2:40 on?"

"Yes." Mathis stood. Craig stayed a step behind him, a twisted smile on his face as if he'd just realized how lucky he was, having that dentist appointment. "Anything else we can do for you ladies?"

Lucy shook her head and walked towards the door. Jenna beat her there, already had it open. Lucy stopped at the threshold and turned back to Mathis. "You've got your hands full with all this, Mr. Mathis. I wonder if maybe Craig could use someone to talk to. Help him cope better."

At first she thought Mathis was going to be offended by her suggestion. But to her surprise, he glanced over his shoulder as if fearful his son was listening in, then leaned forward. "You might have a good idea there. Lately he's been worrying me, leaving him with the younger boys. I'll look into that. Thanks."

Lucy and Jenna returned to the car. No further in finding Marty or Darrin, but maybe they'd helped one kid before it was too late.

—

Deputy Bob rushed over to open the door to the reception area. "Are you okay, sweetheart?"

A little girl, hidden from sight by the deputy's body, answered, "My mommy. She's hurt bad. Please help me."

Adam opened his mouth but couldn't suck in enough air to make a sound. His throat shut tight like he was being strangled. He wanted to close his eyes, knew he should close his eyes, but couldn't even blink.

He wished Bob hadn't told him his name. It was always worse when you knew their names.

"Of course." The deputy squatted to the girl's level. "Where's she at, honey? Tell me what—"

He made a sucking noise. A fish drowning in air. Adam winced at the sound; he'd heard it before.

The deputy rocked back, then fell over onto his side. Both hands clutched at his chest, blood spurting through them. Fast at first, then slower, arching into graceful streams of scarlet.

"Hi there, big brother." Morgan smiled over the deputy's body, still holding her bloody blade. "Daddy sent me to get you."

Adam's blood turned to ice, leaving him breathless and dizzy as he watched the deputy die. The man had been kind. Didn't deserve to die. Not like that.

Nonsense, Dad's voice filled his mind. *He was only a fish. And now he's gutted like one.* Dad's laughter sounded so real, Adam rocked in his chair, looking over both shoulders, expecting Dad to appear.

Morgan was dressed in sky-blue ski bibs and jacket, yellow snow boots, and a jaunty red knit cap with pompoms, making her look younger than she was. She was short enough that she had to make a little leap to clear the still twitching body. She made it look graceful, like something a ballerina would do. Then she spun, bent over, and took the deputy's gun.

"Fleeing felon, you want a gun, right?" she asked, aiming it at him.

Adam scooted his chair back. "I don't want it."

"Sure you do." She pocketed the weapon, grabbed the handcuff keys, and stood. Her eyes widened in a smile that didn't make it down to her lips when she spotted Adam's knife on the counter with his other possessions. She took his cash and keys.

Then she approached Adam, the bloody knife in one hand. He pushed back in his chair as far as he could go. That made her smile.

She stayed just beyond his reach, taking the box of tissues from the desk and wiping her blade clean. The soiled tissues went into her coat pocket along with the now clean knife. She turned to grab Adam's knife.

He wanted to scream, to fight, but what good would it do? He was powerless. And Morgan knew it.

"Just so there's no going back," she aimed her dagger-sharp smile at Adam as she plunged his blade into the deputy's right side and left it there.

She tossed Adam the handcuff keys. He fumbled them, fingers numb, but managed to hang on.

"Okie-dokie. Let's get going. Daddy's waiting."

Chapter 26

They got back into the Taurus, Jenna driving this time. Lucy sat in silence, her jaw making a clicking noise that had Jenna wincing. "Sorry. Guess that was a waste of time."

"Don't worry about it," Lucy said. "Nature of the business. Talk to twenty people to find the one who has the missing piece of the puzzle."

"Weird though. The Caine boy being with the boys yesterday morning."

"Yeah." Lucy's voice sagged in resignation. "We're going to have to have a talk about that."

They reached the blinking light at the base of the mountain. Up at Mathis' place the sunrise made the open meadow look golden, but down here it was all shadows and gloom. As if the clouds conspired with the mountains on either side of the valley to keep it shrouded in darkness.

They pulled into the sheriff's substation and parked beside Bob's patrol car. Lights blazed inside the station. Jenna opened the car door and had no choice but to plant her feet into the unplowed snow. Icy cold ran into her sneakers once again and she wished she'd packed boots like Lucy had.

She danced through the snow trying to minimize the number of footsteps she took. Lucy was already at the door, watching her with a shake of her head that reminded Jenna of her mom.

"What? These are Coach. Probably ruined anyway."

"I was just thinking of the Postal Service's creed. Neither wind nor rain…"

"Oh, shut up. Let's get Caine and get out of here. I'm tired of the country."

Lucy stopped with her hand on the door. "I might stay. Help Zeller."

After the disappointments of the past two days, Jenna merely sighed. She came here thinking she'd learn something from Lucy, maybe even return to Pittsburgh a hero. Instead she'd killed a man, panicked in a cave, and stayed up all night crossing out squares on a map. "Whatever."

She reached past Lucy to pull the door open, anxious to get inside where it was warm, hoping for some of Bob's coffee before they hit the road. Maybe even more of Bob himself if he could get away for a few minutes. She stomped over the threshold, Lucy right behind her, and made it halfway across the reception area before she realized she was mistaken.

It wasn't warm inside the sheriff's station. It was cold. Very cold.

No scent of coffee in the air. Only the smell of feces and blood.

Jenna stopped. Tried to ask Lucy if Lucy saw what she did but the only sound she could make was a gagging noise as if she was being strangled.

Lucy carefully skirted the pool of blood. Squatted and touched Bob's body. Then she backed away, stepping in her own slushy footprints on the linoleum.

"He's dead."

Jenna nodded, still unable to talk. Saw the knife planted in Bob's chest like a flag on top of a mountain. "That knife. It's Caine's."

Suddenly her frozen body felt as if it was being pulled apart, caught in a whirlwind of emotion. Jenna lurched a half step towards Bob's body, then twisted towards the door, then back to face Lucy. "Adam Caine killed him. Sonofabitch! If you hadn't let him go yesterday none of this would have happened. God. This is all our fault."

Lucy ignored her tirade. She held one finger up for quiet as she spoke into her cell phone. Which made Jenna all the more furious. She darted towards the door. "He couldn't have gotten far."

She ran outside, no longer caring about the snow sloshing into her shoes. She unzipped her coat and put her hand on her gun. Until she remembered the holster was empty. And she'd returned Lucy's Baby Glock to her.

The parking lot and street beyond was quiet. Everything was quiet. No motion as far as she could see. Unless you counted the thick white clouds scudding across the sky and a flock of black birds that followed them. Damn country.

Only nice thing about it had been Bob. And now he was gone.

As much as she blamed Lucy, Jenna remembered she'd been the one who pushed to detour and question Mathis. Adam Caine might have never had the chance to kill Bob if they'd gotten here sooner.

Just like Rachel Strohmeyer might still be alive if Jenna hadn't been so ready to try to prove herself to Lucy and get the girl to open up about what really happened in those caves four years ago.

All her fault.

She spotted the footprints in the snow. "There were two of them," she shouted to Lucy who'd hung up her phone and was coming through the door. "Headed that way. Into town."

Jenna tracked the footprints, already disappearing beneath the new snow, across the parking lot. She reached the road as the sirens of the first patrol car roared through the air, shattering the winter silence.

—

The heater died out sometime during the night but it was toasty warm in the down sleeping bags. Until Darrin had to get up and pee. The cold air hit him when he climbed out of his sleeping bag. He used the toilet seat in the corner, glad Sally and Marty weren't awake to watch him.

He returned to his bag, snuggling inside. Then he realized. It was dry. He'd gone the whole night without wetting the bed.

Too bad Dad wasn't here to see. He'd never take Darrin's word for it, so it wouldn't count.

Marty sat up, rubbing his eyes. He looked like he'd been crying. "I'm hungry. I want to go home."

"Adam," Darrin called, the cave walls pitching the name back at him. No answer. He tried again. "We're ready for breakfast." Silence.

Sally woke up and jumped onto Darrin's lap. "Do you think he's okay?" she asked, hugging Miss Priss. "Mommy sometimes is hard to wake up. But," she frowned, "sometimes she isn't even there." She let out a little sigh. "I don't like it when the strangers are there instead of Mommy." She raised her face to the top of the pit. "Adam," she sang out. "C'mon, we're ready to do more 'sploring!"

No answer.

"He left us." Marty's voice sounded like he was about to cry. "We're gonna die down here. Mommy! Mommy!" He shouted over and over, running from one side of the pit to the other, until Sally began to cry.

"Stop it," Darrin said. "You're scaring her." He hugged Sally and wrapped his sleeping bag around her. Then he looked through the Walmart bags scattered around the cave.

"Sally, do you want strawberry Pop Tarts or cinnamon?" he asked as he handed her a juice box. It was a bit gloomy down here but no more than the gray skies visible through the smoke hole overhead. He didn't even need the flashlight but it still made him feel better when Sally cranked it up and began to spin it around.

"Cinmon, please," she said sweetly.

Marty kicked at the stones around the fire pit. "I'm not eating. Not until I get back home." He grabbed a rock and carried it over to the wall. "Maybe we could build some steps. Climb out."

"It's pretty high." Darrin munched his Pop Tart. "Don't worry. Adam will come and get us."

"You're so stupid. Adam's not going to help us. No one is."

Darrin flinched at Marty's words. Watched as the boy built a tower of rocks, then hauled the kerosene heater over to them.

"Aren't you going to help?" Marty asked.

"That's not going to work. Too unsteady." But Darrin got up and helped Marty shove the heater on top of the unstable pile of stones. "It's not high enough."

"Maybe I can jump. Grab the top and climb up."

243

"That's what Boots would do," Sally said, looking up from her coloring.

"This is real life, Sally," Darrin reminded her. And Marty. No way was he going to jump that high.

But Marty was determined to save them. "I'm going to do it," he muttered. "You'll see. My dad said I could do anything."

Darrin's dad never said stuff like that.

Before he could stop him, Marty scampered up the pile of rocks and climbed onto the heater. Darrin rushed to steady it as it wobbled. "Marty, get down. It's going to fall."

Instead of climbing down, Marty stood up on his tiptoes, arms stretched up, reaching for the top of the cliff way over his head. Then he jumped.

And came crashing down. Kicked the heater, which knocked Darrin off his feet, skidded over the pile of rocks that scattered in every direction, and landed with a thud on the rock floor.

Darrin pushed the heater off him and climbed to his feet. Marty hadn't moved.

"Is he dead?" Sally asked, clutching Miss Priss.

Marty's sobs proved otherwise. "My leg, my leg. I think I broke my leg."

—

Morgan wrapped Adam's arm around her, clutching it as if she'd forgotten how to walk. She pressed her body against his as they left the sheriff's station and marched across the snow covered parking lot. It wasn't until they were halfway up the hill to the blinking light that she twirled free, still holding his hand, swinging it between them.

"We've been having so much fun," she said in a singsong tone. "You've missed it all, Adam."

She was just trying to make him feel bad. Morgan's specialty. Getting Dad to smile at her and making Adam feel lousy.

Adam yanked his hand free and shoved it into his pocket. "Where's Dad?"

"Did you really take those kids? Clint's kids?" She stopped, waited until his full attention was on her. "You're either a fool or you have a death wish." Her hat bobbed with her words, the silly pompoms flapping back and forth. "Maybe both."

"I saved them." He said the words to feel better but instead all he saw was Bob's bloody body. Fear kicked him in the throat and he couldn't swallow.

He'd done the right thing. He had.

Now he just had to convince Dad of that. And keep the kids far away from Morgan.

She twisted her fingers in his shirt, forcing him to bend down to her level. Her other hand was in her pocket—the pocket with her knife. He sucked in his breath as panic and anger tangled. He could kill her. He was bigger, stronger.

He didn't want to. But her eyes said that she did. Want to kill. Love to kill. Which gave her the upper hand. As always.

"You saved them. I saved you." Her words came with a bright smile. "Don't forget that, big brother. Don't you ever forget what I did here this morning." She laughed and pushed him away so fast he stumbled back and fell into the snow bank. "I don't care what Clint says. You're just another fish."

"Children, children," came a booming voice from a van that had pulled up beside them. Adam glanced up at the white Econoline. *Guardian Locksmiths*, read the demur gray lettering on the side. *We're there for you when you need us. Day or night.*

"Hop inside," Dad called. "We've miles to go and work to do!"

Morgan leapt over the snow bank, scrambling for the front seat before Adam could get his legs untangled from the cinder-covered snow. He finally made it upright and opened the side door, half anticipating to find a fish inside, naked and bloody.

Instead the rear of the van held two narrow bench seats arranged lengthwise on each side, a small refrigerator and cook top, and neatly stacked plastic containers. The van pulled away from the curb, knocking him onto the seat nearest.

"Pretty sweet, isn't it?" Dad sang out. "All the comforts of home."

"What happened to the truck?"

"Gave it up. Didn't like leaving your sister alone. The new regulations and GPS monitoring cramped my style. Not enough free time for family fun." He and Morgan exchanged a glance and chuckled in unison.

Adam shivered, alone in the back. Realized that's how it had always been. Ever since Dad rescued Morgan from her home in Kansas.

Maybe even before. No, that wasn't true. Dad would take care of him. Family first. He always said.

His vision blurred and he rubbed his thumbs against his eyes, producing red flashes of fatigue. There was no room for doubt, no going back. He had to think about the kids and what was best for them.

Surely that was being with their dad? He remembered Darrin in the basement, Sally freezing, Marty running from his mom, crying. Remembered their smiles and laughter back in the cave.

He'd done the right thing. Of course he had.

The kids needed their dad. They all did.

He opened his eyes and saw they were driving up the lane to Darrin's house. The sun shone down in the valley, but here the west side of the mountain still clung to shadow.

Dad pulled off the road and turned the van around. "You know what to do?" he asked Morgan who took a squirt bottle of ketchup from the glove compartment. She nodded and jumped out.

"Why are we here?" Adam asked.

Dad rested his arm along the length of the front seat, watching Morgan in the rearview rather than looking at Adam. "You have Darrin, right?"

"I saved him. I saved them all." Adam leaned close, waiting for Dad to give him that smile.

It didn't come.

"Figured as much. Now it's my turn to teach that prick Harding a lesson once and for all. There's nothing he has that I can't take."

"He hurt Darrin."

"Don't worry. He's gonna pay. Big time."

Why didn't Dad ask if Darrin was okay? Or any of the others? "I saved Marty and Sally, too."

Dad jerked his head but only to check for movement in the side mirror. "Really? Good for you." His voice was distant and he didn't look back at Adam. Instead, he leaned across the front seat to open the passenger door. Morgan bounded in, breathless, cheeks red with the cold. "Did you do it?"

She nodded. "Of course. Easy peasy. Wrote it on the big windows in the back. No way they can miss it."

"Good girl." Dad drove the van down the mountain. Once they cleared the twists and turns and emerged at the intersection with the main road, he turned to Morgan and rumbled her hair with his long fingers. "I'm so proud of you."

Then he smiled. The smile Adam dreamt of for almost a year. Dad's smile. Aimed at Morgan.

Chapter 27

After giving their initial statements to the responding deputies, Lucy and Jenna were more in the way at the crime scene than helpful, so they drove over the mountain to the main sheriff's station in Huntingdon. Jenna said nothing the entire time. As soon as they arrived, she commandeered a desk in the far corner and collapsed into the chair.

Lucy called Nick while she waited for Zeller to return from his inspection of the crime scene and making notification. Nick listened patiently, as always, and didn't sound upset about her missing the start of Megan's tournament.

"But you know you're going to pay a price," he warned her.

She sighed. Lately there was always a price with Megan. "What?"

"The party tonight."

"Nick—"

"Hear me out. I called the other parents and several of us are attending. Don't call us chaperones, at least not around Megan, but we'll be there. And I talked with Danny. I don't think you have anything to worry about. He has a partner. Named John."

Lucy didn't care about what kind of living arrangements the coach had. Megan was still only thirteen and the youngest attending the party. "You'll be there? The whole time?"

"I promise."

"Okay. Fine."

"Great, I'll let her know. Want her to call you in between games?" If Megan's team won—which they would—they'd have to play a second game today to advance to the quarterfinals.

"Yes. But warn her if I don't pick up—"

"It's not because you don't want to. Love you." He hung up. Lucy turned her attention to tracking down Clinton Caine. Maybe the father could help her understand what the hell was going on with Adam.

When Zeller finally walked in, the few faces of the skeleton staff turned to him, hoping Bob had miraculously risen from the dead.

Zeller met their gazes and shook his head. He shuffled into his office as if carrying something too heavy for a man his age. Lucy waited for him to settle in, then followed.

"Sheriff, I'm so sorry for your loss." Lucy stopped, searching for the right words. There weren't any, but still she had to try.

Zeller said nothing but nodded to the chair before his desk. He reached inside a drawer for a bottle and poured her a paper cup of Macallan's. They toasted in silence and drank. The whiskey slid down smoothly to ignite warm coals in her belly. She shook her head when Zeller tilted the bottle, offering a second shot.

"I can't help but feel responsible," she admitted. "If we'd gotten there sooner—"

"He'd still be dead." Zeller turned his computer monitor so she could see and punched a few keys. "I can't stop watching it."

On the screen there was a grainy black and white surveillance film. The New Hope substation. The time stamp was 6:12 am, before Lucy and Jenna even left the school. The front door opened and a girl came in, looking around. She was bundled for the snow and she looked young, maybe eleven or twelve? She hesitated, then walked to the security door leading to the workspace, and rang the buzzer.

The camera was mounted directly above the security door in order to capture the entire reception area, so all they could see was the girl's head bobbing as she spoke to someone, then her body disappeared as if it had been yanked inside. The heel of her boot flying through the air the last part of her visible.

"What the hell?"

"Keep watching," Zeller said grimly.

A trickle of dark fluid eased into view. "He's already down." Zeller took another drink. "Didn't even have a chance to reach his weapon. Poor bastard."

That was the only motion on the screen for several moments. Then less than two minutes after she arrived, the girl reappeared. Only this time with Adam Caine. Walking behind her, arm wrapped around her, and way too close together. His eyes were wide, expression frenzied as he looked over his shoulder directly at the camera. He shook his head and mouthed a single word, "No."

Then they were gone. Only the growing blood pool remained.

"I know he's your fugitive," Zeller said, his voice rough around the edges. "But that was my man he killed, so I issued a BOLO for Adam Caine. Told my people he's armed and dangerous and to take every precaution when approaching him."

Politically correct way of saying "shoot to kill."

"You don't know it was Adam," Lucy found herself arguing.

Zeller stood, his face filling with disgust and fury. "Then who was it? Houdini? There was no one else there!"

"Who's the girl?"

"You think a little girl got the drop on one of my best men and killed him? Then took Adam Caine—what? As a hostage?" His laugh held no amusement but plenty of scorn. "I may be just a hicksville sheriff in the eyes of the FBI, but I'm not stupid. That boy took advantage of the distraction and didn't think twice. Killed my deputy in cold blood. And now we have another child missing. Once he has no more use for her, she's as good as dead."

"Who is she?"

He jerked his chin up at that. "What?"

"There were no other cars in the lot and no signs any had been there when we arrived. She must have come on foot. Which makes her most likely local. So who is she?"

Zeller shook his head, both hands pressed against his cheeks as if they'd gone numb. Lucy reached across the desk and capped the bottle. It was almost full; he hadn't had much. But she needed his mind clear if they were going to unravel this before some eager-beaver deputy shot Adam.

"I have no idea," he muttered. "One more family will wake up this morning and find themselves devastated." He aimed his gaze at her and it felt heavy. "You know you might be next, right? If Adam Caine killed my deputy because he blamed Bob for his mother's death, that makes you his next target."

Lucy stiffened, halfway out of her chair, ready to defend Adam. Then she checked herself, fought to find that facade of professionalism. "Adam's had plenty of chances to kill me and he hasn't yet."

His shoulders hunched in anger. "Why the hell do you keep denying the truth? Lucy, I just told good people their son died. Don't make me call your husband or tell your daughter the same. Maybe you should leave. Go home. Stay safe. Leave Adam Caine to me. We'll find him, deal with him. One way or the other."

"I appreciate your concern, Sheriff. I really do. And believe me, my family's welfare is my top priority—it's the reason I came here to begin with. But I honestly don't believe Adam is the monster you think he is. We're missing something. Just like last time."

She drew her breath in, knew that by playing her trump card she'd be burning her bridges with him. "Remember what happened then. When your predecessor refused to listen to me, tried to run me out of town."

The past hung in the air. Zeller kicked his chair back away from his desk, putting distance between them. He glanced at the bottle. Grabbed it, shoved it into a desk drawer, then finally looked back at her. "All right. You can stay. But God help us if you're wrong."

Lucy nodded her thanks and stood. "He was a good man, a good officer."

He sighed. "I know."

"We'll find the truth. For Bob."

"Don't make promises you can't keep."

"I don't." Lucy's cell trilled, sounding much too cheerful given the conversation. "Guardino."

"It's me. Olivia. Darrin's sister?" The teen's voice sounded breathless and muffled. "You have to come quick."

Lucy put it on speaker so Zeller could listen as well. "What happened, Olivia? Is it your mom? Are you in danger?"

"Not me. Darrin. I woke up this morning and found— wait, I took a picture of it, I'm sending it to you now. But he's erasing it. They said they'll kill Darrin, but Dad doesn't care. He's going to let them. Please, you have to help. Come now, before it's gone."

"Hang on, young lady," Zeller put in. "This is the sheriff. Calm down and explain what's going on."

Lucy's phone beeped. She had a text. She switched over and found the picture Olivia sent. The kitchen window. Written in red, dripping, still wet.

One million. Or next time it will be HIS blood.

"They want a million dollars for Darrin but my dad doesn't want to pay it. He won't let Mom call you guys, so I snuck out to do it myself."

"We're on our way, Olivia. You just hang tight," the sheriff said, grabbing his coat and hat.

"Is there anyone closer?" Lucy asked. "Maybe from the search?"

"No. We can get there faster."

"Olivia, was there a note? Any instructions?"

"Yeah, a piece of paper slid under the door. I took it. He hasn't figured out it's gone yet, but when he does— oh shit, he's coming!" A loud banging accompanied by shouting echoed through the phone. A girl's scream. And then silence.

Lucy and Zeller were already out the door.

Chapter 28

Jenna still had a list of things to follow up on from the night's SAR operations. One of them was searching the criminal backgrounds of anyone the boys had contact with at home or school.

She barely started when O'Hara, the detective who took her statement after the shooting yesterday, stopped by the desk she was borrowing.

"Thought you'd like to know," he said, "Roy started talking."

"That's good." Somehow the victory felt empty without Bob there to share it. She remembered their encounter in the observation room and sadness engulfed her. A bitter feeling. She was the last person he had sex with and it'd been empty, meaningless sex. How messed up was that?

"Yeah, and more good news. Coroner just called. No signs of a second body at the trailer."

"Second?"

"The little girl, Sally." He shook his head. "I really wasn't looking forward to dealing with a dead kid. Not on top of everything else going on around here."

"Thanks, O'Hara." He left and she stared at her computer screen, not seeing it. All she saw instead was Bob's body, the knife handle, the blood.

"Jenna," Lucy called as she and the sheriff rushed out of the sheriff's office. "With me."

Jenna held her breath for a moment. Better than committing career suicide by telling her supervisor to go to hell. Didn't do much for the burning in her stomach, though.

Lucy was already to the station door before Jenna closed her laptop. She grabbed her bag and slid into her coat. Jenna had the keys to the battered Taurus, so Lucy stood in the snow, parka unzipped, dark hair gathering snowflakes like dandruff, waiting impatiently.

"You hollered?" Jenna asked, taking her sweet time getting the keys out. The sheriff and his driver pulled out past them, showering Lucy with slush.

"Hurry the hell up. We just had a ransom demand."

Shit. Kidnapping for ransom? That was a different story. Jenna jerked the door open and fell into the driver's seat, shoving her bag with the laptop behind her. "Where?"

"Harding's." Lucy gave her directions despite the fact they were tailgating the sheriff's vehicle, its flashing lights cutting swaths of blue and red through the snow. "I don't get it. Why wait until now to make a ransom demand?"

"Waste our time, make us look foolish, spread us thin." The list was endless.

"Give Harding time to get back home."

"He's the man with the money, so yeah." Jenna was getting sick and tired of these conversations about the obvious.

But Lucy kept on talking. As if arguing with herself. "But he's also given us time to pull in resources from all over the state. Surely it would be easier to keep things quiet, just him and the family."

"Maybe it's not about money."

Lucy thought about that. "Maybe. Lord knows, Harding has plenty of enemies."

"Can't attack him publicly. Not with such a sympathetic wife. He's practically tripled his business playing off her tragedy." Something about that nagged at Jenna, but the road took a sharp curve and she had to focus on keeping the Taurus from skidding.

She concentrated on driving for a while before broaching the topic she knew Lucy didn't want to discuss. "Even with this, you can't rule out Caine."

Lucy fiddled with the heat vent. "You think a fourteen year old kid with a fourth grade education and no resources is playing Pied Piper with the children of New Hope? Why?"

"Maybe it is about the money. A million dollars is not a huge ransom demand for a man like Harding, but it's an impressive number to a kid. Or maybe he's angry he grew up without a mom and the rest of these kids had one."

"Wait until you meet Karen Harding, you'll re-think that theory." Lucy shifted in her seat, one knuckle rapping against the window in a senseless rhythm. It was barely noon, but felt like the sun had already abandoned them for the day. "Did they make an ID on the girl with Adam at the sheriff's station?"

"The one he took hostage after killing Bob?" Lucy might insist on living in a fantasyland where Adam Caine could do no wrong, but Jenna sure as hell didn't have to join her there. "No. None of the deputies knew her and they said no one at the school recognized her."

"She looked twelve or so. Definitely school age."

"Maybe she's not from around here."

"Then where'd she come from? Appearing at just the right time in just the right place?" Lucy made a small noise of disbelief. "I don't like it."

"You don't have to like it. It just is. We have it on film, Lucy. Adam Caine is responsible for killing Bob. That's all there is to it."

Gravel sputtered as they turned onto the drive leading up the mountain to Harding's house. The sheriff pulled up the curved area looping around the main entrance. There was a black Escalade parked beneath large steel beams jutting out from the bedrock. Jenna pulled in behind the sheriff. The front door was up several dozen wide flagstone steps, shoveled and salted but still icy.

The steel front door was coated in rust too picturesque to be natural. They rang a doorbell. Zeller waited a short minute before nodding to his deputy who banged on the door with the side of his fist.

The door swung open. Harding scowled at them, then swung his head to shout over his shoulder, "See what you did?"

Olivia scurried from the rear of the house, grabbed Lucy's arm, and pulled her inside. "I don't care what you say. He's my brother and I'll do whatever it takes to save him."

"We don't want or need your help," Harding told Zeller. "And certainly not yours," he added to Lucy.

Too late. Zeller and his deputy were already inside, Jenna on their heels. Harding rolled his eyes and closed the door behind them. He stalked into the kitchen without checking to see if they followed. "I have no idea what she told you—"

"How about that you destroyed evidence in a kidnapping?" Lucy said as they arrived in the kitchen to find the windows clean and a bucket on the deck.

Harding didn't even bother with a glance at the window. He leaned forward, the huge granite topped island between them like an executive's desk, and said, "My wife's in a fragile state. No way in hell I'd let her see that."

"Yeah, right. Ask him about the ransom note. Ask him why he didn't call you, Sheriff. Why I had to."

"Go up and check on your mother." His tone was a threat even without the glare he sent Olivia.

"No. I want to know what you're doing to get Darrin back."

Harding bunched his fists on the countertop. "I'm not discussing important business with a child present. Go. Check on your mother."

"Why is it I'm adult enough to take care of every single person in this house when you're not here, which is like, always, but I'm not adult enough to help get my brother back?"

The tension between father and daughter wasn't helping anyone. Jenna wondered who'd back down first. But then both Zeller and Lucy stepped into the fray. Zeller stood beside Harding and Lucy touched Olivia's elbow and led her into the hall. A moment later footsteps echoed up the stairs and Lucy returned holding a sheet of paper by the corner.

"I doubt we'll get any evidence from it," she said as she laid it on the counter where they could all read it.

One million, small bills, unmarked.

Macy's shopping bag, red ribbon, under Christmas tree, atrium Logan Valley Mall before 1pm today.

No excuses unless you want the next note sent with one of his ears.

"Week after Thanksgiving, that mall is going to be crowded with shoppers," Zeller said.

"Stupid girl. I told her to leave it to me."

"Sounds like she thought you weren't planning to pay," Lucy said.

"Of course I'm not planning to pay. I'm not going to reward a criminal for targeting my family. It would only make them think we're weak." His gaze drifted up in the direction of his wife's room. "But it doesn't mean I'm not going to try to catch these bastards. Get Darrin back."

"Then why didn't you call me?"

"Because, Sheriff, we both know ninety percent of your job is writing tickets and doing foreclosures. I'm not about to entrust the safety of a member of my family to you. I called the Lieutenant Governor and he's arranging for an elite team from the State Police to set up surveillance and manage the ransom drop."

"So you're going through with it?" Lucy asked.

"Of course. Not with my money, though. The State Police are providing fake currency that's specially marked." Harding sneered at Lucy and Zeller, making Jenna glad she'd stayed in the background. "I'm not an idiot." His tone implied they were. "I apologize for my daughter getting you out here. I'm sure you have better things to do with your time."

Zeller ignored him and turned to Lucy. "What should we do about the search? If this is for real, we don't want them stumbling across armed kidnappers holed up somewhere."

"What if it's a hoax? Or a con job? Can we risk losing the time?"

Jenna dared a question. "When did the note arrive?"

"Olivia found it when she got up this morning. Around seven. The ketchup was still wet, dripping."

Lucy glanced at Jenna. "No way it could have been Adam. He was on foot headed in the opposite direction."

"And controlling a hostage. That would have slowed him down even more," Zeller added. "I'm canceling the civilians from the search. We'll keep the local law enforcement agencies on the manhunt for Caine and the boys while the Staties take care of the ransom." He frowned, his eyelids drooping. Jenna had the feeling Harding was right. This was more than a small town sheriff could handle.

"The note says nothing about Marty Brady," Lucy said. "Are you going to tell his mother? There are two missing kids, not just one."

"Actually three, if you count the girl," the sheriff muttered.

"Still no ID on her?"

Zeller shook his head.

Jenna walked away. Let them work things out. She was just along for the ride at this point—no weapon, restricted duty, didn't know the terrain. Useless.

She stared out at the gray on gray vista unfolding below the glass walls of the living room. The ceiling was a good twenty feet high, so the sky loomed overhead. Thick gray clouds pressed down on the house, crushing the tiny

262

humans inside. She'd never felt like less of a hero than she did standing there, useless, tracking snow over immaculate hardwood floors.

This trip was supposed to be her stepping-stone to bigger and better things. Instead she felt small and vulnerable, like a kid up too late walking in on their mom and dad having sex and seeing too much of a world they weren't ready for.

Something the sheriff said about kids… Two kids missing. But there were really three. No, four.

She grabbed her phone and called O'Hara. "The little girl, the one from the trailer?"

"Sally?"

"Yeah, Sally. Where is she?"

He was silent for a moment. "Not really our problem. I suspect social services or the family knows. Probably with a neighbor or one of Rachel's friends. Her grandparents are still here, hold on and I'll ask them."

Jenna pressed her palm against the cold glass. Holding on.

O'Hara came back on the line a few minutes later, sounding breathless. "They have no idea. Social services is still canvassing the trailer park, but as far as they can tell, no one's seen Sally since Thursday night. Roy said she was gone when they woke up on Friday."

"That's when the thief took his stuff, right?"

"And his truck."

"Do me a favor. Put out a BOLO on that truck and Sally."

"Jenna, if you're right…" He hesitated. "I'd better talk to the sheriff. I'm not sure how much more we can stretch the manpower we have. And the media, they'll just cause panic."

None of that was Jenna's problem. But at least she wasn't useless. Because she finally figured out what had been bothering her all morning. What were the odds that two missing kids from the same small town were fathered by the man who killed Adam Caine's mother?

Chapter 29

"You asked Mr. Harding for a ransom, didn't you?" Adam asked as they drove up to the old fire tower on top of Warrior Mountain, right above the Harding house. It was one of Dad's favorite places. From up here he could watch the entire valley, including the traffic on the main roads in and out.

They went as far as they could on the unplowed road, then Dad turned the van around and parked. He didn't bother to answer Adam's question. Instead, he and Morgan opened their doors and hopped out simultaneously, like a pair of synchronized swimmers. All they needed to do was look at each other and they knew what the other was thinking. It'd never been that way with Adam and Dad. But it had between Dad and Mom.

Had Dad already forgotten her? Forgotten his family? He sure wasn't acting like he cared.

They opened the rear doors to the van. Morgan grabbed a pair of binoculars from a shelf while Dad lifted two campstools from behind the seat. Adam hopped out. This high on the mountain there was nothing to cut the wind. If you stood on your tiptoes you could rake your fingers through the clouds.

At least that's what he thought when he was a kid. Now all he could think about was if the kids were warm enough in the cave and what if they spilled their water or one of them was allergic to Dinty Moore or they burned themselves on the heater or...

"I'll never give them to you. Never." Adam hadn't realized he said it out loud until Morgan snickered. He stood apart from her and Dad, could have run, had his feet turned pointing down the mountain like he was going to, but felt like he needed to make that clear first. It was important Dad understood.

Dad finished setting up the stools. Then he turned and looked at Adam. Adam swallowed hard, wishing he'd run while he had the chance. Usually when Dad did the stare and glare, Adam always broke first, filling the silence with an apology or promise to do better next time. Not this time. This time he stood, hands jammed in his coat pockets, and met Dad's gaze.

Finally, Dad said, "That's fine. I don't need them. All I need is that they're someplace where no one can find them."

"I don't understand. How can you hold them for ransom if—"

"You always were slow on the uptake, weren't you, son?"

Disappointment flooded Adam. That he dared to believe. That he ever believed. "You're not giving them back. You just want the money."

"Since I quit driving, we've been a little short on cash."

"But you always said family is everything."

"Yeah, so?"

Adam brightened. "So you're going to let me go, take care of them? Like they're my own family?"

Morgan skipped through the snow between the two of them, breaking the invisible strands of tension. "No, you

266

idiot. You're not going anywhere. And neither are those kids. Wherever you left them, that's where they're going to die."

Adam's vision blurred and his face went cold as if all his blood slipped out of his body, swallowed by the snow. He glanced down, half expecting to see the snow colored red, but no, still white. Pure and sparkling with crystals on top. He remembered the way Sally laughed and played in it last night.

"No. You can't. They're family." Adam stared at Morgan. He'd never hit a girl, but the way her eyes flashed with merriment, as if this was a game…

"Children, children." Dad's voice held a rumble of amusement. "Morgan stop teasing your big brother. Adam, of course you need to take care of the little ones. There's just one thing I need you to help me with first."

"What's that?"

"Lucy Guardino. You and Morgan are going to bring Lucy to me. It's past time she paid for what she did to your mother."

–

Zeller's phone rang and he turned away to take the call. Harding took the opportunity to approach Lucy. "I understand you spoke with my wife last night."

"Yes." Lucy waited. To her surprise, his expression softened.

"Thank you. She seemed—better. More than she has in a long time. Despite," he gestured at the ransom note now encased in an evidence bag on the counter between them, "everything."

"She's a strong woman. She just needs reminding of that."

He bristled at her words. She understood. She was the stranger here. They'd save the boys or not. Either way, she got to go home to her family.

"I have to go. Meet with the State Police." Harding grabbed his car keys.

"The elite ransom drop team."

"Yeah. But," his gaze lifted towards the second floor, "I don't want to leave her alone. Not with a stranger. Could you stay? Just until we know."

Lucy was surprised to find herself nodding. Somehow she felt like she owed it to Karen. She wasn't sure why. There was no way she could have prevented what the woman suffered through seven years ago. But the way things spiraled out of control every time she visited New Hope, she couldn't help but feel responsible somehow. "Of course. I'll stay."

"Thank you." Harding's business-like demeanor returned. "Well, I'd better get going." He headed down the basement steps and closed the door behind him.

The sheriff hung up. "We've another kid missing. This one's only four and she's been gone since yesterday morning."

"Who?" Lucy asked.

"Rachel Strohmeyer's little girl. Sally."

Rachel? Lucy's stomach turned inside out. "She wasn't in the trailer?"

Zeller shook his head. "And they've checked every neighbor. She vanished. Just like the others." His deputy grabbed the evidence bag with the ransom note and headed out. Zeller hesitated. "Lucy, I think you're right. There's something more going on here. Too many things pulling us in too many directions for it to make sense. If you have any answers, now's the time to share them."

Lucy wished she had an answer. Or even a concrete direction to head in.

"Okay." He sighed, his shoulders heaving as he put his hat on and opened the door. "I'd best be going. You okay staying here?"

"Yeah. Someone should."

With Harding and the sheriff gone, the house echoed with quiet. Lucy wandered through the downstairs until she found Jenna in a study beside the dining room. She was buried in her laptop, reading something, forehead wrinkled.

"Did you know we have another missing kid?" Lucy asked.

"Sally. I know. Did you know she's also the New Hope Killer's child? Just like Darrin. It can't be a coincidence. I'm watching the security footage of Bob's killing, trying to see if there's something we can use to identify this other girl. She's got to be the key."

"Any luck?"

"No. I sent it to Taylor in Pittsburgh in the hopes his techy friends could work some magic. But I haven't heard back from them yet."

"Weird we haven't had a missing person report on her. She's young enough someone should have missed her by now."

Jenna looked up from the computer. "Unless her mom isn't in a position to report her missing." She paused. "I know you won't like this, but what if the New Hope Killer isn't dead? At least, not his partner. What if he took this girl's mom?"

"I thought you thought Adam Caine was behind all this? There's no way he can be the killer. He was an infant when the oldest case we found happened."

"Maybe he's working with—no, that doesn't make any sense," Jenna interrupted herself. She did that a lot, Lucy noticed. "He'd never partner with the man who killed his mom. Or got his mom killed. Whatever." She blew out her breath in frustration. "I don't know. It doesn't make sense. But it's too much coincidence not to be tied to what happened here four years ago."

"Keep working it. I'm going to check on Karen."

The way Jenna immediately focused on the computer once more, Lucy had the feeling she thought Lucy had the more difficult task. In a way she did. Waiting was always the hardest part.

Karen wore gray today. The color didn't suit her. Made her look more washed out than the white had. She practically blended into the mist shrouding the windows of her bedroom. Lucy wondered if she'd left the room since yesterday.

"Have you eaten? Can I get you anything?"

Karen shook her head. "Olivia made me eat some eggs a little while ago. I think they were eggs. I didn't really taste them, just spooned them in until the bowl was empty and she was happy."

"You need to take care of yourself."

"I need to take care of my daughter." She inhaled slowly, her body expanding then emptying once again. "Better than I did my son."

Past tense. Never a good sign. "You can't give up hope."

"Hope?" Her voice broke on the syllable as if the word was foreign.

"Yes. Hope." Lucy sat down across from Karen, their knees almost touching. "What you endured, what you survived—that takes a rare kind of strength. But I think you've forgotten that. You've forgotten you have that in you. You need to find it again, Karen. For the sake of both your children."

Karen shook her head at Lucy's words, forbidding them, casting them away. "I'm not like you. I can't just grit my way through the fear. It's like suffocating. The only way to get any air is to surrender to it. Then you find just enough to survive. But that's not enough to share."

"Are you sure? Because if that's true, you've already lost both your children. When Darrin gets back, he's going to need you to be there for him. Olivia, she needs you now."

"They don't need me. They never have. I'm just a burden to them. I'm not strong. Not like you."

"Like hell you aren't. You survived, Karen. You want to forget that along with everything else that happened to you. But if you deny that part of you, there's nothing left."

Karen was silent, knees pulled up to her chest, rocking in her chair as she thought. Lucy waited but she said nothing, so finally she stood to go.

"Lucy." Karen's voice was a whisper. "Do you really think I might get him back? That he's still—alive?"

Lucy knelt before Karen's chair and took both her hands in her own. "I promise you, Karen. We're doing everything possible to find him." Lucy never made promises she couldn't keep, especially not to parents in situations like this. But she knew platitudes weren't going to be enough to give Karen the strength she needed to dare to re-enter her life. "We'll bring him back."

"It should have been me. I would have gone."

Lucy shrank away from the other woman's words. "What do you mean?"

"It was… peaceful. After awhile, I didn't think, didn't exist, didn't feel. There was no fear. Not like here, not like every day since."

Dissociation. Common among victims of prolonged trauma. Lucy wished she could call Nick for a consult. "That was your way of coping. Then. When it was just you. But Karen, that won't work. Not now. Not if you're going to be there for Darrin. Not if you're going to help Olivia get through this. Can you do that? Help your kids?"

Another soul rattling sigh. "I'll try."

"Good. Why don't you get some clothes on, come on down for lunch?" Lucy waited for Karen's reluctant nod, then left, knowing she'd pushed her as far as she could.

She reached the bottom of the steps when the doorbell rang. She opened it, surprised to see Colleen Brady standing there. No coat, no hat, hugging herself against the cold. "Did you know? They called off the search. Just called it off. Where's Kurt Harding? I want to know why he told them to stop looking for my son."

Chapter 30

Jenna heard the commotion at the front door and ran out of the office. Colleen Brady stood there, snow melting in her hair, eyes wide with fear or maybe anger. Lucy escorted the woman inside and closed the door behind her. They sat on the wide leather couch facing the windows. Jenna stayed standing, not liking the waves of panic rippling off the mother.

Somehow Lucy didn't seem bothered. "They had to stop the search. Just temporarily."

"Why? Someone said it was because they heard from kidnappers. Why didn't they call me? Did they say if Marty was okay? Send a picture or video or something? Please—" Colleen collapsed forward, elbows on the large slate coffee table, face buried in her hands. "I can't take this. Not knowing."

Lucy wrapped her arm around the woman and pulled her into a hug. Like she was a friend, not just a victim. "I know. I know."

They sat together crying. Olivia came to the landing and looked down, followed by her mother. Karen Harding whispered something to the girl who nodded, came down the stairs and disappeared into the kitchen. Jenna's phone buzzed and she retreated to the study to answer it.

"I found her!" Taylor's excitement jumped through the airwaves. "Morgan Ames. Lawrence, Kansas. Disappeared two years ago when she was eleven."

"Good work. Are you sure?"

"You only get her full face in a few frames, but the photo from the NCMEC is a dead ringer. Even down to the mole on her left eyebrow."

"Anything on the family or how she went missing?"

"Report says she was last seen walking away from her house with a taller boy, brown hair, hunched posture. No other descriptors. No one got a good look at him or where they went."

Tall, brown hair, hunched posture. "Caine. Sonofabitch." So he and this girl were accomplices? But he would have only been twelve when he took her. "All the way from Kansas? There has to be an adult."

"You asking me or telling me?"

"Anything pop on that background check I asked you to do earlier? Colleen Brady?"

"Found a report alleging an assault. Filed almost seven years ago. Closed as unfounded."

Seven years ago? And Marty Brady was six. Too much of a coincidence. "What kind of assault? Where did it take place? Who were the suspects?"

"Sorry. All it says is unfounded, complaining witness emotionally unstable."

"What the hell? What kind of report is that?"

"Military Police. Fort Rucker, Alabama. Can't find any other records about it. Either they scrubbed it or maybe junked it before an investigation was begun. Couldn't tell you. Have to go through the Army. And you know how much they like to share."

Assault. Too vague. Could be a simple attempted mugging or even a drunk soldier getting frisky. Hell, could be a fellow army wife pissed off about something. Who knew?

One person knew. "Thanks, Taylor. Call me if you find out anything more about the Ames girl."

"Yeah. But," he hesitated, "shouldn't we call the family? Let them know we found her? They've been waiting for two years."

"Not yet. Not until we actually have her."

"You don't really think she killed that deputy, do you? Such a tiny thing. She looks so, well, sweet. Innocent."

She shook her head. She might be the rookie on the team, but she sure as hell wasn't the most naive. "Just call me. Thanks."

Jenna pocketed her phone and peeked outside to the living room. Lucy and Colleen still huddled on the couch facing each other, cups of tea steaming from the slab of slate that served as a coffee table. Damn, this was going to be hard. Should she let Lucy take the lead?

Last time she let Lucy take the lead, a police officer ended up dead.

She walked out to the living room and sat in a leather chair perpendicular to Colleen. "Mrs. Brady, I don't think we've been introduced. I'm Inspector Galloway. I work with Special Agent Guardino."

Lucy cut her a look filled with warning. Tread lightly.

"Ma'am," Jenna continued, trying to keep her voice even and non-threatening. "I was wondering if you could tell me about an assault you reported seven years ago at Fort Rucker in Alabama?"

Colleen didn't gasp or faint or anything dramatic. She just vanished. Her body frozen, her expression an absolute blank. Lucy leaned forward and placed one hand on her knee. "What is it, Colleen?"

It took a moment before Colleen's thousand-mile stare retreated. Her shudder rocked her entire body. "I hoped I'd never have to think of that night again."

"What happened?"

"I went shopping. Off post. Must have picked up a nail or something, because on the way back, it was dark and Rucker is in the middle of nowhere. Tire went flat just as I was passing Lake Tholocco. Couldn't reach anyone on my cell, so I was getting ready to change it myself when this mail truck pulled up."

"A delivery vehicle?" Jenna asked.

"No. A semi. But the trailer was marked US Mail. He said he was headed to Rucker, would be happy to drop me off at the gate. Or he could send someone back for me. He even offered to change the tire himself, but I could tell he was on a schedule and he seemed so nice and so I said I'd wait in the car if he could send help as soon as he got to an area with cell phone reception. He said fine, but first we better push the car farther off the road so no one hit it in the dark and so we both went to the back to push and—" The headlong rush of words fractured into silence.

Colleen gasped for air, hands clenched around her knees, hanging on tight. "He used a stun gun on me. Next thing I knew I was in the dark, in a compartment on his truck. I knew we were moving, I could feel the vibration below me like I was just above the road. It was so noisy, but I couldn't see anything. My hands were tied with plastic loops. They were so tight, it hurt so bad." She dragged in a breath. "He pulled off the road and came inside and..."

"He raped you?" Jenna asked, despite Lucy's warning scowl. Hell, they weren't ever going to court with this, and they didn't have time to waste.

Colleen nodded. "Over and over. All that night. And—" The thousand mile stare was back. "Other things." Then she straightened. "But I got the better of him. He thought I was unconscious, left for a while. I'm not sure how long. I was ready for him when he came back. Broke those plastic zip ties just like Martin taught me to. I waited by the door and when he came inside, thinking I was in the front of the trailer where he left me, I ran out, slammed the door, and kept on running.

"He'd parked near a roadside bar at the edge of the camp. Place with a few rooms out in back where guys would go to blow off steam, you know, with hookers. I was naked, half crazed, and I guess the owner thought it best to call the MPs instead of the county sheriff. By the time they came, the truck was long gone. They took me to my car and the tire wasn't flat any more.

"So," she shrugged, "they said if I was lonely because Martin was busy training or I was trying to cover up a one night stand or affair, there were better ways to do it. As a favor to Martin, to protect his career, they were going to close the case. Even said I was lucky they didn't press charges against me for filing a false report."

Jenna didn't blame her for the bitterness that colored her voice. She'd spit nails if anyone tried to do that to her. "Did you see your attacker?"

"Yes, a little. Had a ball cap on and a very full beard. Wore tinted glasses even though it was night. My description was pretty worthless. He could have been any one."

"Did you go to the hospital? Have an exam done?"

Colleen glared at her, her gaze clear for the first time since she began telling her story. "I'm a nurse. Of course I did. Even talked to the county attorney, but no one wanted to pursue it. The chain of command was too tangled. The truck was parked on Army property, but they wanted no part of it. And…" Another shrug. "Without evidence, what could they do?"

"I'm so sorry you went through that." Lucy nodded to Jenna. She finally got where Jenna was heading.

"One good thing came of it. In the ER they did a pregnancy test—didn't want to give me the Ovral if I was already pregnant. And that's when I found out about Marty."

Jenna sat up. "So he's not the rapist's child?"

"No. He's Martin's. Through and through." Colleen looked at them. "Why did you need to know? I mean, my case couldn't have anything to do with what happened here or to Karen Harding, could it? He was just a sick truck driver, not a serial killer." Despite her words, she hugged herself and pulled back into the corner of the couch.

Lucy comforted the woman. "Thanks for sharing with us, Colleen. You know how important it is that we cover every possibility." She stood and beckoned to Jenna. They left for the study.

"The kidnapper couldn't know Marty wasn't his. That makes three for three," Jenna said in a rush as soon as the door was closed. She took a breath, half jazzed with adrenalin and half terrified by the enormity of it all. "Three missing kids, all the product of rape."

Lucy called both Karen Harding and Colleen Brady down to the living room and sent Jenna to keep Olivia occupied in the kitchen. If what she suspected was true, the teen didn't need to be privy to her mom's secrets.

"I know this is hard," she said as both women took seats on the opposite ends of the long couch. They glared at each other as if opponents in a championship fight. Nothing like having both your boys' lives at the mercy of a kidnapper to make you wary. After all, a mother would do anything to save her child. But maybe not another woman's child.

"Time is short, so I'm going to be blunt," Lucy continued. "You both were the victims of a sexual assault seven years ago. And you both have ties to New Hope."

Colleen jumped, leaning forward, bracing herself on the slate coffee table. "Wait. You're not saying—" She turned to stare at Karen who was curled up, knees hugged to her chest, looking frail and vulnerable. "It couldn't be the same man. It just couldn't be."

"I think we need to explore that option."

"No," she persisted, shaking her head. "No. Her," she didn't use Karen's name, "attacker is dead. You saw him die. Four years ago. It's one of the reasons I brought Marty back home when Martin redeployed. I figured no town would be safer. The danger was gone." She gulped so loud, Lucy heard it. "Are you saying… Are you saying, Marty was kidnapped because I came back home?"

Lucy sidestepped the question. "Karen, you and your husband are both from New Hope. Did you return home seven years ago? You, too, Colleen. Any visits to your mom?"

"That summer," again it was Colleen answering, "was our tenth high school reunion. She probably doesn't remember me," another nod in Karen's direction, "but I remember her and Kurt. King and Queen of the prom. Again. But Martin and I still had a grand time." She touched her cheek, a soft touch as if remembering her husband's hand. "That's probably when Marty was conceived."

"Tell me about the reunion. Anything memorable?" Lucy looked to Karen, trying to get her to join in on the conversation, but she stared vacantly out the rapidly darkening windows.

"Martin got into a fight. Guy I dated in high school. We went out twice, that's all. I wouldn't even call him a boyfriend since both times we were with a group of kids. He tried to hit on me. Clint was drunk, it was no big deal, I was handling it. But Martin, well, he's an Army pilot, testosterone was pretty much what he lived on."

"Clint?" Lucy pounced on the name. "Clinton Caine?" Adam's father. The long distance truck driver. A shiver shook her as shadows crowded the room. But she kept her voice calm. "Karen, did you know Clinton Caine?"

Karen froze, not even breathing for a long moment. Then she let out her breath and said, "He proposed to me. On the night of the prom. We'd never even talked before, but he said he loved me. Wanted to marry me. I thought it was sweet. Had a crush on me since second grade, always shadowing me around. Never daring to even talk to me before that. But," she closed her eyes, wincing, "but, Kurt and the other football players overheard him. They beat the crap out of him. He missed prom and never came back to school. Not even for graduation."

Two women, the objects of Clinton Caine's affection. Two men who'd ridiculed him. The perfect fuel to feed a grudge. Or obsession. And it explained why Caine took so many risks with Karen. He not only wanted to humiliate, but wanted to own every part of her. Steal her from Kurt.

"Clinton Caine," Lucy murmured. She'd once met the man. Hadn't had a clue. Thought he was a loving husband and father. Grief-stricken.

Adam said he wanted to bring his father back to New Hope. Maybe he'd succeeded. Too well. Maybe Caine had returned. Only now he was collecting his children. His trophies.

But what did he want with them?

She needed to see if Morgan Ames could also be one of his children, the product of another rape-abduction. If Morgan was involved with Deputy Bob's death, did Caine teach her how to kill?

Adam had lived with the man his entire life. Did that make him a victim? Or an accomplice?

Maybe killing was in his blood.

Chapter 31

Lucy was an adult. And an FBI agent. She could take care of herself. Marty, Darrin, and Sally couldn't. They needed Adam.

That's what he told himself after Dad gave him a gun and sent him and Morgan down the mountain to Darrin's house. They had Bluetooth earpieces so Dad could hear everything they did and talk to them. Well, talk to Morgan. Adam was too busy thinking to pay much attention.

He couldn't stand up to Dad. He couldn't even stand up to Morgan. Look what happened to Deputy Bob. He should have stopped it. He knew what was happening, but he just sat there and watched like a dope. Helpless, stupid, dope. That was Adam.

Would he let that happen to Lucy? His boot heel caught on a tree root hidden by the snow on the trail and he slipped banana peel style. Morgan's laughter cut through the air, silencing the birds. Even the wind hushed when faced with Morgan. She owned any space she moved through. Even if Adam stood in her way.

Especially if Adam stood in her way.

Dad gave her a gun, plus she had her knife. And Dad whispered last minute instructions to her after Adam started down the trail, thought Adam too stupid to notice. Or suspect that maybe once Dad had what he wanted, he might not need Adam anymore. Just like in Cleveland.

Maybe Dad hadn't come back to save Adam. Maybe he'd come to silence Adam.

Adam pushed back to his feet, wiping the snow from his jeans before it could melt. The house was just ahead. Dad would be pulling the van around, ready to pick them up as soon as they had control of things.

"Should be just Lucy, Karen, sweet Olivia, and that red-haired girl," Dad had said. "Everyone else is headed over to the ransom drop. You have plenty of time, but don't waste it. I want to be long gone before anyone squawks to the cops."

The approach was simple: Adam in through the basement, Morgan at the front door. No one knew her. They'd open the door to her and that was all they needed.

They reached the end of the trees. Morgan did a little dance as she pulled her gun out and unzipped her coat so she could reach her knife easily. "You ready, big brother?"

No. Not at all. He still hadn't figured a way out of this. He needed to save Lucy and he needed to tell her where the kids were before he ran. New Hope wasn't safe for him. Not anymore. Not with the cops ready to shoot to kill and Dad and Morgan ready to go fishing.

With Adam as bait.

–

Lucy rushed into the kitchen where Jenna and Olivia were making spaghetti for dinner. "Yesterday I asked you to locate Clinton Caine. Did you find him?"

Jenna kept chopping tomatoes, not even looking up. "No. Sorry, it wasn't a priority, what with trailers blowing up and—" She dropped the knife and whirled. "Oh shit. You're not saying—"

The doorbell rang.

"Lucy, is it Caine? Why? How?" Jenna sputtered.

"I'll get the door." Olivia headed down the hall.

"I think it's Caine." Lucy had her cell out to call Taylor. Adrenalin flooded her veins. She was right. She knew she was right.

"Put down the phone, Lucy." The muzzle of a gun pressed against the back of her head. It was Adam. He drew her weapon, put it on the counter across from Jenna. "I said put it down."

She obeyed.

Jenna was staring, back pressed against the cooktop. The knife she held just a few moments ago out of reach.

"Yours, too," Adam ordered Jenna. "And your gun."

Jenna slid her phone from her pocket, carefully set it on the counter. "I don't have a gun."

"Adam," Lucy said, her voice calm. She knew this boy, she could reason with him. He wasn't like his father. She may have been mistaken about Clinton Caine, but not about Adam.

She was staking their lives on it.

"Adam. I know it was your dad. And your mom. She was his partner, wasn't she?"

"Of course." His tone was wistful. "She loved him so much," he said in a singsong. "She could never say no to him."

"Adam!" A girl's voice called from the other room. "Bring your fish in. Stop fooling around."

"You heard her. Into the living room." Jenna backed down the hall, hands raised in the air. Adam prodded Lucy forward.

Lucy tried to think of a way to get to her backup weapon. "Is it just you and Morgan?"

"Yeah. How'd you know her name?"

"I know everything, Adam. I know you took the boys and Sally. Your way to get your father back. But now that he's here, now that he's made you kill—"

"I didn't, it wasn't me—"

"She killed for you. Take responsibility for your actions. Be your own man. Not your father's puppet."

He stiffened at that. "You don't know anything."

They entered the living room. The girl from the security tape stood near the open front door, the gun in her hand aimed at the three women cowering on the couch.

"Good boy," she told Adam. "Red," she waved her gun at Jenna, "you sit over there." She nodded to the chair on the far side of the slate coffee table.

Jenna glanced at Lucy, did as instructed. Then Morgan aimed at Lucy. "Now you," she smiled so wide, all her teeth showed, "you're coming with us. Adam promised you to Clint. A special fish to play with."

Lucy stood her ground. "No."

Morgan looked at her in surprise. "Excuse me?"

"I said no. I'm not going anywhere."

The girl considered her options. Then shrugged. "Fine. Adam, shoot her."

The muzzle knocked against the side of her skull as he trembled. She forced herself to breathe slow deep breaths, knowing he was almost there, almost ready to give up.

"I can't, I can't," he sobbed, throwing the gun down and collapsing onto his knees.

Jenna lunged for the pistol as Lucy threw her weight down and pinned Adam to the floor, the couch between her and Morgan.

Lucy drew her back up weapon from her ankle holster, but didn't have a shot. One of the women from the couch dove to the ground, plowing into Lucy, knocking her gun away.

"Don't shoot him. He knows where Darrin is," Olivia cried, clutching Lucy's arm.

"Everyone freeze. His gun might be not be loaded, but mine is," Morgan shouted.

Jenna aimed Adam's gun and fired. Nothing. Morgan laughed. "Told you."

Lucy shook Olivia off and inched towards her weapon. Morgan shifted position and fired a shot into the floorboard near Lucy's hand, splinters spraying the air. Lucy used her body to cover Adam, twisting to keep Morgan in sight.

Morgan tilted her head, a mad gleam in her eye. From where Lucy lay on top of Adam, she heard a voice murmuring through the Bluetooth he wore.

"No," Adam cried, not talking to them but to whomever's voice spoke in his ear.

Morgan smiled. "He wants you." She aimed the gun at Olivia. "He says to take you. Just like he took your mother."

An unearthly screech emerged from Karen as she lunged for Morgan. Colleen threw herself on top of Olivia, tumbling them both behind the coffee table. Morgan fired again and hit Karen in the leg.

Jenna caught Lucy's eye and made a diversionary move. Lucy sprang from the floor, hoping to catch Morgan off balance. She grabbed the girl's gun hand. It was a move of desperation, but when you had an active shooter you didn't sit around and wait for them.

Jerking Morgan's gun into the air, she used her weight to twist the arm, keeping the weapon aimed away from her. Morgan anticipated her move and turned into Lucy's body, ending up with a knife to Lucy's throat, drawing blood.

Lucy relinquished her hold on the girl's other hand. She barely felt the burning sting of the shallow cut, but saw the red trickle of her own blood slip down the knife blade. The girl quickly repositioned herself with Lucy as a shield, the gun held steady at the base of Lucy's spine.

"Okay, maybe for once we don't get the fish. But we'll still get who we came for." Morgan pulled Lucy back, heading for the open door. Lucy had no choice but to comply. "Pull it shut," she ordered.

As soon as Morgan and Lucy stepped over the threshold and the door clanged shut with Adam, Jenna, and the others safely behind it, Lucy straightened, ready to make another move. That's when she saw the man. The man with the stun gun.

Everything sparked red as electricity jolted through her, disconnecting her brain from her body with the force of a pilot being ejected from his jet. Pain fired through her muscles and she fell to the ground. The man laughed as he grabbed her up in a fireman's carry.

"Adam's telling them he'll take them to the kids," Morgan said, listening to her earpiece. "Should I kill him?"

"No. Follow them. I want Adam." Even as he jostled Lucy down the steps and threw her into the back of a waiting van, the man sounded relaxed. As if he abducted federal agents at gunpoint every day. As soon as her body hit the floor, he grabbed her wrists and handcuffed them behind her. Her leg was twitching but she couldn't control any movements other than forcing her chest muscles to let air in and out.

"See," he beamed at the girl, "I told you. You can have it all. You just need the balls to go after it."

The girl ran off beyond Lucy's limited line of sight from her face down position. The man rolled her over. Lucy managed to blink her eyes into focus. Clinton Caine.

"Nice to see you again, Lucy. We have a lot to talk about. Like how you got my wife killed." He zapped her again with the stun gun and the world went black as her body blazed with pain.

Chapter 32

As soon as the door shut behind Lucy and Morgan, Jenna made her move. She scrambled under the couch, coming up with Lucy's backup weapon, and ran to the door, listening. Damn thing had no sidelights, only a worthless peephole, and this was the only wall in the room without windows.

"Call 911," she told Olivia as she handcuffed Adam. No other weapons on him. She took his Bluetooth and listened but the line was dead. Grabbed his phone. Colleen was already assessing Karen's wound.

Olivia ran to her mom's side. "I can't believe you did that. For me."

Karen grabbed her daughter into a one-armed hug and kissed her forehead. "I should have stood up for you a long time ago. From now on everything is for you. And Darrin."

"Get on the phone," Jenna ordered as she tried to get a line of sight out the window. Stupid things were angled so sharply it was hard to see down to the driveway.

"The kids," Caine said, rolling to his knees awkwardly with his hands cuffed behind him. "We need to get to the kids. Let me take you there."

Jenna saw the van pull down the drive, couldn't see the plate in the dark. She could try to follow in the Taurus. They hadn't disabled it. She wasn't sure why, seemed like they'd be smarter than that, but if they spotted her, they'd kill Lucy. Better to wait for backup. That was procedure. But with the sheriff's department stretched so thin, it might take time. "Are the kids in danger?"

"They are if he finds them. I'm sorry, so sorry. I thought I was saving them. But he—" Adam sputtered to a halt.

"What does he want with the kids?"

"He's their father. He-he's my father." He squeezed his eyes shut as if the truth was too painful. "I think he might hurt them. Or let Morgan hurt them. She killed Deputy Bob. Right in front of me. And," he took a breath, opened his eyes again, "and she liked it. She laughed. He didn't deserve that. He was a nice man. But she gutted him like a fish."

"Where are the kids?"

"In a cave. I have to show you, you'll never find them otherwise. Please. Don't let her do that to the kids. Please."

Olivia came in, holding the phone. "They're sending an ambulance from Alexandria. They want to know if the scene is safe."

Jenna made her decision. Someone had to save the children. She took the phone. "This is Inspector Galloway. The scene is safe. Tell Sheriff Zeller that Agent Guardino was taken hostage. They're in a white van, Ohio plates, marked Guardian Security on the van's side. The man is Clinton Caine, five-ten, one-eighty, brown, brown. Wearing a black jacket, jeans, work boots. The girl is Morgan Ames, thirteen, wearing a light blue ski jacket and jeans. She killed Deputy Bob."

"Zeller here," the sheriff's voice interrupted her. "What the hell's going on?"

"I have Adam Caine in custody. His father just abducted Lucy. We also ID'd the girl as Morgan Ames, from Lawrence Kansas."

"Clinton Caine is behind all this—"

"Adam knows where the children are. He's going to take me there. I'll call you with directions as soon as I get there." She looked over her shoulder at Caine. "How long will it take?"

"Driving or walking?"

Like she was going to hike through the woods with a prisoner. "Driving."

"Fifteen, twenty minutes. Tell him it's near the old Stolfultz barn. He'll know where I mean."

"Did you get that?"

"Yeah. I shut down operations at the school. All the mutual aid from Blair and Cambria County are providing back up for the Staties at the Mall."

"The Mall was a diversion. Just like Lucy thought." Seemed like Lucy had been right about a lot of things.

"I'll get the State Police, see if they can get a helicopter searching for the van, as well as set up roadblocks. It'll be thirty minutes or more before I can get someone over to that side of the county. There's a pile-up with injuries on Route 45."

Adam shook his head, panic straining his features. "No. They can't wait. We need to go save them. Now!"

"Have them meet me at the barn. As soon as they can." She hung up and gave the phone back to Olivia. Then she hauled Adam to his feet. "Come on. We're going for a drive."

–

Well at least she hadn't wet herself, was Lucy's first clear thought once she regained control of her body. That was one of the most common side effects of being tasered—and Clint's stun gun seemed to have been modified for extra voltage.

And this was just the start, a grim voice in her head reminded her.

The van rocked and rolled around sharp turns and bumps in the road. Then it stopped. The main road, she thought, trying to get her bearings. But when she looked out of the section of the windshield she could see, it was just sky and the tops of trees. Then the van lurched onto even rougher road, its wheels slipping against the snow covered ground.

Not the main road. Probably a logging trail. Which meant they could be anywhere on the mountain. Another lurch and she rolled onto her side, her face against the floorboards. The stench of diesel made her nauseous. She forced it aside, just like she had her fear. Think, dammit. Think.

He wouldn't take her too far. He needed to stay in cell range of Morgan. Which, from the Hardings' house, meant staying on this side of the mountain and the south end of the valley. Which also meant she was in range of help if she could grab a phone.

She pressed her hip against the floor. No telltale feel of her keychain and the small knife she kept there. He must have taken them. Her backup gun? No, Jenna had it.

"You back with us?" Clint called from the front of the van. "Wouldn't want you to miss any of the fun." The van stopped and he turned the ignition off. He turned around in the front seat, his arm draped over the back, and stared at her.

Just sat and stared.

The van was dark. The only light was the feeble sunbeams fighting through the snow that quickly covered the windshield. With the engine off, it quickly grew chilly.

Yet Lucy was sweating. Her shirt stuck to her and she could smell the acrid stench of her perspiration. She forced herself to lie still, keeping eye contact with Caine. He was used to total control and power over his captives, body and mind.

But this time was different. She wasn't in the dark. She knew what he was capable of. She had no hope of anyone finding them. Which in a way was freeing. It was just her and him. And she had a helluva lot more to live for than he did.

Caine did what he did for mere pleasure. Lucy was fighting to get back to her family alive.

An unbidden smile twisted her lips. He laughed at the sight of it. "This is gonna be fun."

Chapter 33

Jenna moved his restraints to the front and made the kid drive. Technically a no-no, but what choice did she have? Not like she trusted him behind her or even beside her. To her relief, he didn't give her any trouble.

"Used to drive all the time for my dad," he told her, as if they were taking a trip down memory lane instead of to rescue the kids he kidnapped. "I'm tall for my age, so it was easy."

"Did you help your dad in other ways?" She didn't add: Like rape and torture his victims?

Adam swallowed hard, his hands tightening on the wheel. "I helped him find fish. Yeah. Wasn't very good at it. He never let me touch any of them. Said I would ruin it. But he made me watch a few times. Before we got Morgan. After that," he shrugged, "it was their thing. I was in charge of stuff like getting food, stealing cash."

He sounded remorseful, but Jenna wasn't buying it. How could anyone—even a kid—not know what he saw was wrong?

They pulled up to the barn where Bob had brought her yesterday. "We're not going in there, are we?"

"No. There's another cave. Smaller. Just through those trees." He pointed to the forest that spread out from the side of the barn at the base of the mountain. The sun was gone now and in the light of the car's headlights, the trees swayed in the wind looking as if they weren't too happy about anyone trespassing.

Jenna wasn't happy either. Especially not about another cave. She called the sheriff's station. Backup was delayed at least another half an hour. Maybe more.

Well, hell. Sit and let those kids freeze to death? Or worse, let Caine Senior find them? Or play the hero and rescue them?

She wanted to do the first. Play it by the book. That way anything that happened wouldn't be her fault.

But all she thought was what would Bob do? What would Lucy do?

They wouldn't play it safe. They'd save those kids and not care about being a hero. Easy for them. They already were heroes. Even with a gun at her head, Lucy hadn't been afraid. Jenna wanted to run away and hide. Of course she didn't, her training wouldn't let her. But that didn't erase the fear she felt when Morgan aimed that gun at her.

"Please," Adam begged. "We can't wait. He'll find them. I know he will. He's too smart—and when he wants something, he always gets it."

Jenna made her decision. "Okay, let's go. But if you try anything, I'll shoot you like a dog."

Not so heroic, but kids or no kids, she was coming out of this alive.

–

It was so easy. The redhead's car had a safety latch inside the trunk, making it child's play for Morgan to hide there, hear everything they said, then slip out again. Easy peasy to follow their trail through the snow after that.

She watched from beneath a hemlock, shielded by its low hanging branches. Adam sidled behind a rock and vanished, followed by the redhead. Another cave. One so well hidden, no one, not even the search teams, would ever find it. Clever boy, her big brother. Maybe more clever than she gave him credit for.

She pulled out her phone. The reception here was lousy. A single bar, but good enough for her needs. "I found them." She gave Clint directions to the cave. "You can't miss their trail. Now that the snow's stopped, it's obvious."

"That means the cops will find it."

"They're half an hour out. So you need to hurry."

"We're ten minutes away. No worries, baby girl. We'll have plenty of time to have some fun."

She wasn't sure about that. Lately Clint had been taking way too many risks. Almost like he wanted to be caught. No, that wasn't it. Like he needed the *rush* of almost being caught.

Fine for him. But not her. She liked her freedom, being able to blend in, go anywhere, do anything. She'd always be grateful to Clint for giving her that freedom, showing her how powerful she was. But that didn't mean she was ready to rot in prison for the man.

She pulled out her knife and followed Adam's footsteps into the cave. She owed big brother for his betrayal back at the house. And she'd smelled the fear radiating off the redhead.

She'd be long gone before the cops came.

Plenty of time for fun.

Jenna swallowed the urge to scream as she followed Adam into the cave. She didn't have Bob's hand to hold this time, so she clutched Adam's arm instead. Had to keep her prisoner close. Although she already felt like an idiot for not thinking of another way to save the kids. As it was, she made Adam hold the flashlight. She didn't like giving him a potential weapon, but it was the only way to keep her gun hand free.

He was docile enough so far. But they were on his territory. And totally out of her comfort zone. The blackness closed in on her as it had yesterday. Not so bad, thanks to the light Adam held, but bad enough.

All he had to do was turn the light off and she'd be a goner.

"Keep moving," she snapped at him when he hesitated. They were in a large cavern at the front of the cave with two paths in sight: one leading down and one leading to another chamber to the side.

Her blood pounded in her throat and she thought he was going to make a move. She raised her weapon, ready to pull the trigger. But all he did was clear his throat.

"I wasn't sure—would you, I mean, there's a lantern in the bedroom. We could set one in here. It's pretty bright. If that's okay."

Thank God his back was to her. She'd almost shot him. "Yeah. Get it."

He handed her the flashlight and bowed his head to step into the side chamber. He emerged a second later holding a Coleman lantern. He lit it and moved to the second path. "If I leave it here, you'll always know your way out."

"Don't you need the light?" she asked as he led her down the path and across a small stream.

"No ma'am. I know my way around here light or dark. Sometimes it's easier in the dark. Not so scary."

She doubted his father's victims would agree.

They passed through a chamber with pale white rock formations and cave art scattered at shoulder height, reminding her they weren't the first humans to pass this way. Then she saw what he meant about scary. There was another stream—or a branch of the same one—but this one was riotous, white water rushing and she had no idea how deep.

Marion Caine's body had been lost in an underground stream like this. Swallowed by the mountain and never seen again.

"Usually not so high or wide," Adam said, backing up a few steps before leaping across the water, the flashlight bobbing with the motion. "Must be the snow. It's warm enough inside here to melt." He stood on the other side and held his handcuffed hands out to help Jenna across.

He could have just run. Could have pushed her into the water before he crossed. Could have done a lot of things. Still, she wasn't about to trust him. "How much farther?"

He nodded to a cavern on the other side of some tumbled boulders. There was a faint light coming from it. "In there."

They must have been close because suddenly there were cries of help from beyond the boulders. "Help! Help us, please! Marty's hurt bad!"

Jenna grit her teeth, took three steps back and leapt, flying through the air and remembering doing the same on her horse when she was young. She landed hard, almost slipped back into the water, but Adam caught her and set her onto her feet.

"This way." He hurried up the path and stooped low to make it into the next cavern. Jenna followed him. It was smaller than the area at the front of the cave but the air was crisp, less stale. A faint glow came from an area below a drop off. Camping supplies littered the ledge including another lantern Adam knelt to light. Beyond him was a wooden ladder.

"Lie down, face down," she ordered Adam, not trusting him at her back when she got close to the edge. Who knew how far down the bottom was.

"Help! Help us!"

Adam complied. Even laced his fingers behind his head. Jenna inched forward and craned her head over the edge. About ten feet down she saw three kids surrounded by flashlights. One of them lay flat, his leg splinted with two mountain pie makers tied with fabric.

"Hi guys! We're going to get you out of there," Jenna called. "Everyone okay?"

"Marty fell," one of the boys called. Darrin. "I think his leg is broke."

Adam twisted his head around. "Sally, are you okay? Told you guys I'd come back for you."

"Adam! Adam, you came back! I don't want to 'splore any more." The little girl clutched a toy cat to her chest and sounded close to tears.

"Don't worry, sweetheart," Adam shouted. "Everything's going to be fine." He turned his head to Jenna. "Please. Let me help. You'll never get them all out by yourself."

Jenna stood at the edge of the pit. Adam was right. But she couldn't trust him down there with three potential

299

hostages. Who knew what was down there to be used as a weapon.

"Tough choice, isn't it?" a girl's voice came from behind Jenna. Just before she pushed Jenna over the edge and into the pit.

Chapter 34

"What are you most afraid of, Lucy?" Clint asked as they drove down the mountain.

Face down in the back of the van, Lucy couldn't see where they were going. All she knew was a phone call had changed Clint's plans. After he hung up, he put away the stun gun and hopped into the driver's seat.

Not that she was complaining. Clint knew his anatomy. The repeated blasts of electricity to the nerves of her neck and face left her jaws locked in spasm as fire danced beneath her skin. A ferocious headache made even blinking painful.

"That last blast was your trigeminal ganglia. People have gone insane from those nerves firing, so it's obviously not pain that you fear," he continued, his tone amiable as if they were discussing the Steelers' chances in the playoffs. "I don't think even death. Not the way you saved those children in September. Or the way you look at me. Never had a fish look at me like you do."

Lucy ignored him. Better to concentrate on finding a tool. She could pick the handcuff lock if she had a piece of wire. Better yet would be finding a weapon to use on Caine. That would solve everything.

They stopped. A lot sooner than the ten minutes she overheard him promise Morgan. He must not trust the girl. Maybe Lucy could use that. Drive a wedge between them.

The van door opened. He hauled her out by the arm. She could barely stand. Only sheer stubbornness kept her from surrendering to the nausea roiling her gut. The sun had totally set, leaving her shivering since she had no coat.

He parked the van behind the school where it wouldn't be seen. Smart, Lucy realized as he led her across the playing field and into the woods. An easy escape away from the path the cops would take.

Sending two kids to do his work, making sure no one saw his face. He definitely cared about getting caught. She'd wondered about that, given how risky it'd been for him to keep Karen for so long or to take Rachel so close to home. If he'd picked up stakes and left, just killed her quickly, his family could have started over without anyone ever knowing there was a killer in their midst.

But instead, he'd stayed. Determined to break Rachel's devout faith.

Not stupid, but definitely driven more by his needs than safety or security.

"You kept Karen longer than anyone," she mused as he pushed her into the trees. The only light came from a small LED flashlight he clipped to the visor of his ball cap. "What did Marion think about that?"

"She understood. She was just getting back on her feet from her first bout with cancer. She liked that I stayed home. Understood I needed something to occupy my free time."

"You kept Karen here all those months?"

He chuckled. "Down in the root cellar. She wasn't the first—or the last. Marion's idea. She liked to watch. To take care of the fish when I was gone. But it was hard for her to go far while she was getting her radiation and chemo. She got tired so easily."

Lucy remembered the basement of the Caine house. The small dirt-floor room with the shelves of preserves. The strange configuration of the rest of the space. "Adam. He stayed down there a lot, too?"

"When she was feeling okay, Marion came on the road with me. Fishing trips. Couldn't risk the boy hurting himself or someone seeing him. So we got him all squared away down in the basement." He sounded as if Adam's time living among the spiders and shadows was better than a trip to summer camp.

They came across fresh tracks in the snow. "Should be right over here. Ah, I see what she was talking about. Funny, I've been past those boulders a thousand times, never realized there was an opening back there." He shoved Lucy into the narrow space. "You first."

Squeezed between two rock faces, hands cuffed behind her, Lucy still wanted nothing more than to run screaming into the snow. No matter that it would get her killed. Anything was better than dying in a cave, buried under the weight of the mountain, maybe not even a body for Nick and Megan…

Nick and Megan. Their faces appeared before her, their laughter squelched the panic ringing through her brain, and she was able to keep going.

She had to make it out alive. For Nick and Megan.

They emerged into a cavern lit by a lantern at the far end. "Nice," Clint said appreciatively. He prodded Lucy down the path and across two streams. The second one was wide and he forced her to wade through it, laughing when the water reached her knees and the current threatened to drag her down. "Careful there, Lucy. Hard to swim with your hands cuffed behind you."

When she was almost to the other side, gasping with cold, her feet and legs numb, he leapt across the water and hauled her out. Her teeth chattered uncontrollably.

"Little taste of what Marion got," he muttered. He wrenched her arm and dragged her past the boulders to a cavern. Just as he forced Lucy's head down to push her through the opening, a woman screamed.

Lucy scrambled into the cavern in time to see Morgan push Jenna off a cliff. "No!" She rushed forward.

Jenna and the three kids were at the bottom of a pit. Not very far down, in fact, Jenna was already pushing herself up to her knees.

"You okay?" Lucy asked.

"Just bruised. But Marty has a broken leg."

Clint dragged her away from the edge before she could answer. "Good job, Morgan. And we still have plenty of time before the cops get here."

"Let's take them somewhere where we can play, Clint," Morgan said. "Where we won't be rushed."

"Yeah, but I don't really want to be bothered with two to watch. We'd have to stay up, guard them while we travel. Not like the old days with your mom, Adam. We had three fish at once a few times in Echo Cavern. Used to play them off each other. Got to the point where they'd fight for the chance to torture each other just to live another day." He walked around the cavern, assessing possibilities.

Lucy spotted a ladder lying on its side. If she could get it down to Jenna… She edged towards it, thinking she could kick it in, when Clint whistled.

He raised a can of Coleman fuel. "Give me a hand here, Morgan." She rushed to his side, kicking Adam on her way. She and Clint whispered for a moment, then Morgan danced away, holding the fuel can.

"Stand up, Adam. You're not going to want to miss this," Clint said. Adam climbed to his feet. Clint pulled him to the edge of the cliff. Morgan opened the fuel can and doused the children and Jenna with it.

Jenna grabbed a sleeping bag and tried to shield the children from the volatile liquid, but it was too late. Thankfully the kerosene heater was out and there were no open flames.

Clint handed Morgan a silver cigarette lighter. She flicked it and held it above the pit, directly over where Marty lay unable to move because of his injury.

"Now, this is what I love. A real moral dilemma. Shows you the truth about a person." Clint laughed. A small, mean noise coming from a man his size. He took out a handcuff key, unlocked the bracelet on Lucy's left wrist and joined it to the bracelet he removed from Adam's right wrist, securing Lucy and Adam by eight inches of steel.

"Here's my proposition. We're going to have a little duel. Right here, right now. Winner gets to live."

Lucy glanced at Adam. "I won't do it."

"Then I let Morgan have a wiener roast."

Morgan smiled and flicked the lighter again.

"The sheriff is on his way," Lucy tried to reason with them. Morgan seemed more receptive to the idea of escape. "If you go now, you have a chance."

"Don't worry. This won't take long. Adam's bigger but hasn't the guts to kill a woman. So, Lucy, it's up to you. Faster you kill Adam, faster we'll leave and these kids and your friend down there can live to tell the tale."

Now Adam dug in. "It doesn't take guts to kill a woman. I won't do it either. She's right. You better just run. Leave those kids alone."

Clint shook his head. "Not going to happen, son. I'll sweeten the pot. Lucy, if you want to save your daughter, Megan, all you need to do is kill Adam. Adam, if you want to save your brothers and sister, all you need to do is kill Lucy."

Lucy stared at him, straining against the chains, wishing she was close enough to wrap them around his neck. "If you so much as look at my daughter—"

"That's the spirit, Lucy! Just one catch." He pulled out his cell phone. "I'm going to film the whole thing. When I'm done it will go online. And if Lucy wins, I'm taking Olivia."

He turned the camera to film himself. "Let's make sure Megan knows what's at stake. Megan, darling, if you're watching this, then your mom killed an unarmed boy to save your life. And right now I'm killing a sixteen-year-old girl. Slowly. Taking my time." He winked. "Savoring every minute of it. She's gonna scream for days. Weeks."

"Sick sonofabitch!" It didn't take any acting skills to give Clint the desperation he wanted. But even as she hurled the words at him, Lucy was frantically thinking. How could she reel him in?

Rule number one in dealing with predators: they always lied. No way in hell he had any intention of letting either her or Adam live. Or Jenna and the kids.

He *tsked* at her. "Lucy, Lucy. I thought your job was understanding sick bastards like me. Getting into our heads."

Exactly. And Clinton was all about asserting control. Power.

Dominance.

"My job is hunting you down. Which is exactly what I'll do." She lunged at him, but the chain pulled her short.

Adam started to move with her, then Morgan flicked the lighter again and he froze.

Another laugh, and Clint turned the camera on Adam. "For anyone watching, this is Adam Caine. If he's still alive at the end of this, he'll have murdered a federal agent."

He peered around the camera. "That's the death penalty right there, Adam. Only way to save yourself is to go on the run. With me. Helping me fish. Doing everything I tell you."

Ahhh. Her hook. Why had Clint kept Adam alive this long? He had other children to replace him with. And obviously Adam didn't fit his father's idea of the perfect son.

Because Adam hadn't broken. Same way Clint kept Rachel alive far longer than was safe or expedient. He wanted to break her. He needed to break Adam as well.

But Adam would never become the monster Clint wanted. Lucy wouldn't give him the chance. Even if it meant sacrificing herself to save him. She'd kill Clint with her bare hands before she let Adam follow in his father's footsteps.

Megan and Nick's faces floated through her vision. She blinked them back with regret.

"Are you willing to do that, Adam? Become the son I deserve? Follow wherever I lead?"

Adam squirmed. Clint aimed the pistol at him and he froze in place. "No. I won't. You said you'd let the kids go. Someone has to take care of them."

"You don't come with me and I'll let Morgan take care of them. Imagine the fun she'll have, teaching them everything I taught her. Stay here and go to death row, abandoning the kids, or come with me and be the man I know you can be. Which will it be?"

Adam said nothing. His face tightened. Then he stared at Lucy, eyes narrowed. Assessing her vulnerabilities. Deciding where to aim the kill strike.

Clint's laughter echoed through the blackness. Morgan chimed in, dancing along the edge of the cliff, chanting, "Adam, Adam, Adam..."

"Adam, don't listen to him—"

He shook his head and looked away from Lucy, his fists tight, face a blank mask.

The face of a man who had decided. Life or death.

Chapter 35

Jenna wiped the foul Coleman fuel from her face, then turned to the kids. Sally was crying, rubbing her eyes as if they burned, while Darrin hovered over Marty, his face turned up to where Morgan taunted him with the lighter. Jenna couldn't believe she'd let a thirteen-year-old girl get the drop on her.

Worse, she saw the gleam of anticipation in Morgan's eyes and knew she would eventually light the fire.

"Help me move everything that got wet away from this side," Jenna whispered to the kids. "Fast as we can, stack it all over there, as far away as possible." She wadded the sleeping bag she'd grabbed to shield herself and took off her tie-dyed New Hope sweatshirt that reeked of kerosene. It was chilly, but better than burning. Darrin quickly followed suit, shedding his jacket and taking the fleece blanket that covered Marty, adding them to the bundle on the other side of the pit.

Sally kept crying, not willing to let go of the stuffed cat, despite the fact it was soaked.

"Darrin, help her," Jenna ordered. She had no time for tears as she scoured the pit for anything to help them get out of here. She found Lucy's Glock. She'd dropped it when she fell, but it was useless. One spark and the fumes from the fuel would ignite the air around them.

She sat back on her heels, realizing the futility of their position. It wasn't the fuel she had to worry about; it was the fumes. And she just succeeded in spreading those all over the bottom of the pit.

There had to be a way, she thought, only half listening to what Clint was saying. Crazy talk was no help either. Although this duel might be enough of a distraction—if she could find something to climb on. She dragged the heater to the base of the cliff. It wasn't very big and only stood about two feet high, but it might be enough.

"Here," Darrin said. "Put these under it." He held a stack of coloring books and magazines. Another six inches.

"Good. Anything else?"

"The rocks from the fire ring. But they're not very level."

"That's okay. Sneak a few of the flattest ones over here and we'll give it a try." The overhang partially hid them from Morgan, who was watching Clint anyway, but the fire ring was directly in her line of sight.

Whatever Clint had been talking about began. There was a thud. Someone hit the ground hard. Morgan turned away and clapped. Darrin saw his chance and dragged over the flattest rock he could find.

"Be careful," Marty whispered as Jenna climbed the precarious tower.

Darrin leaned his weight against her legs helping her keep her balance. If she could just get one hand over the edge, she might be able to reach the ladder she'd seen up there.

The sound of pounding feet came her way. Pebbles showered down on her and Darrin but the boy never lost his grip. She glanced down and saw that Sally figured out what they were doing. She had dropped her cat and helped steady the wobbly heater. Jenna stretched, only a few more inches, but her balance wavered and she fell back with a crash, narrowly missing the kids.

Morgan caught the movement and turned back to the pit. "Are we boring you?" she said with a sneer. "Here's something to keep you busy."

She flicked the lighter, used it to set flame to a rag she stuffed into the mouth of the fuel can, and flung it into the pit.

—

Clint threw a knife down between Adam and Lucy. "Three minutes," he said, making a show of looking at his watch. "Go."

At first both Lucy and Adam froze, their gazes locked.

Clint nodded to Morgan who flicked her lighter. "She'll do it. I'll give you to the count of three. Three—two—"

Adam lunged forward, knocking Lucy to the ground. He grabbed the knife. She was dragged across the harsh limestone by the chain connecting them. She couldn't let him get the upper hand. She had plans for that knife. Plans that included Clint.

Just as he turned to pounce on her, she kicked his leg out from under him, tripping him to the ground. She rolled, scrambling to get on top of him and pin his knife hand. They were face to face, their breath clouding the chilly air between them, when he whispered, "Trust me."

Morgan said something Lucy couldn't hear over the roaring in her brain. But she saw the flaming fuel can fly past her into the pit.

No choice. No time. She nodded to Adam, let him take the lead. Prayed her instincts hadn't condemned her.

—

Adam feinted with the knife, almost sliced Lucy's cheek—just close enough to make it look good as he tumbled them both to the ground again. Lucy didn't need to be told to kick the ladder into the pit.

To mask her movement, she punched Adam in the face, pulling it at the last minute and rolled her weight, sending them both over again, towards Clint. He ended up on top and sat up, reaching back, jerking his chin to signal Lucy. She kneed him in the thigh, just missing his groin.

He leapt up, hauling her halfway to her feet with the chain. Clint was only a few feet away, standing in the shadows, his back to the stalagmite formation with a two foot furrow at its base where Adam once found shards of clay pots. Not enough of a drop to kill him, but enough to give Adam and Lucy a chance.

Adam raised the knife, aiming a killing blow at Lucy as she rose to her feet. "Now!"

Lucy pivoted in unison with him and together they rushed Clint. The gun went off, the noise combining with the screams of the kids in the pit.

Chapter 36

Morgan watched as the flames danced merrily. There was even a tiny fireball when the fumes exploded. Not much of a blast, only a little whoosh of sound, but it made the kids scream in terror. She clapped her hands and hoped for another fireball, but there was more smoke than flames.

The ladder clattered into the pit. She glanced up, angry that Lucy and Adam were trying to spoil her fun. She watched them grapple and realized they were working together. Clint didn't even notice. He leaned forward, the gun slack in his hand, tongue darting out to lick his lips. Oh yeah, she knew that look. Like he was in a trance, anticipating the fun yet to come.

Adam and Lucy rushed Clint. The gun fired, the bullet ricocheting and sparking overhead. They pushed Clint over a small outcropping. He went down hard. He hit his head on a rock formation, then Lucy and Adam used their chain to throttle him.

Easy to see what came next. And it wouldn't be any fun.

Smoke billowed over the top of the pit. Morgan took advantage of the cover to slip away.

After all, there were other fish in the sea. Just waiting for her.

-

The ladder hit Jenna on the head. She set it upright, almost losing it when a pouf of fire ignited just above the pile of fuel-soaked material on the other side of the pit. Then the flames began in earnest, creating waves of black, oily smoke.

"Up the ladder," she told the kids.

Sally scrambled up, not even looking back for her stuffed cat. Darrin stood there, gaping at the flames and smoke coming at them like a tidal wave.

"Now!" She yanked him by the arm, set his hand on the rung.

"What about Marty?"

"Don't worry. Just go."

Still he hesitated. Jenna pushed him half way up, but he froze again, looking down at his friend. She scrambled up the ladder, forcing him to the top and over the edge. As soon as she cleared the top Adam climbed over her to head down. The smoke roiled over the edge of the pit, choking her vision. But she saw Morgan run past, escaping.

No way. No way in hell.

Jenna pulled her gun and followed.

—

Lucy and Adam held Clint pinned down while Lucy used her free hand to search his pockets. She found the handcuff key, uncuffed them, then cuffed Clint instead.

"The kids," Adam breathed as soon as he was free and vanished into the smoke.

A moment later Darrin and Sally appeared, holding hands, looking frightened but unharmed. "Marty," Darrin gasped. "He's still down there."

"Don't worry. We'll get him."

Before Lucy could move Jenna crashed past her, gun aimed at Morgan's fleeing form. The girl's back disappeared through the entrance to the outer passage.

"Jenna, no." Lucy lay her hand over Jenna's arm, forcing her gun down.

"But she's getting away." Jenna pushed Lucy away and aimed once more.

Lucy wrenched the Glock from Jenna's grasp. "She's a thirteen-year-old kid. You going to shoot her in the back?"

Morgan's laughter filled the air as she vanished from sight.

"She's no kid," Jenna muttered. "She's a monster."

"Yeah," Lucy agreed. "But you aren't."

—

Adam's eyes teared with smoke. There weren't a lot of flames, but the ones that blazed through the thick, oily smoke had found the wooden ladder. They sparked over its surface, hungry for more.

Marty's cry for help was choked short by a coughing spasm. Adam couldn't even see the boy, but that was okay. He didn't need to see, he could find his way around the pit blindfolded.

He pulled his sleeves down over his hands to protect them from the flames snaking around the ladder's rungs. No structural damage yet as they danced along the surface of the old, dry wood, but it wouldn't last long.

Smoke curled around him, wrapping him in black. He was surprised when his feet hit the ground sooner than he expected.

"Marty," he shouted. Just the one word and he was gasping for air, the thick smoke impossible to choke down.

He ended up on his knees. Marty should be right here, if his sense of direction was—got him. He grabbed the boy's shirt and pulled Marty to him. The boy barely flinched even though Adam knew the movement had to hurt his broken leg. But there was no time to waste.

"Adam!" Lucy's voice came from above. "Hurry!"

He retraced his steps, totally blinded. The bottom rung of the ladder was burnt through but the second and third looked only charred. Hefting Marty over one shoulder, the mountain pie makers clanging against his side, he reached for the ladder. Heat scorched his palms but he hauled himself up the first rung. His foot broke through and he almost dropped Marty as a coughing attack overtook him.

No way. He wasn't going to let Marty die. It was his fault the kids were down here in the first place. He had to save them.

He hauled in a breath, his throat filling with bile, trying to expel the noxious air. Reaching as high as he could, he pulled himself up to the third rung, then as quick as possible the fourth. Now he was high enough the flames found him, jumping onto his sleeve as he climbed. He couldn't stop to put them out, so he clenched his jaw and forced his legs to push harder, his arms to pull faster.

Then someone lifted Marty's weight from him. He sagged against the ladder, so close to the top but without any strength left to make it over. That was okay, a voice cut through the fog in his brain. You saved them. It's okay to let go.

His fingers relaxed their grip and the ladder began to sway back away from the wall. Then it bumped forward and Lucy grabbed him, hauling him up and over the edge of the cliff to safety.

He lay there coughing, vision choked with red. He rolled over and vomited. Then everything went black.

Chapter 37

Adam sat at the table in the small room. It smelled of sweaty socks, just like the juvenile detention facility, but there was also an undercurrent of something else. Something sweet and bitter, acrid and damp, that permeated the cinder blocks. Fear.

The heavy metal door opened, allowing the sounds of the men beyond to escape into the room. They didn't sound like men but like wild beasts foraging, grunting, sniffling as fresh prey passed by.

One guard held the door open while another escorted his father inside. Clint shuffled. The chains cobbling his ankles extended up to a wide leather belt where they joined to the handcuffs around his wrists. The first guard watched as the second undid the handcuffs, positioned him in the chair, then reattached the chain running between the handcuffs to a ring on the table. Their movements were quick and efficient. All done without eye contact or words, as if his father wasn't even human.

Throughout it all, Clint rolled his eyes and made faces at Adam. Like this was some kind of game. He didn't even notice it was exactly the same kind of game he played on those women. Controlling them. Positioning their bodies. Chaining them in place.

A strange calm descended over Adam, easing the flutter of panic he'd felt when he first sat down. He wasn't his father. He wasn't anything like him.

The guards turned to leave, one of them stopping to put a hand on Adam's shoulder. "You need anything, you just hit that button." He pointed to a doorbell button fastened to Adam's side of the table. "We'll be watching. Okay?"

Adam nodded. "I'm fine."

The guards left. The door closed and silence descended on the room. Adam sat up. Realized all that time hunched over, trying to make himself small, he'd never noticed that he'd grown taller than his father.

The chains rattled as Clint leaned forward and talked in hushed tones. "I'm glad you came to your senses, boy. I've got it all figured out. See, they have no bodies. No proof anyone was even killed. So, poof, no murder charges."

Adam cringed and drew away from the fetid odor of rotting fish that colored Clint's breath.

Clint leaned closer, bouncing with excitement. "And those women? Their word against mine it wasn't consensual. You know David Parker Ray, the guy who almost got away with that stuff in New Mexico? Same deal as me. Only they even had an actual video of him having fun with a fish. Slicing and dicing and electrocuting her and everything, right there on film. Plus, he let her live, so she actually testified in person. Even with all that, it was a hung jury and they let him go. I'm gonna see if I can get his lawyer. I figure if he can do that for Ray, my case should be a walk in the park.

"So, here's the plan. All you have to do is exactly what you always do: stay quiet and act dumb. You didn't see anything, you didn't hear anything."

Clint reached across the table. The chains felt cold when he covered Adam's hand with his own and squeezed. "There's nothing to be afraid of. Just don't say a word and everything will be fine. I'll be out of here before you know it. It'll just be you and me, kid. Like it was meant to be."

His smile was blindingly wide. The smile Adam had been waiting for all his life. But all Adam could focus on was the piece of meat stuck between Clint's upper teeth, dangling, flicking up and down as Clint licked his lips and refreshed his smile.

"What's wrong, son? This is no time to have second thoughts. I need you to be a man. Make me proud. I know you can do it."

Adam finally found the courage to ask the question he came here to ask. "What about Mom?"

"Mom? What's she got to do with anything?"

"You never even asked how she died. What happened in that cave. Is that because you told her what to do?"

"Did I—" He pulled away, slouched back in his chair, his dark eyes squinting at Adam, assessing, plotting. Like Adam was a fish. "Your mom was a brave woman. Smart. I didn't have to tell her what to do to protect the family. She figured it out all on her own."

"She killed that man. Killed herself. Just to save you."

"She was dying anyway. Doctor said maybe a month or less. She knew we pushed things too far in New Hope. Problem with your hometown, everyone remembers everything, like who you asked to the prom and got turned down, or who tormented you in the locker room. Small stuff, but if anyone put things together, we were sunk. Lucky I decided to keep that Penn State student alive long enough to frame him. Your mother's idea, by the way.

Good thing, too. He was there, drugged out of his mind, so your mom could use him as a fall guy. Literally."

He chuckled and the sound made Adam's skin shiver. "Guess she figured it would sell better if she went with him. Like I said, she was smart. Smartest fish I ever got."

Adam jerked up straight, halfway out of his chair. "She was no fish."

"She never told you?" Defiance glittered from his eyes. "Before her, they were all hit and run jobs. She was so sweet, special somehow. I kept her longer. Took her away instead of finishing the job. Oh the things we did. And she loved every minute. Begged for it. She needed me. To tell her what to do, how to think. She wouldn't blink without my permission. Best fish I ever had."

He sighed. "It was good while it lasted. So don't you let her down. You do as you're told. Stay quiet. And everything will be fine. I'll be out before you know it. Things will go back to the way they always were."

Adam shook his head. "No."

"What do you mean, no? I own you, boy. You're just as much a part of this as I am. Don't you forget that."

"No."

The chains stretched as he raised a hand to slap Adam. Before it could make it halfway, Adam caught it, twisted his thumb back, and shoved it away. As if Clint was weak. Powerless.

The word felt right. Adam pressed the button to call the guards. He pushed his chair back and stood, towering over his father.

"Don't do this, son! You'll regret it. I have friends in here, powerful friends. You're going to jail, too, and I'll make your life a living hell." Saliva speckled the tabletop as

Clint ranted, enraged by Adam's rebellion. "You'll be back, begging me to protect you. But I won't, I won't, because you're a fish like all the rest. Worthless, no good—"

The guards came, one pressing Clint's face down hard into the table, keeping pressure on the back of his neck so he couldn't resist.

"You done here, son?" the other guard asked Adam.

"I'm done."

They escorted Adam back outside to where Lucy waited. She'd arranged this final visit before he went into supervised custody. They made him stay in juvie until the psych eval was done, but after, the judge said he could have an ankle monitor and stay in a foster home.

Mrs. Chesshir, his old teacher had volunteered—which surprised Adam. He didn't think anyone in New Hope would want him anywhere near their home, not after what he did. Figured he'd stay in juvie for the duration. Even thought maybe that was better for everyone.

He didn't want to hurt anyone ever again. Didn't want to end up like his father. Or Morgan.

"Amanda's waiting," Lucy said as they walked out to her car. He was still getting used to the idea of calling Mrs. Chesshir by her first name. "Said the monitoring folks will be there by ten."

They passed an area with picnic tables. For families waiting to visit—or maybe the guards ate out here when the weather was nice. He stopped. "I need to tell you something."

She looked at him, nodded slowly. He used his sleeve to wipe a spot at a table clean for her, then took a seat on the other side. He wasn't sure he could face her when he told her his secret, but he knew he should try.

"What is it, Adam? Did your father upset you?"

"No. He wanted me to not say anything, but I don't care. I want to tell you and the judge and everyone everything. It's the least I can do if it helps those families. I can't take you to any bodies, my dad always took care of them, but maybe I can help you figure out who they were. And what happened to them."

She covered his hand with hers. "That's very brave of you."

He shrugged with one shoulder. "Least I can do. Try to make up for," he jerked his chin at the red brick jail behind them, "what he did. I know I was just a kid, but I should've known better."

"You never had a chance to know better. They raised you to be a part of it your entire life. There's no way a kid could have fought against everything he'd ever known."

"But I'm not a kid anymore." He sucked in his breath. The cold felt sharp, scratchy against his throat. "I need to be a man and own up to what I did. Everything I did. Including what happened in the cave four years ago."

"I know your mom set that up. She faked the carjacking and told you to lead us there, didn't she? She wanted to give your dad an alibi." She paused. "Who was the man? Was it Rachel's boyfriend?"

"How'd you know?"

"He was a geology major. Into caving."

"He just showed up one day when Mom was feeding the fish. She hit him on the head and had me help her drag him to one of the back chambers. Dad said he kept him alive so he could frame him when Dad was ready to leave New Hope."

"But then Rachel came looking for him."

"Rachel." He sighed, his breath emerging in a puff of steam quickly whisked away by the breeze. "She was too much for Dad to resist. Kept saying how defiant she was, all her praying and faith in God. Mom wanted him to leave, take me. Let her clean up after him, but he refused. Said he wouldn't leave New Hope until he broke Rachel. Showed her what God really was, who was in charge."

They were both silent for a long moment. "I guess Rachel won in the long run," Lucy said. "If it wasn't for her and you, we never would have caught him." She rubbed her finger against the tabletop, tracing letters in the moisture left behind by the melted snow. "Did she mean to kill herself or was that an accident? Your mom."

"She was dying. Her cancer was back. I guess it was one last way for her to show how much she loved him." He swallowed hard against the knot in his throat. Not from thinking about Mom, but thinking about what else had happened that day. "But…" This was the hard part. The part he never told anyone. "I'm the one who stabbed you."

Lucy jerked her chin up at that. "You?"

"When I ran into the cave, Mom grabbed me, said she needed more time to get things ready. She gave me one of his knives. Told me to slow you down anyway I could." He blinked back tears. Wished this was easier. Better to get it out as fast as possible. "She wanted me to kill you then run and get the other cops. But, but, I couldn't. I knew how to do it right, where to put the knife, but I just couldn't. I wimped out. Just like a fish."

He watched in agony as she gazed past him, eyes clouded with memory. Goodbye house arrest. Hello jail. For a long, long time. You didn't admit to trying to kill a FBI agent and get to walk free.

Worse, he'd lose Lucy.

"You were ten years old, Adam. And you didn't really hurt me."

He looked up in surprise. "You're not mad? I mean—"

"Don't get me wrong, I don't recommend the experience. And we definitely have to tell your counselor and the judge. You don't get to keep secrets like this. Not anymore."

"No. No ma'am. I…" he stammered into silence, not sure what to say.

"Truth is, you probably saved my life. If you hadn't slowed me down, it might have been my body Marion threw off that cliff. Then my husband and little girl would have never known what really happened to me."

He hadn't thought of it that way. "So, we're like, cool? You're not going to leave me, are you?"

The desperation coloring his voice shamed him, made him look down, waiting for her answer.

"No, Adam. I'm not leaving you. Why would I when you're turning out to be such a fine young man?" She stood and brushed off the back of her pants. "But we need to leave here or we'll be late for your appointment with the monitoring company. And I have to get home. I've a soccer game to get to."

—

The final soccer game between the league all-stars. Lucy stood on the sidelines, not worried about the rain or the mud the players sprayed over her as they scrambled after the ball. She held a red umbrella, big enough for two, waiting for Nick, and bright enough for Megan to spot no matter where she was on the field.

Unlike the other soccer moms and dads, she held her umbrella in her left hand. Leaving her weapon hand free and her parka unzipped, but it was only force of training.

The crowd cheered and laughed and shouted, Lucy right there with them, not even looking more than twice when two dads pushed in behind her for a better view of a penalty kick. She ignored her phone the first three times it rang, but finally picked it up after the fourth to see if it was Nick canceling.

It was John Greally. Just like the other three times.

There was a time out on the field, so she relented and took the call. "Guardino."

"Where the hell are you? The shrink's been calling here. You missed your appointment. Again."

"Couldn't help it. Megan's game went late."

"How's she doing?" John's daughter played on Megan's regular team but hadn't made it to the all-stars.

"Kicking butt and taking numbers." Pride rang through Lucy's voice.

Greally laughed. "Just like her mother. You sound better. More like yourself."

Lucy cradled the phone between her ear and shoulder as she moved to the parking area, standing with her back to the Subaru and keeping an eye on Megan. Not in panic, but because she didn't want to miss any of the game.

"I feel better," she admitted. "I know what happened in New Hope wasn't by the books and I'm willing to take whatever OPR throws at me. But John, we both know being chained to that desk was killing me. I belong out in the field. I can lead my people from the front lines. You know I can. And it will get the job done better. Plus keep them safe." She pled her case. For the last time. If the Office of Professional Responsibility wanted to kick her to the curb, then so be it.

She'd done what needed doing and she'd do it again. Not just for the victims she fought for every day. For herself. To give Megan a mother she could be proud of. A mother she could respect.

"Given the public support and media behind you, I think the brass will back off. Again." His voice held a tone of warning Lucy almost missed as Megan stole the ball and ran down field. She leaned forward, fist clutching the umbrella, urging her on, then sighed as the ball flew out of bounds.

"Do me a favor, though," Greally said, "don't miss another psych eval. And I'll see about getting you help to deal with the administrative duties. But you'll be a man short."

"Why? Who am I losing?" Lucy's focus returned to the phone.

"Galloway. Failed her own psych eval."

Lucy turned her back on the field for a moment, gaze searching the parking lot and the cars zooming past. No threats. In fact, the car slowing and turning in was the one she'd been waiting for.

"Don't say 'failed.' She didn't fail anything," she told Greally. "It's a tough job. Not everyone is cut out for it."

Nick parked beside her and hopped across the puddles of melted snow to reach the shelter she provided, taking the umbrella from her so she could have both hands free. She tilted her face to him and he kissed her beneath the cover of the umbrella.

"Gotta go," she told her boss. "Family time."

She hung up the phone, shoved it deep inside her pocket, intertwined her left arm in Nick's right, and they strolled back to the soccer field just in time to see Megan dive headfirst into the mud as she blocked what would have been the winning goal.

Behind them stood a girl in a black raincoat, watching. Not the game, but Lucy and Nick. Lucy caught a glimpse of dark curls, just before the girl turned and ran splashing through the puddles.

No. Couldn't be. No reason why Morgan would risk showing her face anywhere around Lucy. Just her imagination running wild.

Lucy tightened her arm around Nick and edged closer to the sideline to keep Megan in sight, one hand resting on the butt of her gun. More than training, this time. But less than panic.

Maybe it was Morgan watching. Maybe it wasn't. Didn't matter. Lucy was ready.

Also by CJ Lyons

Lucy Guardino FBI Thrillers

Snake Skin
Blood Stained
Kill Zone
After Shock
Hard Fall
Bad Break

Beacon Falls Novels Featuring Lucy Guardino

Last Light
Devil Smoke
Open Grave

Caitlyn Tierney FBI Thrillers

Blind Faith
Black Sheep
Hollow Bones